Edward S. Ellis

Footprints in the Forest

Edward S. Ellis

Footprints in the Forest

ISBN/EAN: 9783337252489

Printed in Europe, USA, Canada, Australia, Japan

Cover: Foto ©Andreas Hilbeck / pixelio.de

More available books at **www.hansebooks.com**

FOOTPRINTS IN THE FOREST.

BY

EDWARD S. ELLIS,

AUTHOR OF "NED IN THE BLOCK-HOUSE," "NED IN THE WOODS,"
"NED ON THE RIVER," "THE LOST TRAIL," ETC.

———◆———

CASSELL & COMPANY, LIMITED:

LONDON, PARIS, NEW YORK & MELBOURNE.

1886.

FOOTPRINTS IN THE FOREST.

CHAPTER I.

RETROSPECTIVE.

THOSE of my friends who have done me the honor of reading "Campfire and Wigwam," will need little help to recall the situation at the close of that narrative. The German lad Otto Relstaub, having lost his horse, while on the way from Kentucky to the territory of Louisiana (their destination being a part of the present State of Missouri), he and his young friend, Jack Carleton, set out to hunt for the missing animal. Naturally enough they failed : not only that, but the two fell into the hands of a band of wandering Sauk Indians, who held them prisoners.

Directly after the capture of the lads, their captors parted company, five going in one

direction with Jack and the other five taking
a different course with Otto. "Camp-Fire and
Wigwam" gave the particulars of what befell
Jack Carleton. In this story, I propose to tell
all about the hunt that was made for the honest
lad, who had few friends, and who had been
driven from his own home by the cruelty of
his parents to engage in a search which would
have been laughable in its absurdity, but for
the danger that marked it from the beginning.

The youth, however, had three devoted
friends in Jack Carleton, his mother, and
Deerfoot, the Shawanoe. But for the compas-
sion which the good woman felt for the lad,
she never would have consented that her
beloved son should enter the wilderness for the
purpose of bringing him home.

One fact must be borne in mind, however, in
recalling the two expeditions. In the former
Jack and Otto were the actors, but now the
hunters were Jack and Deerfoot, and therein
lay all the difference in the world. Well aware
of the wonderful woodcraft of the young
warrior, his courage and devotion to his friends,
the parent had little if any misgivings, when

she kissed her boy good-by, and saw him enter the wilderness in the company of the dusky Shawanoe.

Something like a fortnight had gone by, when Deerfoot and Jack Carleton sat near a camp-fire which had been kindled in the depths of the forest, well to the westward of the little frontier settlement of Martinsville. The air was crisp and cool, and two days had passed since any rain had fallen, so the climate could not have been more favorable.

The camp was similar to many that have been described before, and with which the reader has become familiar long ago. It was simply a small pile of blazing sticks, started close to a large tree, with a little stream of water winding just beyond. More wood was heaped near, and Jack was lolling lazily on the blanket which he had brought with him, while his friend sat on the pile of sticks opposite.

"Deerfoot, you remember I told you that while I was in the lodge of Ogallah, an Indian came in who was one of the five that had taken Otto away?"

The Shawanoe nodded his head to signify he recalled the incident.

"He made some of the queerest gestures to me, which I could no more understand than I could make out what his gibberish meant, but when I described his actions to you, you said they meant that Otto was still alive—that is, so far as the Indian knew?"

"My brother speaks the truth: such was the message of the Sauk warrior."

"They say all the red men can talk with each other by means of signs, but, without asking you to explain every word of the Sauk, I would like to hear again what it was he meant to tell me."

"He said that Otto had been given to a party of Indians, and they had started westward toward the setting sun with him."

"But why did they turn him over to the strangers?"

"Deerfoot was not there to ask the Sauk," was the reply of the young Shawanoe.

"That is true, for if you had been, you would have known all about it; but, old fellow, you can explain one thing: why do you not make your way to the Sauk village and get those warriors to give you the particulars?"

Such it would seem was the true course of the dusky youth, on whom it may be said the success or failure of the enterprise rested. He was silent a minute as though the question caused him some thought.

"It may be my brother is right, but it is a long ways to the lodges of the Sauks, and when they were reached it may be they could tell no more than Deerfoot knows."

Jack Carleton did not understand this remark.

He knew how little information he had given his friend, and it seemed idle to say that the real captors of Otto Relstaub could not tell more of him.

Strange things happen in this life. Several times during the afternoon Deerfoot stopped and glanced about him, just as Jack had seen him do when enemies were in the wood. He made no remark by way of explanation, and his friend asked him no question.

"It seems to me the Sauks can tell a good deal more than I ; for instance—"

Deerfoot suddenly raised his forefinger and

leaned his head forward and sideways. It was
his attitude of intense attention, and he had
signaled for Jack to hold his peace. The
tableau lasted a full minute. Then Deerfoot
looked toward his friend, and smiled and nodded, as if to say it had turned out just as he
expected.

"What in the name of the mischief *is* the
matter?" asked Jack, unable longer to repress
his curiosity; "you've been acting queer all
the afternoon."

"Deerfoot and his friend have been followed
by some Indian warrior for many miles. He
is not far away; he is now coming softly
toward the camp; I have heard him often; he
is near at hand."

"If he wants to make our acquaintance,
there is no reason why he should feel so bash-
ful," remarked Jack, glancing at different
points in the darkening woods; "I don't see
any reason why he should prowl around in that
fashion."

The lad's uneasiness was increased by the
fact that Deerfoot was manifestly looking over
his head and into the forest behind Jack, as

though the object which caused his remarks was coming from that direction.

"The Indian is not far off—he is coming this way—he will be in camp in a breath."

"And, if I stay here, he will stumble over me and perhaps break his neck," remarked Jack, who caught the rustle of leaves, and springing to his feet, faced toward the point whence the stranger was approaching.

It can not be said that the youth felt any special alarm, for he knew the sagacious Deerfoot would take care of him, but the knowledge that an armed stranger is stealing up behind a person, is calculated to make him nervous.

At the moment Jack faced about, he caught the outlines of a middle-aged warrior, who strode noiselessly from the wood and stepped into the full glare of the camp light. Without noticing Jack, he advanced to Deerfoot, who shook him by the hand, while the two spoke some words in a tongue which the lad did not understand.

But when the visitor stood revealed in the firelight, the boy looked him over and recognized him. He was the Indian who came into the hut of Ogallah, the Sauk chieftain, when Jack was a captive, and who went through the odd gesticulations, which the lad remembered well enough to repeat to Deerfoot, who, in turn, interpreted them to mean that Otto Relstaub had not been put to death, as the two youths had feared.

It was strange indeed that he should come to the camp of the lads, at the very time they were in need of such information as he could give.

While Jack identified the visitor as that personage, Deerfoot recognized him even sooner as Hay-uta, the Man-who-Runs-without-Falling. It was he who, while on a hunt for scalps, came upon the young Shawanoe and engaged him in a hand-to-hand encounter. You will recall how he was disarmed and vanquished by the younger warrior, and how the latter read to him from his Bible, and told him of the Great Spirit who dwelt beyond the stars, and whose will was contained in the little volume which was the companion of the Shawanoe. Hay-uta showed he was deeply impressed, and abruptly went away.

It will be remembered, therefore, that there were peculiar circumstances which caused the two red men to feel friendly toward each other and which led them to spend several minutes talking with such earnestness that neither seemed aware that another party was near. Jack did not object, but busied himself in studying the two aborigines.

Hay-uta has been already described as a middle-aged warrior. He was strong, iron-limbed and daring, but was not to be compared as respects grace, dignity and manly beauty to Deerfoot. What specially attracted Jack's attention was the rifle which he idly held with one hand while talking, the stock resting on the ground. It was the finest weapon the lad had ever seen—that is so far as appearance went. The stock was ornamented with silver, and the make and finish were as complete as was ever seen in those days. It was a rifle that would awaken admiration anywhere.

" I shouldn't wonder if he shot the owner so as to get it," thought the lad.

But therein he did the Sauk injustice. The savage gave all the furs and peltries that he was able to take during an entire winter to a white trader from St. Louis, who with a similar weapon bought more supplies enough to load him and his animal for their return trip to that frontier post.

While Hay-uta and Deerfoot talked, they smiled, nodded and gesticulated continually. Of course the watcher could not guess what they were talking about, until he noticed that Hay-uta was making the same motions that he saw him use in the lodge of Ogallah, adding, however, several variations which the youth was unable to recall.

"By George!" muttered Jack, "they're talking about Otto; now I shall learn something of him."

When the conversation had lasted some minutes, the talkers appeared to become aware that a third party was near. A remark of Deerfoot caused Hay-uta to turn and look at the young man, as though uncertain that he had ever met him before.

"Hay-uta has traveled a long ways since my brother saw him," said Deerfoot, who did not deem it worth while to explain why it was he had made such a journey : "he followed us a good while before he knew I was his friend ; then he came to the camp that he might talk with me."

Hay-uta, though unable to understand these words, seemed to catch their meaning from the tone of Deerfoot, for they were scarcely spoken, when he extended his hand to Jack, who, of course, pressed it warmly and looked the welcome which he could not put into words that would be understood.

These ceremonies over, all three sat on the ground, Hay-uta lit his pipe and the singular conversation continued, Deerfoot interpreting to his friend, when he had any thing to tell that would interest him.

"What does he know about Otto ?" asked Jack.

"He can not tell much : the warriors who made him prisoner walked slowly till the next morning ; they took another path to their lodges ; on the road they met some strange Indians, and they sold our brother to them for two blankets, some wampum, a knife and three strings of beads."

"How many Indians were there in the party that bought Otto?"

Deerfoot conferred with Hay-uta before answering.

"Four: they were large, strong and brave, and they wanted our brother; so he was sold, as the young man was sold by his brothers and taken into a far land, and afterward became the great chief of the country, and the friend of his brethren and aged father."

Astonished as was Jack Carleton to hear these tidings, he was more astonished to note that the young Shawanoe was comparing the experience of Otto Relstaub with that of the touching narrative told in the Old Testament of Joseph and his brethren.

CHAPTER II.

"BUT who were the Indians?" asked Jack Carleton.

Deerfoot shook his head, smiled in his faint, shadowy way and pointed to the west.

"They came from the land of the setting sun ; Hay-uta knows not their totem ; he never saw any of their tribe before and knows not whither they went."

" I should think that even an Indian would have enough curiosity to ask some questions."

" He *did* ask the questions," replied Deerfoot, "but the strange warriors did not give him answer."

"Then all that we know is that Otto was turned over to four red men who went westward with him."

Deerfoot nodded his head to signify that

B

such was the fact, and then he continued his conversation with Hay-uta.

Jack Carleton recalled that when he and Deerfoot were guessing the fate of Otto, the suggestion was made that probably such had been the experience of the poor fellow. He had been bartered to a party of red men, who had gone westward with him, and beyond that important fact nothing whatever was known.

My reader will remember also that I spoke in "Campfire and Wigwam," of the strange Indians who were sometimes met by the hunters and trappers, and well as by the red men themselves. They were dusky explorers, as they may be termed, who like Columbus of the olden time, had the daring to pass beyond the boundaries of their own land, and grope through strange countries they had never seen.

The four warriors had come from some point to the west, and Hay-uta said they could not speak a word which the Sauks understood, nor could the Sauks utter any thing that was clear to them. But the sign-language never fails, and had the strangers chosen, they could have given a great deal of information to the Sauks.

A little reflection will show how limitless was the field of speculation that was opened by this news. Beyond the bare fact, as I have said, that the custodians of Otto Relstaub came from and went toward the west, little, if any thing, was known. Their hunting grounds may have been not far away on the confines of the present state of Kansas or the Indian Nation, or traversing those hundreds of miles of territory, they may have built their tepees around the headwaters of the Arkansas, in Colorado (as now called), New Mexico or the Llano Estacado of Texas. It was not to be supposed that they had come from any point beyond, since that would have required the passage of the Rocky Mountains—a feat doubtless often performed by red men, before the American Pathfinder led his little band across that formidable barrier, but the theory that Otto's new masters traveled from beyond, was too unreasonable to be accepted.

Yet from the little camp where the three persons were lounging, it was more than half a thousand miles to the Rocky Mountains, while the territory stretched far to the north and south, so that an army might lose itself beyond recovery in the vast wilderness.

The task, therefore, which faced them at the beginning was to learn whither the four warriors had gone with the hapless Otto.

It need not be said that none understood this necessity better than Deerfoot himself. Consequently he drew from Hay-uta, the Sauk, every particle of knowledge which he possessed ; that, however, amounted to little more than has already been told. But that which the Shawanoe sought was a full account of their dress, their looks, arms and accouterments—such an account being more important to the young warrior than would be supposed.

The information he gained may be summed up : the strangers were taller, more powerful and better formed than Sauks. Each carried a rifle, tomahawk and knife as his weapons ; they had blankets, and their clothing, while nearly the same as that of the Sauks, was of a darker and more sober color. They had no beads or ornaments ; their leggings, moccasins, and the fringe of their hunting shirts, were less gaudy in color than those of the other party. Their moccasins were well worn, from which it was fair to infer they had traveled a long distance.

Hay-uta stated another fact which should be known : when the two parties discovered each other, the strangers showed a desire to engage in a fight, not that there was any special cause for so doing, but as may be said, on general principles. Though the Sauks were five to their four, they were afraid of the strangers, and they opened the negotiations for the transfer of Otto, with a view of diverting hostile intentions. The Sauks had the reputation of being brave and warlike, but they did not feel safe until many miles of trackless woods lay between them and the strangers.

So much, therefore, was known, and surely it was little enough. Hay-uta added the remark that as nearly as he could tell, Deerfoot and Jack were close to the very path which the strangers had taken on their way home. It might be they were on the trail itself, if such a thing be deemed possible, where no footprints

in the forest existed, for since the passage of
the four dusky aliens and their prisoner, the
wilderness had been swept by storms which
had not left the slightest trace on the leaves
that could be followed, and, though our friends
might be stepping in their very tracks, it was
hardly possible that the lynx eyes of the young
warrior could detect it.

When Deerfoot and Hay-uta had talked
awhile longer, the former turned to Jack and
amazed him by the remark :

"Hay-uta will go with us to give what help
he can to find our brother who is lost."

The news was as pleasant as it was surprising. It did seem singular that the one who
had helped take Otto Relstaub prisoner, and
then sold him to strangers, should now offer to
do what he could to bring back the lad to his
friends. He could not fail to be a valuable
ally, for, though vanquished by Deerfoot, he
ranked among the best warriors of his people.

"I wonder what led him to volunteer?" said
Jack.

"Deerfoot asked him, and he was kind
enough to do so."

" That's because you overcame him."

The young Shawanoe had given a short
account of his extraordinary meeting with
Hay-uta, when the older warrior tried to take
his life, but Jack knew nothing more than the
main incident. He had not been told of the
aboriginal sermon which Deerfoot delivered on
that "auspicious occasion".

It was only natural that the Sauk should feel
a strong admiration for the remarkable youth,
but the Word which Deerfoot expounded to him
had far more to do with his seeking the com-
panionship of the Shawanoe.

The latter made no answer to the remark of
Jack, but turning toward Hay-uta continued
the conversation which had been broken several
times. Young Carleton, believing there was
nothing for him to do, spread his blanket near
the fire, and, lying down, so as to infold himself from head to feet, was not long in sinking
into slumber.

Ordinarily his rest would not have been
broken, for his confidence in Deerfoot was so
strong, that he felt fully as safe as if lying at
home in his own bed, but, from some slight

cause, he gradually regained his senses, until he recalled where he was. He was lying with his back to the blaze, but the reflection on the leaves in front, showed the fire was burning briskly. He heard too, the low murmur of a voice, which he knew belonged to Deerfoot.

"What mischief can be going on?" he asked himself, silently turning his head, so that he could look across to his friend.

The scene was one which could never be forgotten. Deerfoot was lying or rather reclining on one side, the upper part of his body resting on his elbow, so that his shoulders and head were several inches above the ground. In the hand of the arm which thus supported him, was held his little Bible, the light from the camp-fire falling on the page, from which he was reading in his low, musical voice—that is he was translating the English into the Sauk tongue, seeking to put the words in such shape that the listener could understand them. It would be hard to imagine a more difficult task.

Between Deerfoot and Jack was stretched the Sauk, his posture such that his features were in sight. He lay on his face, his arms

half folded under his chest, so that his
shoulders were also held clear of the ground.
His dark eyes were fixed upon the countenance
of the Shawanoe youth, with a rapt expression
that made him unconscious of every thing else.
Into that heart was penetrating the partial
light of a mystery which mortal man has never
fully solved ; he was learning the great lesson
beside which all others sink into insignifi-
cance.

Jack Carleton moved as softly as he could,
so as to view the picture without bodily discomfort. Deerfoot glanced at him, without
checking himself, but Hay-uta heard him not.
Watchful and vigilant as he was, an enemy
might have stolen forward and driven his tomahawk through his brain, without any thought
on his part of his peril.

"I wish I could understand what Deerfoot is
saying," was the thought of Jack, whose eyes
filled at the touching sight.

"A full-blooded Indian is urging the Christian religion on another Indian. Even I, who
have a praying mother, have been reproved by
him, and with good cause too."

By and by the senses of the young Kentuckian left him, and again he slept. This time he did not open his eyes until broad daylight.

CHAPTER III.

THE expedition on which Jack Carleton entered with his two companions promised to be similar in many respects to those which have been already described. It looked indeed as if it would be more dull, and, for a while, such was the fact, but it was not long before matters took a turn as extraordinary as unexpected, and which quickly led the Kentuckian to conclude that it was, after all, the most eventful enterprise of his life.

For nearly three days the westward journey was without incident which need be given in detail. They swam several streams of water, climbed and descended elevations and shot such game as they required. The weapon of Hay-uta proved to be fully as excellent as it looked. Though its flintlock and single muz-

zle-loading barrel would have made a sorry
show in the presence of our improved modern
weapons, yet it was capable of splendid execu-
tion. Jack Carleton was a fine marksman, but
in a friendly contest in which the three
engaged, the Sauk beat him almost every time.
That this was due to the superiority of his gun
was proven by the fact that when they
exchanged rifles, the young Kentuckian never
failed to beat the other, and the beauty of the
whole proceeding was that when Deerfoot took
the handsome weapon, he vanquished both;
in fact he did it with the gun belonging to Jack
Carleton.

Though the young Shawanoe clung to his
bow, it was clear to his companions that he
admired the new piece. He turned it over and
examined every part, as though it possessed a
special attraction.

"Deerfoot," said Jack, pinching his arm,
"you could beat William Tell himself, if he
were living, with the bow, but what's the use
of talking? It can't compare with the rifle and
you know it. Just because a gun of yours
once flashed in the pan, you threw it away and

took up the bow again, but it was a mistake, all the same."

" One of these days Deerfoot may use the rifle," he answered, as if talking to himself, "but not yet—not yet."

Little did he suspect how close he was to the crisis which would lead him to a decision on that question.

Toward the close of the three days referred to, the trio were in what is to-day the southwestern corner of Missouri. Had the time been a hundred years later, they would have had to go but a short distance to cross the border line into Kansas.

A remarkable feature of their journey to that point, was the fact that, while making the distance, they had not seen a single person besides themselves. Not once, when they climbed a tree or elevation and carefully scanned the country, did they catch sight of the smoke of a solitary camp-fire creeping upward toward the blue sky. They heard the crack of no gun beside their own, and the keen eyes which glanced to the right and left, as they trod the endless wilderness, failed to detect the figure of the stealthily moving warrior.

This was singular, for there were plenty of Indians at that day west of the Mississippi, and it would be hard to find a section through which such a long journey could be made without coming upon red men. But at the end of the three days, our friends could not complain that there was any lack of dusky strangers.

It was near the middle of the afternoon, when finding themselves in a dense portion of the wood, on a considerable elevation, they decided to " take another observation ". To Jack Carleton it looked as if they were engaged on a hopeless errand, and, but for his unbounded faith in Deerfoot, he would have turned back long before in despair; it would be more proper indeed to say, that he never would have entered alone on such an enterprise.

There was no need for the three to climb a tree, so two stood on the ground while Deerfoot made his way among the limbs with the nimbleness of a monkey.

He went to the very top, and balancing himself on the swaying limb carefully parted the branches before his face. His penetrating glance was rewarded by a sight which caused an amazed "hooh!" to fall from his lips.

A little ways to the westward flowed a rapid stream, a hundred yards wide. The other shore, for a rod or two, was bare of trees and vegetation, except some stunted grass, and in this open space was encamped a party of Indians. The sentinel in the tree counted eleven, and suspected there were others who just then were not in sight. Though it lacked several hours of darkness and the air was pleasant, they had started a fire, big enough to warm a large space. Some of them seemed to have been fishing in the stream, for they had broiled a number of fish on the coals, and the nostrils of the young Shawanoe detected their appetizing odor.

Under ordinary circumstances there would have been nothing specially interesting in the group, but Deerfoot had studied them but a minute or two when he became convinced that they belonged to the same tribe which held Otto Relstaub a prisoner. Their dress, looks, and general appearance answered the description given by Hay-uta.

The heart of the youth beat faster over the thought that probably the four warriors whom he was seeking to follow were among them, and the fate of the German lad was about to be solved. He glanced down the trunk of the tree, and saw Jack Carleton and the Sauk standing on the ground and looking up at him, as though they suspected from his manner that some important discovery had been made. Without speaking, Deerfoot beckoned to the warrior to join him. The next instant the fellow was climbing among the limbs with such vigor that Deerfoot felt the jar at the very top.

Their combined weight was too great for such an elevation, and the younger perched himself somewhat lower, so as to give Hay-uta the advantage. A few words made known what Deerfoot had seen and that he wished the elder to answer the questions which the Shawanoe had asked himself.

Hay-uta was as guarded in his actions as Deerfoot could have been. He spent several minutes in a study of the group on the other side of the stream. Had he and the Shawanoe suspected they were so close to a camp of red men, neither would have climbed the tree, for little, if any thing, was to be gained by doing so ; the strangers could have been scrutinized from the ground as well as from the elevation. It was a noteworthy fact that two such skillful woodmen as Hay-uta and Deerfoot should approach so close to another party without discovering it.

While Hay-uta was inspecting the warriors, Deerfoot quietly awaited him on a limb some ten feet below, and Jack Carleton, peering aloft from the ground until his neck ached, wondered what it all meant.

The Sauk softly withdrew the hand extended in front of his face, and the leaves came together with scarcely a rustle. With several long reaches of his arms and legs, he placed himself beside his friend below and told what he had learned. The two of course talked in the Indian tongue and I give a liberal translation :

" What does my brother know ? " asked Deerfoot.

" They belong to the tribe who took the
C

pale-face ; Hay-uta knows not their name, but their looks show it.''

" Then their village can not be far away.''

" We must learn that of a surety for ourselves ; two warriors among them are the same that gave us the wampum and blankets for the pale-face boy.''

" Does my brother make no error ?'' asked Deerfoot, surprised to be told they were so close upon the heels of a couple of the very red men whom they scarcely hoped to find.

But the suspicion that such was the fact caused the Sauk to keep up his scrutiny until no doubt was left. He assured Deerfoot of the truth, adding that the taller was the one who handed over the wampum, and who showed such a willingness to draw the Sauks into a fight without waiting for provocation.

This was news of moment and raised several questions which the friends discussed while perched in the tree. If two of the original warriors were present, where were the others ? Was it not likely they were out of sight only for the time being? It seemed probable that the four while journeying toward their own hunting grounds, had joined a company of friends, with whom they were making the rest of the trip.

Then followed the question, *What of Otto Relstaub?* Varied as might be the answers to the question, all the probabilities pointed to his death, and that, too, in the most painful manner ; but it was idle to grope in the field of conjecture. It was for the friends to decide on the means of learning the truth.

In the hope of getting more knowledge, Deerfoot again climbed to the highest point, and studied the group on the other side of the stream ; but was disappointed, and he and Hay-uta made their way to the ground, where Jack Carleton was told all.

The eyes of the young Kentuckian expanded, and, when the story was finished, he exclaimed in a guarded voice :

"They've got Otto—of course they have."

The expression of the Shawanoe's face showed he was not sure of the meaning of his friend, who added :

" The whole four that had charge of him are with those fellows, and, if Otto isn't there also we may as well give up and go back, for he is no longer alive."

Deerfoot made no answer, but Jack was sure he shared the fear with him.

A discussion of the situation and the difficulties before them, led the two warriors to decide on a curious line of action.

It was agreed that one should cross boldly over and mingle with the strangers, while the other should reconnoitre the camp and learn what he could, without allowing himself to be seen.

It would be supposed that, inasmuch as Hayuta was acquainted with two of the Indians, and had parted from them on friendly terms, he would be selected to enter camp, while Deerfoot's matchless woodcraft would lead to his selection to work outside ; but these situations were reversed.

Since the strangers had journeyed far to the eastward into the hunting grounds of the Sauks and Osages (probably to the very shore of the great Mississippi), it followed that no surprise should be felt by them to find that some equally inquiring red man had travelled toward the

Rocky Mountains, with a view of seeing the strange land and its people. It was the intention of the young Shawanoe to assume such a part. Should any mishap befall Hay-uta, he would give out that he was engaged on a similar mission, and not knowing he was near friends, he was reconnoitring the party from a safer distance.

There were several reasons for this reversal of duties, as they may be called, but it is necessary to give only one or two. The appearance of Hay-uta among them most likely would raise suspicion that it bore some relation to the captive Otto. The red men, therefore, would be put upon their guard and the difficulty of securing him—if alive—greatly increased.

But the strongest reason was that Deerfoot would be sure to do better when brought in contact with the Indians. He was greatly the superior of the Sauk in mental gifts, and, with his remarkable power of reading sign language, would be sure to extract knowledge that was beyond the reach of Hay-uta.

Having decided on the course they were to follow, no time was lost in talking over the plan agreed upon. Jack Carleton was informed of the particulars by Deerfoot.

"I suppose it's the best thing to be done, though my opinion don't amount to much in *this* crowd. What am *I* to do?"

"My brother may sleep," said the Shawanoe, with that slight approach to humor which he sometimes showed.

"Yes; I would do a great deal of sleeping; but go ahead and I'll be on the lookout for you. I don't suppose you can tell when you are likely to get back?"

Deerfoot shook his head, but intimated that he hoped to learn all that he sought to know before the coming night should end.

A few minutes previous to this, Hay-uta had walked down the stream, keeping so far back that he could not be seen by any one on the other side. The Shawanoe took the opposite direction, the purpose of each being to act independently, and, in case circumstances brought them together in the presence of the aliens, the agreement was that Sauk and Shawanoe should comport themselves as though they had never met before.

When the time should come for the scouts, as they may be called, to return to the shore from which they started, they would have no trouble in finding Jack Carleton, with whom it was easy to communicate by means of signals. The most trying task was that of the young Kentuckian himself, who was left without any employment for mind or body.

Deerfoot walked several hundred yards up stream until he had passed a bend, where he swam across. He kept his bow so far above surface that the string was not wetted.

When he had surveyed himself, as best he could, he walked in the direction of the camp of the hostiles, as he more than suspected they should be classed. Had any one noticed him just then, he would have observed that the Shawanoe walked with a limp, as though suffering from some injury.

The readers of "Ned in the Block House," will recall that Deerfoot once saved his life by feigning lameness, and the youth saw nothing to lose and possibly much to gain by such strategy in the enterprise on which he was engaged.

CHAPTER IV.

D EERFOOT was by no means free from misgivings when he limped from the woods, and, crossing the narrow space that lined the stream, advanced to the camp-fire around which the warriors were lounging.

Their appearance showed they were doughty fighters, and what Hay-uta had told proved the same thing. But the Shawanoe had no fear that they would rush upon and overwhelm him, and he had been in too many perilous situations to hesitate before any duty.

The Indians turned their heads and surveyed him as he walked unevenly forward, holding his bow in one hand, and making signs of comity with the other. They showed no surprise, for such was not their custom; but stoical and guarded as they were, Deerfoot could see they felt considerable curiosity, and the fact that he carried a bow instead of a gun

must have struck them as singular, for he
came from the East, where the white men had
their settlements, and such weapons were
easily obtained. These strange Indians had
firearms, though beyond them in the far West
were thousands who had never seen a pale-
face.

Deerfoot's friendly salutations were answered
in the same spirit, and he shook hands with
each of the eleven warriors, who seemed accustomed to the civilized fashion. He seated himself a short distance from the fire, so as to
form one of the dozen which encircled it. No
food was offered the visitor, but when one of
the strangers handed him his long-stemmed
pipe, Deerfoot accepted and indulged in several
whiffs from the red clay bowl.

The two warriors whom Hay-uta had pointed
out as members of the party that had bought
Otto Relstaub from the Sauks, were objects of
much interest to the youth. They could not
have observed it, but he scanned them closely,
and when he sat down, managed to place himself between them—one being on the right,
and the other on the left.

Thus far, hosts and guest had spoken only by signs, but a surprise came to Deerfoot when the warrior on his right addressed him in language which he understood.

"My brother has journeyed far to visit the hunting grounds of his brothers, the Pawnees."

The words of the warrior made known the fact that the party belonged to the Pawnee tribe, but the amazing feature of his remark was that it was made in Deerfoot's own tongue —the Shawanoe. The youth turned like a flash the instant the first word fell upon his ear. He knew well enough that no one around him belonged to that tribe, but well might he wonder where this savage had gained his knowledge of the language of the warlike people on the other side of the Mississippi.

"My brother speaks with the Shawanoe tongue," said Deerfoot, with no effort to hide his astonishment.

"When Lone Bear was a child," said the other, as if willing to clear up the mystery, "he was taken across the great river into the hunting grounds of the Shawanoes; he went with a party of Pawnee hunters, but the

Shawanoes killed them and took young Lone Bear to their lodges."

"The Shawanoes are brave," remarked Deerfoot, his eyes kindling with natural pride.

" Lone Bear staid many moons in the lodges of the Shawanoes, but one night he rose from his sleep, slew the warrior and his squaw, and made haste toward the great river; he swam across and hunted for many suns till he found his people."

If this statement was fact, it told a striking story, but Deerfoot doubted its truth. The reason was that, judging from the age of the warrior, the exploit must have taken place when Deerfoot was very young, if not before he was born. The capture of a Pawnee youth and his escape in the manner named, formed an episode so interesting that it would have been spoken of many times during the early boyhood of Deerfoot, who ought to have heard of it, but he was sure that this was the first time the story had fallen on his ears. Deer-foot's sagacity told him that Lone Bear, as he called himself, was the only Pawnee who understood a word of their conversation ; that much was evident to the eye. It might be, too, that there was a good deal of truth in the words of the warrior. At any rate, it was easy to test him.

"Did Lone Bear dwell with Allomaug?"

"Allomaug was a brave chief; he was the father of my brother Deerfoot, who is fleeter of foot than the wild buck."

That settled it. The reader will remember that Allomaug was the parent of the youth, and that he was a noted sachem among the Shawanoes. Lone Bear had told such a straight story that Deerfoot was convinced that he must have dwelt at one time among his people.

All this was supplemented by the fact that Deerfoot himself was recognized and addressed by the name he had received from the white people. The young Shawanoe half expected the other to make some reference to the youth's escape from Waughtauk and his revengeful warriors, but Lone Bear had no knowledge of that episode, which took place long after his flight from the tribe. Deerfoot was puzzled to know by what means the

warrior identified him, when he was certain
he had never seen Lone Bear until he surveyed him a short time before from the tree-
top.

Deerfoot noticed that during their conversation, the others seemed to listen with as much
interest as the American Indians ever allow
themselves to show, and Lone Bear, now and
then, turned and addressed them in their own
tongue. When he did so, he spoke to the
whole group and every word was strange to
Deerfoot. While the latter could understand
a number of dialects used by the tribes west
as well as east of the Mississippi, he knew
nothing of that of the Pawnees.

" Why does Deerfoot wander so far from his
hunting grounds?" asked Lone Bear.

" Deerfoot has not wandered as far as the
Pawnees," was the truthful reply of the
Shawanoe. " He once lived beyond the great
river, but he lives not there now."

The Pawnee looked as though he suspected
Deerfoot was telling him fiction, but he was
too shrewd to express any such thought.

" Where are the companions of my

brother?" was the pointed question of Lone Bear.

"Deerfoot is alone and his companion is the Great Spirit."

The reader will observe that the reply of the Shawanoe partook of the nature of a falsehood, inasmuch as it was accepted by Lone Bear (and such was Deerfoot's purpose), as a declaration that he had travelled the whole distance alone. Enough has been told to show the extreme conscientiousness of the young Shawanoe, and no danger could lead him to recoil from duty. He had imperilled himself many a time from that very motive, but he believed it right to do his best to deceive Lone Bear. In fact, his visit was of itself a piece of deception.

"Why does Deerfoot come to the camp of the Pawnees?" continued Lone Bear, as though his guest was on the witness stand.

"Not many suns ago the Sauk warriors made captives of two pale-faced youths; one of them has come back to his people, but the other has not. He was a friend of Deerfoot; he went among the Sauks, but his friend was

not there ; he was told that he had been bartered for wampum and blankets and beads to
the Pawnees. Can Lone Bear tell Deerfoot of
his friend ? "

This was coming to the point at once, but it
was the wiser course. Deerfoot saw that any
other statement he might make would be
doubted, as most probably was the explanation
itself. He looked into the face of Lone Bear,
so as to study his expression, while answering
the question.

"The words of my brother sound strange to
the ears of Lone Bear ; he has not seen his
pale-faced friend."

"Has not *he* seen him ? " immediately asked
Deerfoot, pointing to the Pawnee on the other
side.

Lone Bear exchanged words for two or three
minutes with the latter, and then replied to
the visitor.

"Eagle-of-the-Rocks has not seen the pale-
face friend of my brother ; he and Lone Bear
have staid with their Pawnee brothers ; they
have met no pale-faces in many moons."

Here was a direct contradiction of what

Hay-uta had told. It might seem that the
Sauk had mistaken the identity of Lone Bear
and Eagle-of-the-Rocks, and had there been
but one of them in question, it was possible ;
but Deerfoot was satisfied that no such error
had been made. Hay-uta was positive respecting both, and he could not have committed a
double error.

Furthermore, the study of the Pawnee's
face convinced Deerfoot that Lone Bear was
lying to him, though to ordinary eyes the expression of the warrior's face was like that of
stone.

Why this falsehood should have been used
was beyond the power of the Shawanoe to
guess. The band was so far from the settlements that they could feel no fear from white
men. Nevertheless, Deerfoot was sure that,
had Lone Bear chosen, he could have told every
thing necessary to know about Otto Relstaub.

Two answers to the query presented themselves : the poor lad had either been slain or
he had been turned over to the custody of still
another party of Indians. As for escape, *that*
was out of the question.

The probability that the Pawnees had put Otto to death occurred to Deerfoot more than once, and while seated on the ground, he had looked for signs that might show what had been done. There were several scalps dangling at the girdles of the warriors, but the hair of each was long, black and wiry, showing that it had been torn from the crown of one of their own race. The yellow tresses of the German lad would have been noticed at once by Deerfoot.

The latter was angered by the course of Lone Bear, who had told an untruth, without, so far as Deerfoot could see, any proper motive. So sure was the youth on this point, that he did not hesitate to tell the Indian his belief.

"My brother, Lone Bear, has spoken, but with a double tongue. He and Eagle-of-the-Rocks have seen my pale-faced friend ; they gave the beads and wampum for him ; Deerfoot knows it ; Deerfoot has spoken."

Lone Bear, like all his race and the most of ours, was one of those who looked upon the charge of falsehood (especially if true) as a deadly insult. His dull, broad face seemed to crimson beneath its paint, and turning partly toward the daring youth, he grasped the handle of his knife.

"Dog of a Shawanoe! Who bade you come to the camp of the Pawnees? Do you think we are squaws who are ill, that we will let a dog bark at our heels without kicking him from our path?"

Lone Bear talked louder and faster with each word, until when the last passed his lips, he was in a passion. He had faced clear round, so that he glowered upon the youth. He now rose to his feet and Deerfoot, seeing that trouble was at hand, did the same. As he came up, he took care to limp painfully and to stand as though unable to bear any part of his body's weight on the injured leg.

"Lone Bear is as brave as the fawn that runs to its mother, when it hears the cry of the hound; he is in the camp of his friends and it makes him brave; but if he stood alone before Deerfoot, then would his heart tremble and he would ask Deerfoot to spare him!"

No more exasperating language could be framed than that which was uttered by the young Shawanoe. He meant that it should fire Lone Bear and he succeeded,

CHAPTER V.

WHY it was Deerfoot sought a quarrel with the Pawnee can not be made fully clear. I incline to believe that his quick penetration detected signs among the warriors that they did not mean to let him withdraw, when he should seek to do so, and his plan was to use the quarrel as a shield to thwart their purpose. This may seem a strained explanation but let us see how it worked.

It is not impossible that the wonderful young warrior brought about the disturbance in what may be called pure wantonness ; that is, his confidence in his own prowess led him to invite a contest, which scarcely any other person would dare seek.

His last words were the spark to the magazine. The knife griped by Lone Bear was snatched from his girdle, and he sprang forward, striking with lightning-like viciousness at the chest of the Shawanoe, who avoided him with half an effort.

In dodging the blow, the youth moved backward and to one side, so as to bring all the warriors in front, and to leave open his line of retreat. He had been as quick as Lone Bear to draw his weapon, but he did not counter the blow— that is to an effective extent. He struck his antagonist in the face, but only with the handle of the weapon. Perhaps a pugilist would have said that the younger "heeled" the other.

The stroke was a smart one, and delivered as it was on the nose, intensified, by its indignity, the fury of Lone Bear. He lost all self-control, as Deerfoot meant he should do.

This flurry, as may be supposed, centred the interest of the others upon the two. The quarrel started as suddenly as it sometimes does among a group of fowl, and, before it was understood, the combatants, with drawn knives were facing each other. Few sights are more entertaining to men than that of a fight. The Pawnees in an instant were on their feet, with eyes fixed on the scene.

It must be believed that every one of the eleven Pawnees was sure it was out of Deer foot's power to elude the vengeance of Lone Bear. The only fear of the ten was that he would dispatch the youth so quickly that much of their enjoyment would be lost. When they saw him strike Lone Bear in the face, a general shout of derision went up at the elder antago- nist, for permitting such an outrage. This did not add to the good temper of Lone Bear, who compressed his lips, while his eyes seemed to shoot lightning, as he bounded at Deerfoot, intending to crush him to the earth and to stamp life from him.

But even though the youth seemed to be lame, he leaped backward and again escaped him. Lone Bear dashed forward, to force him down, but Deerfoot kept limping away just fast enough to continue beyond the reach of his enemy.

"Lone Bear runs like the fowl that has but one leg," was the odd remark of Deerfoot, who pointed the finger of his left hand at the other's face by way of tantalizing him.

But the fierce Pawnee was now pursuing so

swiftly that Deerfoot had to whirl about and run with his face from him. He still limped, though had any one studied his gait, the trick would have been detected ; but the sight of Lone Bear chasing a lame youth and failing to overtake him, did not calm his rage.

The warrior, however, was fleet, and marvelous as was the speed of the young Shawanoe, he was compelled to put forth considerable exertion to keep beyond his reach. His course took him quite close to the edge of the wood, along which he ran, so that, should it become necessary, he could leap among the trees. He watched his pursuer over his shoulder, to prevent his coming too close. His plan was to keep just beyond his reach and tempt him to the utmost effort.

Faster and faster went the fugitive, while the pursuer desperately put forth every effort, maddened beyond expression that the outstretched hand failed only by a few inches to grasp the flying Deerfoot. The spectators were amused to the last degree. Expecting quite a chase, they ran forward, as persons along shore follow a boat race, so as not to lose a phase of the struggle.

In the depths of his wrath, Lone Bear regained something of his self-command, and called to mind the stories he had heard of the fleetness of the young Shawanoe. That, with the fact that there was no longer the least halt in his gait, told the disadvantage in which the pursuer was placed.

If he could not reach the Shawanoe with his knife, he could with his tomahawk or his rifle. Hastily thrusting back the knife, he whipped out his tomahawk and raising it over his shoulder, hurled it with might and main at the crown surmounted by the stained eagle feathers and streaming black hair. At that moment, pursuer and fugitive were scarcely ten feet apart.

But Deerfoot knew what was coming, and the instant the missile left the hand of Lone Bear, he dropped flat on his side, as if smitten by a thunderbolt. The shouting Pawnees, who were some distance behind, supposed his skull had been cloven by the fiercely-driven tomahawk, but it was not so.

Lone Bear did not see the trick of Deerfoot in time to escape its purpose. The fall was so sudden, that before he could check himself, his moccasin struck the prostrate figure, and he sprawled headlong over him, heels in the air, and with a momentum almost violent enough to cause him to overtake the tomahawk that had sped end over end several rods in advance.

Before the Pawnee could rise, Deerfoot bounded up, sprang forward, and, placing one foot on the head of Lone Bear, leaped high in air and spun around so as to face the party. Brandishing his bow aloft, he emitted a shout of defiance and called out :

"Why do not the Pawnees run ? Is none of their warriors fleet enough to seize Deerfoot when he is lame?"

The only one of the company who could understand these questions was the slightly stunned Lone Bear, who just then was climbing to his feet ; but the gestures and manner of the fugitive told the meaning of the performance.

The young Shawanoe stood still on the edge

of the wood, as if to show his contempt for the Pawnees, who before Lone Bear could recover from his discomfiture, sped forward in pursuit. One of them emitted several whoops, which Deerfoot half suspected were meant as a signal, though of course he could not be sure of their meaning.

It seemed like tempting fate to stand motionless, when only a few seconds were required to bring his enemies to the spot, but Deerfoot waited till Lone Bear was erect again, when he called to him,

"The heart of Deerfoot is sad because Lone Bear can not run without falling ; let him go to the lodges of the Pawnees and ask the squaws to teach him how to run."

Lone Bear made no reply, for it is safe to say he could not "do justice to his feelings". Few Indian tongues contain words that answer for expletives, which in one sense was fortunate and in another unfortunate for Lone Bear.

When several of the pursuers brought their guns to their shoulders, Deerfoot shot like an arrow among the trees and vanished. It was time to do so, for his enemies were close upon him.

Though the Pawnees had learned of the swiftness of the young Shawanoe, they had no thought of abandoning the attempt to capture him. The flying tresses would make the most tempting of scalps to dangle from the ridge-pole of the wigwam, and because he could out-run all their warriors was no proof that he could not be overcome by strategy.

When the fugitive disappeared, the same signal of which I have spoken was repeated, and the Pawnees scattered—that is to say they plunged into the wood at different points : they did not try to overhaul him by direct pursuit.

Two of the Indians declined to join in the chase, but walked toward Lone Bear, who hav-ing assumed the perpendicular again, was look-ing around, as if uncertain of the best course to pursue.

The American Indian, as a rule, is melancholy and doesn't enjoy innocent fun as much as he ought, but, as I have shown, there are few or none in which the element of humor is alto-gether wanting. The two of whom I am just now speaking, shook with laughter, as they saw Lone Bear sprawl over Deerfoot, his heels flying in air, and their mirth became so great when the young Shawanoe used his crown as a stepping stone, that they paused from weakness.

Lone Bear knew nothing of this, and when he saw them approaching, their faces were as long and grave as if on the way to attend the funeral of their dearest friend. Perhaps he expected to receive a little sympathy, but he must have felt some misgiving.

"Lone Bear runs like the wild buck," was the remark of one of the warriors, though the observation itself did not amount to much, nor could the one to whom it was addressed see why it should be made at all. He, therefore, remained silent, feeling as though he would like to rub some of the bruised portions of his body, but too dignified to do so.

" If the wolf or buffalo crosses the path of Lone Bear, he does not turn aside."

" No ; he runs over him."

Even though he be a warrior, Lone Bear goes over him, as though he were not there."

The party of the third part began to see the

drift of these comments, and he glared as though debating which one to slay first.

" Lone Bear has a kind heart; it is like that of the squaw that presses her pappoose to her heart."

"He is kinder than the squaw, for he lies still and lets the Shawanoe rest his weary foot on his head."

Lone Bear glowered from one to the other, as they spoke in turn, and kept his hand on his knife at his girdle, as if to warn them they were going too far. They seemed to hold him in little fear, however, and continued their mock sympathy. One walked to where the tomahawk had lain untouched since it left the hand of the Pawnee, and, picking it up, exam ined it with much care.

"There is no blood on it," he remarked, as if talking to himself, but making sure he spoke loud enough for the other to hear ; " we were mistaken when we thought it went through the body of the Shawanoe ; the hand of Lone Bear trembles like that of an old man, and he can not drive his tomahawk into the tree which he reaches with his hand."

The black eyes of the Pawnees sparkled, and they seemed on the point several times of breaking into laughter, but managed to restrain themselves.

Still resting his hand on his knife, Lone Bear directed his first remark to the last speaker.

"Let Red Wolf keep his tongue; he talks like the pappoose."

Red Wolf, however, did not seem to be alarmed. He glanced into the face of his companion and added :

"Though Red Wolf talks like the pappoose, his heart is not so faint that he lies on the ground, that his enemy may have a *soft place* where he may rest his moccasin."

This, beyond question, was a severe remark, and, as the two broke again into laughter, Lone Bear was almost as angry as when he took a header over the body of the Shawanoe ; but the warriors were as brave as he ; without reply, he turned sullenly away, and walked toward the camp fire which he had left a short time before.

CHAPTER VI.

DEERFOOT the Shawanoe darted among the trees and ran a hundred yards with great swiftness. He seemed to avoid the trunks and limbs with the ease of a bird when sailing through the tree tops.

Coming to a halt, he looked around. He had not followed a direct course into the woods, but turning to the right, ran parallel to the open space which bordered the stream. He knew the Pawnees would do their best, either to capture or kill him. So long as there was a chance of making him prisoner, they would do him no harm, for the pleasure of acting as they chose with such a captive was a hundred fold greater than that which could be caused by his mere death. The American Indian is as fond of enjoying the suffering of another as is his civilized brother.

The burst of speed in which the youth indulged gave him a position where it would require some searching on the part of the Pawnees to discover him ; but they were at work, as speedily became evident.

A few seconds only had passed, when he caught sight of several forms flitting among the trees. While they were separated from each other by two or three rods, they were not far off, and their actions showed they had observed him at the same moment he detected them. They made no outcry, but, spreading still further apart, acted as if carrying out a plan for surrounding him.

Deerfoot was too wise to presume on his fleetness of foot, and he now broke into a loping trot which was meant to be neither greater nor less than the gait of his pursuers. Glancing back he saw they were running faster than he, whereupon he increased his speed.

Suddenly one of them discharged his gun, and a moment later another shot was heard. The first bullet sped wide, but the second clipped off a dead branch just above the head of the fugitive. There was no mistake, therefore, as to the purpose of those who fired.

It was not the first time that Deerfoot had served as a target for the rifle of an enemy, and though never wounded, his sensations were any thing but pleasant. Where a good marksman failed, a poor one was liable to succeed: for the most wonderful shots are those made by chance.

Deerfoot now ran as fast as he dared, where branches and tree trunks were so numerous. Glancing to the rear, as he continually did, he noticed that two of the Pawnees were leading in the pursuit. The thought came to him that no better time could be selected for teaching them the superiority of the bow over the rifle.

As he ran, he drew an arrow from the quiver over his shoulder and fitted it to the string. This was difficult, for the long bow caught in the obstructions around him and compelled him to slacken his pace. Then, like a flash, he leaped partly behind a tree and drew the arrow to a head.

The Pawnees must have been amazed to discover, while in full pursuit of an enemy,

E

that he had vanished as through swallowed by some opening in the earth ; for the action of the fugitive was so sudden that it was not observed. They ran several rods further, during which Deerfoot made his aim sure. As they had discharged their guns, and had not yet slackened their pace to reload them, he had no fear of being hurt.

All at once the foremost Pawnee saw the long bow, with the gleaming eyes behind the arrow, whose head was supported by the right hand which grasped the middle of the bow.

"Whoof !" he gasped, dropping to the earth as if pierced through the heart. His action saved his life, for a second sooner would have enabled the matchless archer to withhold the shot, which was as unerring as human skill could make it. Though the flight of the feather-tipped missile could be traced when the spectator stood on one side of the line, yet the individual who was unfortunate enough to serve as a target, could not detect its approach.

Just as the leader went down, a quick whiz was heard, and the arrow clove the space over him. Had his companion been in line he would have been pierced, but he was just far enough to one side, to be taught a lesson.

The strongly-driven missile went through the fleshy part of his arm, and sped twenty feet beyond, nipping several branches and twigs before its force was spent. No doubt the American race as a rule is hardy and stoical, but the stricken Pawnee acted like a school-boy. Dropping his gun, he clasped his hand over the wound, and emitted a yell which surpassed every thing in that line that had been heard during the day.

Even the warrior on the ground called to him to hold his peace, and the wounded Pawnee, awaking perhaps to a sense of the unbecoming figure he was cutting, compressed his thin lips and became silent.

But the other took good care to reload and prime his rifle before rising, and even then he came up with the utmost slowness, peering toward the tree from which had come the missile. He was not surprised because he saw nothing of the Shawanoe. Having discharged the weapon, it was natural that the latter should shelter himself from the bullet that was to be expected in return. Deerfoot (so reasoned the Pawnee), would not dare show himself again; but therein the warrior made a mistake.

The latter slowly came up, his form in a crouching position, his head about four feet above ground, while his eyes were fixed on the tree from behind which had sped the well nigh fatal missile.

"He will soon show himself," must have been the thought of the Indian, "the bullet can travel faster than the arrow."

At that moment his companion, who was still clasping his wounded arm, uttered a warning cry. He had discovered the Shawanoe behind another tree, aiming a second arrow at the breast of the leader.

With incredible dexterity, Deerfoot had run to a trunk fully twenty yards from the one which first sheltered him. He crouched so low and passed so swiftly that he reached the shelter before there was a possibility of discovery. It was accident which led the second warrior to detect the long bow, bending almost like a horseshoe, with the arrow aimed at the other.

The latter could not grasp in an instant the full nature of the peril which impended, though, as a matter of course, he knew it must be at the hands of the Shawanoe. He cast one glance around him, and again dropped on his face, but this time the arrow was quicker than he.

Zip came the missile straight for the brawny chest which never could have dodged from its path in time to escape; but, as if fate had determined to interfere, the pointed flint impinged against a tiny branch protruding from the tree nearest the Pawnee, clipping off enough of the tender bark to leave a gleaming white spot, and glanced harmlessly beyond.

Deerfoot was astonished beyond measure. He had discharged two arrows at the foremost foe, and had failed to harm a hair of him. Such a double failure had never before taken place in his history.

But the cause was self-manifest. The Indian dodged the first, and the twig turned the second aside. All this was natural enough, but the fact which impressed the young Shawanoe was that it would have taken place in

neither case had he used a rifle. Was it a
wise thing, therefore, when months before, he
had flung aside his gun and taken up his bow
again ?

Deerfoot had asked himself the same question more than once since that time, and the
doubt had deepened until he could no longer
believe he was wise in clinging to his bow and
arrow, great as was his skill in their use.

But a third arrow was quickly drawn, and
stepping from behind the tree, so that he stood
in full sight, he swung his hand aloft with a
defiant shout, and coolly walked away, as
though the warriors were too insignificant to
be noticed further.

The wounded Pawnee was so much occupied
with his hurt that he was willing the youth
should leave the neighborhood without further molestation from him. Taking care to
keep an oak fully a foot in diameter between
them, he was content to let him depart in
peace.

Not so with the other, who, waiting only long
enough to make sure the back of the youth
was toward him, straightened up and brought

his rifle to his shoulder. The distance was considerable, but he ought to have reached the mark, and probably would have done so, had not a disturbing cause prevented.

While sighting along the barrel, the startling fact broke upon him that the face of Deerfoot was toward him, and he was in the act of drawing a third arrow to the head. He had whirled about almost at the same instant that the Pawnee levelled his gun. To say the least, it was very disconcerting, and, anxious to anticipate the Shawanoe, the other fired before he could be certain of his aim. The bullet went so wide that Deerfoot heard nothing of its passage among the branches around him.

Although it looked as if the Shawanoe had the other at his mercy, yet he refrained from discharging the arrow. In fact, his whole action was designed rather to disconcert the Pawnee than to injure him. Not only had Deerfoot's confidence in his bow and arrow weakened, but the two escapes of the Pawnee gave him a half-superstitious belief that it was intended the latter should not be injured. He, therefore, relaxed the string of the bow, but,

without replacing the arrow in the quiver, he
strode off, continually glancing back to make
sure the Pawnee did not use the advantage thus
given him.

CHAPTER VII.

YOU will understand that the pursuit of Deerfoot the Shawanoe was not confined to the two Pawnees, whom he thwarted in the manner described. Their superior activity simply brought them to the front and hastened the collision.

It will be seen, therefore, that the incidents must have taken place in a brief space of time : had it been otherwise, Deerfoot would have been engaged with the entire party. No one could have known that better than he. The whoops, signals and reports of the guns could not fail to tell the whole story, and to cause the Pawnees to converge toward the spot. In fact, when Deerfoot lowered his bow and turned his back for the second time on the warrior, he caught more than one glimpse of other red men hastening thither.

Dangerous as was the situation of the youth, he did not forget another incident which was liable to add to the difficulty of extricating himself. From the moment he began his flight several of the Pawnees gave utterance to shouts which were clearly meant as signals. These had been repeated several times, and Deerfoot could form no suspicion of their full meaning. Had the red men been Shawanoes, Wyandots or almost any tribe whose hunting grounds were east of the Mississippi, he would have read their purpose as readily as could those for whose ears they were intended.

The interpretation, however, came sooner than was expected.

Deerfoot ran a little ways with such swiftness that he left every one out of sight. Then he slackened his gait, and was going in a leisurely fashion, when he came upon a narrow creek which ran at right angles to the course he was following. The current was swift and deep, and the breadth too great for him to leap over.

He saw that if he ran up or down the bank too far, he was likely to place himself in peril again. He could have readily swam to the other side, but preferred some other means, and concluded to take a minute or two in looking for it.

A whoop to the left and the rear made known that no time was to be lost. He was about to run in the opposite direction, when he caught sight of the bridge for which he was hunting. A tree growing on the opposite side had fallen directly across, so that the top extended several yards from the shore. The trunk was long, thin, covered with smooth bark, and with only a few branches near the top, but it was the very thing the fugitive wanted, and, scarcely checking his gait, he dashed toward it, heedless of the Pawnees, a number of whom were in sight.

He slowed his pace when about to step on the support, and placing one foot on the thin bridge, tested it. So far as he could judge it was satisfactory, and, balancing himself, he began walking toward the other shore. Only four steps were taken, when a Pawnee stepped upon the opposite end, and advanced directly toward the Shawanoe.

It began to look, after all, as though Deer-

foot had presumed too far on his own prowess,
for his enemies were coming fast after him, and
now, while treading the delicate structure, he
was brought face to face with a warrior as
formidable as Lone Bear or Eagle-of-the-Rocks.

But there was no time to hesitate. The
Pawnee had caught the signals from the other
side the stream, and hurried forward to intercept the enemy making his way in that direction. He advanced far enough from the spreading base of the tree to render his foothold firm,
when he braced himself with drawn knife, to
receive the youth. He had flung his blanket
and rifle aside, before stepping on the trunk,
so as not to be hindered in his movements.

His painted face seemed to gleam with exultation, for, if ever a man was justified in believing he had a sure thing it was that Pawnee
warrior, and if ever a person made a mistake
that Pawnee warrior was the individual.

Instead of turning back Deerfoot drew his
knife, and grasped it with his right hand, as
though he meant to engage the other in con-
flict where both had such unsteady footing.
Had the young Shawanoe held such a purpose,

however, he would have held the knife with his left hand, but the Pawnee, having never seen him before, could not know that, and he was confident that the slaying of the youth was the easiest task he could undertake.

Deerfoot not only continued his advance, but broke into a trot composed of short, quick steps, such as a leaper takes when gathering on the edge of a cliff for his final effort. He still held his bow in his left and his knife in his right hand, and tightly closing his lips, looked into the eyes of the Pawnee.

Just as the latter drew back his weapon with the intention of making the decisive blow, and when two paces only separated the enemies, the Shawanoe dropped his head and drove it with terrific force against the chest of the Pawnee. The latter was carried off the log as completely as if he had been smitten with a battering ram.

He went over with feet pointing upward, and dropped with a splash into the stream. The blow was so violent indeed that the breath was knocked from him, and he emitted a grunt as he toppled off the support. As he disappeared,

Deerfoot, too, lost his balance, but he was so close to land, that he leaped clear of the water. Then, as if he thought the Pawnee might need his blanket and rifle, he picked them up and tossed them into the stream after him.

Incidents followed each other with a rush, and the report of two guns in quick succession reminded the youth that it would not do to linger any longer in the vicinity ; but assured now of the meaning of the signals which he had heard, he scanned the woods in front, as much as he did those in the rear. It was well he did so.

By calling into play his magnificent fleetness, he rapidly increased the distance between him and his enemies, but was scarcely able to pass beyond their sight, before, to his astonishment, he found he was confronted by two other warriors, coming from the opposite direction. They were doubtless on a hunt when signaled by the large party to intercept an enemy flee-ing from them.

It began to look to Deerfoot as though he had struck either a settlement of Pawnees, or a very large war party, for, beyond question, the "woods were full of them". To have continued straight on would have brought about an encounter with the two, and there was too much risk in that, though from what the reader learned long ago of Deerfoot, it is unnecessary to say that he would not have hesitated to make such a fight, had there been a call to do so.

Truth to tell, the red men were firing off their guns too rapidly to allow the fugitive to feel comfortable. Thus far, although he had swept his foes from his path, as may be said, he had refrained from slaying any one. He would not take life unless necessary, but he began to doubt whether he had acted wisely in showing mercy. Had he pierced two or three of his foes through and through, the others would not have been so enthusiastic in pursuing him across stream and through wood.

At any rate, he decided to be more resolute, and when necessary, drive a shaft "home".

The moment he observed the two Pawnees advancing from a point in front, he made another change in his course. This time it was to the right, and again he put forth a burst of speed the like of which his enemies had never seen. He passed in and out among the trees, and through the undergrowth, with such bewildering swiftness, that, though he was within gunshot, neither would risk firing, where it was more difficult to take aim than at the bird darting through the tree tops.

The last act of the fugitive had, as he believed, thrown all his pursuers well to the rear. When he made the turn, the two whom he last encountered tried to head him off by cutting across, as it may be called, but they relinquished the effort when they saw how useless it was.

Thus far, though Deerfoot had been placed in situations of great danger, he had managed to free himself without any effort that could be deemed unusual for him, though it would have been remarkable had it been performed by any one else. But now, when it began to look as if the worst were over, he was made aware that the most serious crisis of all had come.

At the moment when he began to lessen his speed, simply because the intervening limbs annoyed him, he made the discovery that still more of the Pawnees were in front. He caught the glimmer of their dress between the trees scarcely more than a hundred yards in advance, and, instead of one or two, there were at least five who were drawing near.

These were what may be called strangers, since they and Deerfoot now saw each other for the first time. Had they known the exact circumstances, they would have kept out of sight until the fugitive had run, as may be said, into their arms; but, like the rest, they were moving toward the camp, in obedience to the signals, keeping a lookout at the same time for the enemy that they knew was somewhere in the neighborhood. The reason they had not put in an earlier appearance was because they were further off than the rest.

At the moment Deerfoot observed them, he was not far off from the winding stream over which he had passed on the fallen tree. Like a flash, he turned about and ran with his own extraordinary fleetness, directly over his own trail.

It will be seen that the peril of this course reached almost a fatal degree, for the other

F

Pawnees could not be far off, and a very brief run would take him in full sight of them.

The last comers showed more vigor than the others. The glimpse they caught of the strange warrior dashing toward them, told the whole truth. The sight of a man running at full speed with a whooping mob a short distance behind, is all the evidence needed to prove he is a fugitive. Besides, when the Pawnees bore down on Deerfoot they knew far more of the neighborhood than he, and were sure he was entrapped.

The purpose of the Shawanoe was to put forth his utmost swiftness, hoping to place himself, if only for part of a minute, beyond sight of his enemies. Though he made the closest kind of calculation, circumstances were against him, and he not only failed to disappear from the last two, but, short as was the distance he doubled on his own trail, it took him into the field of vision of the parties whom he had eluded but a few minutes before. So it came about that he was in full view of a number of enemies, rapidly converging toward him, while a deep, swift stream was flowing across his line of flight.

The success of the pursuers now looked so certain that their leader emitted several whoops, a couple of which were meant as a command for none to fire : the Shawanoe was cornered and they meant to make him prisoner.

It need not be said that under the worst conditions the capture of the young warrior would have been no easy matter. He could fight like a tiger when driven into corner, and his great quickness availed him against superior strength. He had bounded out of more desperate situations than any person of double his years, and, knowing that no mercy was to be expected from the warlike Pawnees, it must have been a strange conjunction of disasters that could compel him to throw up his hands and yield.

Deerfoot had crossed one stream on his way to the Pawnee camp, and it was no task to swim one of double the width ; but the skillful swimmer can advance only at a slow rate through the water, and, before he could reach the other shore, a half dozen Pawnees would be on the bank in the rear, waiting for him to reappear. He was a master of the natatorial art, but he was not amphibious, and soon would have to come to the surface or die. The watchers would be quick to detect him, and their position was so much the superior of the fugitive that his capture was inevitable.

Suddenly Deerfoot seemed to see that there was but the one thing to do; turning again, he faced the stream which was but a few rods distant, and ran toward it. The undergrowth was abundant, but his head and shoulders were seen, as under the swift doublings of his limbs, they shot forward as if borne on the back of an invisible express engine.

The thrilling run lasted but a second or two; then, having reached the margin of the stream, the fugitive was seen to gather himself and rise like a bird on the wing. He had made a prodigious leap toward the other shore.

The Pawnees uttered several cries of exultation, for no doubt remained of their success. For one instant the figure was suspended in mid air, and then it descended. The pursuers heard the loud splash, and were on the spot before the most skillful swimmer could have taken three strokes or forced his body an arm's length through the water.

The leading Pawnee saw the ripples made in the swift current by the Shawanoe, whose body was out of sight, for he had not been given time in which to rise. As the current was too powerful to permit any one to swim against it (besides which such an expenditure of strength could gain nothing), it followed that the youth must either come up near the spot where he went down, or some distance below it.

The supposition would be that, helped by the momentum of his own body, Deerfoot would aim for the other shore. Fearful of attempting to climb the opposite bank with a half dozen standing just behind him with loaded guns, he would try to keep out of sight by thrusting just the point of his nose above the water, so as to gain a breath of the indispensable air.

But two facts rendered this impossible. In the first place, the water was remarkably clear, so that a body only a fractional part of the size of the youth, could not come within a foot of

the surface without being seen. Besides, the
vegetation on the other side did not overhang
the current (as it did in one or two instances
which perhaps my readers will recall), so nothing there could serve to screen such a movement. A third obstacle to such strategy may
be mentioned: the stream along shore was
shallow, while with the two conditions first
mentioned in his favor, water to permit the
most absolute freedom of movement was indispensable. Enough has been said, however, to
prove that the feat was beyond the reach even
of such a marvel as Deerfoot the Shawanoe.

The leader of the Pawnees repeated his warning against shooting the fugitive—that is,
against killing him. If there seemed to be
danger of his getting away, they were to fire so
as to disable without slaying him. It would be
an easy matter to bring him down without
endangering his life.

As if to shut out all hope for the Shawanoe,
three of the warriors who seemed to be wandering everywhere through the woods appeared
at this moment on the other shore. They were
given to understand the situation, and joined

the parties that waited for the reappearance of the youth, who seemed to have disported himself like a very demon since coming into that vicinity.

The Pawnees were so distributed along the bank that the very instant a swimmer should approach the surface from below, he would be observed by several spectators. And thus stood and waited the swarthy warriors for the sight which was never to come to them.

CHAPTER VIII

THE FLIGHT OF DEERFOOT.

NONE could know better the length of time it is possible for a person to live under water than did the Pawnees who lined the shore of the stream from which they awaited the young Shawanoe to rise and surrender himself.

At such times the seconds seem long, but in due time they grew into minutes, until one, two, three, four, and fully five had gone by, and still nothing was seen of the Shawanoe, who, they were assured, had leaped into the river. Before this, the warriors looked wonderingly at each other, unable to guess what it could all mean.

Had he bounded across the creek? Wide as it was, the possibility had been considered from the first, and, when the seconds were well along, the leader called to those on the other side to examine the margin for the imprints of the Indian's moccasins. Striking with such force, the dents would be in sight from across the stream. As it was easy to identify the spot where he made the leap, it was equally easy to determine the precise point where the telltale footprints should appear.

But the minute scrutiny of the edge of the creek proved that no moccasin had touched it. And that being the case, the question came back as to what had become of the fugitive.

"The dog of a Shawanoe is at the bottom," was the natural remark of the leader. "He has gone down, and the Great Spirit is so angry with him that he will not permit him to rise."

That was a curious explanation of the occurrence, but it appeared to be about the only one left to the pursuers, who were not fully satisfied even with that. We are aware that a person who springs into the water, even if he can not swim a stroke, is pretty sure to come up once or twice. The Pawnees knew of a verity that the Shawanoe must be an excellent swimmer, and it certainly was inexplainable if he did not reappear.

"Did he leave the shore?" asked one of those who had approached from the side toward which Deerfoot had sped.

" We saw him run for it as runs the deer," was the reply.

"But the Shawanoe is like the weasel; he may have turned aside and sped up or down the stream, with his head bent so low that he could not be seen."

" The eyes of Wimmoroo were open," said the leader, who, in spite of his assurance, began to feel suspicious that some trick had been played upon them, though, as yet, he could not define its nature.

" What did the eyes of Wimmoroo tell him?" asked the other, showing a Yankee-like persistency in his questions.

"They showed him the dog of a Shawanoe, as he bounded high in air and strove to reach the other shore."

" Can Wimmoroo make sure the Shawanoe did not leap in the air and then place his feet on the ground where they were before?"

Could it be possible that such a strategy had been used? He began an examination, two of his warriors helping him. There were the footprints of the delicate moccasins in plain sight, showing where he had leaped clear from the ground, but not the faintest impression was visible either to the right or left of the spot. Inasmuch as the fugitive could not have fled in either direction without leaving a trail, and the closest search failed to show any thing of the kind, the conclusion was inevitable that no such flight had taken place.

Besides—how came Wimmoroo to forget it?—all caught the splash of the body as it dropped in the water. As might be expected witnesses were not wanting to declare they had seen the spray fly upward, and had caught sight of the eagle feathers in the crown of Deerfoot as he swam for the other side.

All which being so, the question came back again—where could Deerfoot be?

It is not often that a group of red men are so at their wit's end as were the Pawnees. They stood looking about them, silent and bewildered. Wimmoroo took a sly glance at the tree tops as though he half expected to see the missing Shawanoe perched in the branches.

But among those red men was one at least with quick intelligence. He was the last to approach the stream from the side toward which Deerfoot leaped. He had not yet spoken, but when told the facts, he glanced here and there, so as to take in all the points, and it was not long before a suspicion of the truth dawned upon him.

Several facts, which were patent to the others, took connection in his mind. Let me name one or two—Deerfoot possessed a fleetness which no Pawnee could equal ; he was seen to run toward the stream with the utmost speed of which he was capable ; he was observed to make the jump, and the creek itself was a little more than twenty feet in width. The conclusion, therefore, was certain—he had bounded across.

The leap, while a great one, was not beyond the attainment of the Pawnee himself, who was studying the question. He was sure that with a running start he could clear the water, though he could do no more. Still there were no footprints on the margin that could have been made by the fugitive ; but, recalling the prodigious activity of the fugitive, the Pawnee scrutinized the ground further back. He had done so only a half minute when he discovered the truth. Making it known to the others, they refused for a minute or two to believe him, but the proof was before their eyes and they disputed no longer.

The young Shawanoe, finding that his only escape from the Pawnees, who seemed to spring from the ground all around him, was by placing himself on the other side the creek, turned and made for it, as I have already told, with all the speed he possessed. The stream was of a width varying from twenty to forty feet or more. Where he had crossed it before, it was too wide for him to think of leaping. In fact, his hasty search along shore failed to show a spot across which he could jump, and he did not expect to do so in the present instance.

But the extremity of good fortune attended the fleet-footed Deerfoot, who struck one of the narrowest portions. He anticipated falling into the water, quite close to the other side, whence he meant to crawl hastily out and continue his flight. Gathering his muscles, he made one of the most terrific efforts of his life, and, rising in air, described a parabola, which carried him fully six feet past the water, striking the ground beyond a clump of bushes. There, as I have said, when the search was made, his footprints were seen too plainly to leave any doubt as to the exploit he had performed.

At the instant of alighting, he whirled around, stepped close to the water, and struck it a sharp blow with his long bow. It was his quickness of resource which led him to do this without a second's delay. Well aware of the great leap he had made, he caused the splash, so as to lead his pursuers to think he had dropped into the current. It has been shown how he succeeded.

Crouching low, so as to keep his body hidden so far as it was possible to do so, he ran along the stream, sometimes almost on his hands and knees, until a point was reached where he was able to straighten up without detection. His keen vision showed him the Pawnees advancing from the side on which he had taken refuge, but he easily avoided discovery, and had not far to go, when he felt that all danger was over.

It will be admitted that, from the moment when he entered the Pawnee camp and fell into a dispute with Lone Bear, he had been given little time to rest. It may be said that the sweep of incident kept him on the jump, from the opening to the close. He was given no time to think of Hay-uta nor of Jack Carleton, from whom he was separated by still another stream of water, across which he was forced to swim, in order to reach the war party. He had done his utmost to gather some information respecting Otto Relstaub, for whom the three were searching, but had not picked up the first grain of knowledge. Lone Bear, who could have told him one or two surprising facts respecting the young German lad, sought to mislead him. What his reason was for such a course was beyond the power of Deerfoot to guess.

It can not be said that the Shawanoe felt any misgivings as to the situation of the two who had come with him. The Sauk was skillful, and would be quick to learn the peril in which the young warrior had become involved. Such knowledge would enable him to guard against similar slips himself.

Convinced that at last he had shaken off his enemies, Deerfoot resumed his moderate pace, ' while he debated with himself the best course to pursue.

He was back again on the side of the stream where he had first seen the Pawnees encamped, and doubtless a number of them were scattered at different points through the wood. There must have been twenty of them in the neighborhood, for, when summoned by signal, they appeared to come from all points of the compass. But none now was in sight, and who of them all was able to outwit the Shawanoe in woodcraft and cunning?

The clothing which had been saturated by his plunge into the larger stream was nearly dry, and an examination showed he had suffered no damage in person or property. More than one bullet had been fired at him, but not a hair of his head was harmed. The stained eagle feathers still projected from his crown ; the quiver of arrows rested behind his right shoulder ; the string of his bow was free from moisture ; the red sash around his waist, the fringes of his hunting shirt, his leggings, his moccasins and even the double string of beads around his neck and the golden bracelet which clasped one wrist, showed no evidence of the ordeal through which their owner had so recently passed. Knife, tomahawk and bow were as ready as ever for any emergency which might call for them.

Deerfoot reflected that, so far as he was con-cerned, the result of his enterprise was a failure—in truth, it was worse than a failure, for, having learned nothing of the fate of Otto, he had put the Pawnees on their guard against giving such information. Lone Bear showed an unwillingness to tell any thing, and now it was to be expected that he and his compan-ions would take care to thwart the wishes of the Shawanoe and what friends he might have.

The young warrior asked himself whether he must recross the stream and join Jack Carleton with the confession that he had not been able to learn any thing about Otto, and that he saw

G

no chance of doing so. He was loth to make such acknowledgment, and he determined not to do so, until after making at least one more attempt to force the truth from some member of the war party.

The afternoon was well advanced when he appeared in the camp of the hostiles, and it would seem that the incidents which took place ought to have carried him close to nightfall. But I must repeat that on account of their hurricane-like rush, they took a small amount of time, and now, when he found himself free of his pursuers, the sun was yet a couple of hours above the horizon. Enough daylight remained for him to do a large amount of work, always provided the work presented itself to be done.

He decided to take another survey of the camp before returning, in the hope that possibly some "material" for labor awaited him. A quick survey of his surroundings caused him to locate himself. The camp was not far off, and he began making his way toward it.

In doing so he did not steal forward with the slow caution which his race generally show when approaching an enemy, but he advanced briskly among the trees, though his motion was as noiseless as that of the shadow of the cloud overhead.

CHAPTER IX

A MONG all the chagrined Pawnees, there was none so humiliated as Lone Bear, who had been thrown headlong by the trick of the young Shawanoe dropping in front of him. That was bad enough, but it was made a hundred-fold worse when Deerfoot stepped on the crown of his head before he could rise, or prevent it. It was Red Wolf who cruelly remarked that the reason for the youth taking that step was that he might have a *soft place* whereon to rest his moccasin.

Instead of replying to the chaffings of his two companions, Lone Bear sat on a pile of fagots in the deserted camp, and smoked his pipe in silence.

Red Wolf and the other Pawnee sat near, but neither lighted his pipe. They had done all they cared to do in the way of tantalizing their comrade, who had spent a part of his early boyhood among the Shawanoes on the other side of the Mississippi. They saw he was in an ugly mood, and would be likely to fight if provoked further. Though they did not hold him in fear, they did not seek a quarrel. Besides, too, they saw the serious side to the business : Deerfoot had already proved that he was a remarkable warrior, for, amid the shooting and firing of guns, which came from the forest beyond, there was heard no signal which told that the daring youth had been shot or captured. The moment such a result should take place, it would be made known by the exultation whoop from the one fortunate enough to bring it about.

The question which presented itself to Red Wolf and his companion was, whether it was probable the wonderful Deerfoot was alone. The Pawnees were returning from a long excursion eastward, which had led them across and into new hunting grounds, where their presence was sure to arouse enmity whenever discovered. On that journey toward the Mississippi, the Pawnees had come in collision with other parties of red men ; guns had been fired and one or two scalps taken, including one lost. In addition, the invaders had destroyed much game, so that abundant ground for complaint rested with the strangers. What more probable than that some of those aggrieved tribes had determined on a retaliatory policy, by sending a strong party to chastise the Pawnees ?

Before Red Wolf could start a discussion on this question, the one at his side became so interested in what was going on deeper in the woods that he sprang to his feet and was off like a shot. This left Red Wolf and Lone Bear alone, and the former felt much less disposition to pick a quarrel than before.

"Are not the hunting grounds of the Shawanoes beyond the Great River?" asked Red Wolf.

Lone Bear glared at him, as if doubting the sincerity of the question, but, satisfied a moment later that the inquirer was in quest of truth, he shook off his surliness and answered :

"Two suns' travel beyond the Great River

lie the hunting grounds of the Shawanoes and Wyandots."

" The Shawanoes are brave warriors?"

"Only the Pawnees excel them," was the reply of Lone Bear, who in those words uttered the greatest compliment possible to the warlike tribe which did more than any other to give Kentucky its baptismal name of the Dark and Bloody Ground.

" Why is the Shawanoe whom you call Deerfoot journeying toward the hunting grounds of the Pawnees?"

This was a pertinent question, which Lone Bear would have been glad to have some one answer for him, but which, as might be expected, he sought to solve without hesitation.

" He has come to look upon the woods and streams and prairies so favored by the Great Spirit, where the bravest warriors, the Pawnees, are born, and from which they drive all strangers."

Had Red Wolf chosen, he might have reminded the speaker of the bad taste of this remark, when he had been so recently overthrown and disgraced by one of the tribe which he placed lower in rank than his own ; but Red Wolf was disposed to take a more practical view of matters, and it was natural he should go to the Pawnee who had once lived among the Shawanoes.

"We saw only one Shawanoe, but there may be more hiding among the trees, and waiting to fire at the Pawnees when they have their eyes closed in slumber."

"Red Wolf has seen no Shawanoe!" exclaimed the other, wrathfully. "There has been none here."

"Why does Lone Bear speak in riddles? What is the totem of the young warrior called Deerfoot?"

"He *was* a Shawanoe ; his father was Allo-maung the great chief ; but Deerfoot became a pale-face ; he listened to the prating of the missionaries, and turned away from the wigwams of his people ; he has not consorted with the Shawanoes for years ; they would give a hundred scalps if they could tear his from his crown. If the warriors of the Shawanoes were in the woods," added Lone Bear, with a sweep

of his right arm, "Deerfoot would not be here,
for he is a dog that runs when he hears the call
of his masters."

None could be more aware of the falsity of
this than Lone Bear, who, though he left the
tribe before Deerfoot did, had heard of his
exploits since then, and knew him to be one of
the bravest youths that ever lived. And,
again, he lost sight of his recent experience
with him.

But when he reminded Red Wolf that the
Shawanoe dwelt beyond the Great River,
whither the Pawnees had not penetrated, and
that Deerfoot had made known that his errand
was to look for the captive pale-face, all fear
of his being in the company of a war party was
removed.

However, no matter what explanation was
given, it brought forward other questions which
could not be explained away. One of these
was the natural one, that, if the Pawnees had
happened to have the German lad in their
custody, by what means did he hope to recover
him? He brought with him nothing in the
shape of a ransom, so far as could be seen, and

it was hard to imagine what other method he expected to employ.

When Otto was bought of the Sauks, a pretty fair price was paid for him, and it was not to be expected that his purchasers would discount that compensation. The conclusion that the daring Shawanoe relied upon other means, which were not apparent, gave a vague misgiving to Lone Bear and Red Wolf, as they sat near the camp-fire talking over the stirring incidents of the last half hour.

Now and then they ceased and listened to the sounds which came from the forest, wherein the efforts were pushed to make prisoner the young Shawanoe, who was dodging hither and thither as if running a gauntlet. The temptation was strong to mingle in the general melee, as it may be called, but the treatment Lone Bear had received at the hands of the Shawanoe filled him with a fear that he had never known before, for there was a tinge of superstition in it, as appeared in the next remark he made.

" Deerfoot calls himself a Shawanoe; he was born with the people, but when he left them he became an Evil Spirit."

This was Lone Bear's method of saying that the devil bore an active part in the exploits of the youth, an opinion which was shared by Red Wolf.

"The Evil One is his friend : if he was not, he would have fallen by the bullets that were aimed at him. Lone Bear would have slain the greatest warrior, when he was running before him as Deerfoot ran, but he could not slay Deerfoot, because the Evil One was his friend."

This was the kind of remark to please Lone Bear, for it implied that the best possible reason existed for his failure ; his enemy was of the supernatural class, and, therefore, beyond the power of any human being to overcome.

Lone Bear turned his head toward the woods, while he held his lips closed over his pipe-stem. The sharp report of a rifle had reached their ears, and the two Pawnees listened for a minute without moving or speaking. Deerfoot just then was doing wonders in the way of dodging and running, and the warriors sitting by the camp-fire could almost read the narrative, as you have done from these printed pages.

Red Wolf leaned forward and lighted his pipe from the glowing coals, and then seated himself a little closer than before to his companion. They were at the end of the fire, as may be said, and so near each other that when they talked and gesticulated their heads almost touched.

"They will not harm the Shawanoe," was the truthful remark of Lone Bear, though in his heart he hoped they would bring his reeking scalp into camp. "The Evil One runs at his side, and when the bullet is aimed by the brave Pawnees, he catches it in his hand and holds it that it may not harm the Shawanoe."

This was an ingenious explanation, for it helped to release the warrior from a questionable situation. Red Wolf, who was sitting cross-legged, like a tailor, sent an enormous puff of smoke over his shoulder, and nodded several times with much vigor, to signify that he indorsed the sentiments of his comrade.

"He can not be harmed until the Good Spirit shall drive the Evil One away; then the bullet of Lone Bear and the tomahawk of Red Wolf and the knives of the Pawnees shall reach him.

He shall then die as dies the rattlesnake coiled in our path."

At intervals the two ceased speaking, and, looking toward the wood, listened, but an interval of silence followed. Both began to hope that in spite of the armor they had thrown around the Shawanoe, he had been brought down by some of the Pawnees, who were making such efforts to destroy him.

It will be remembered that the wood from which Deerfoot had caught sight of the Pawnee war party came down to the edge of the broad stream over which he swam in order to reach them. On their side, the growth of the forest ceased some rods away from the water, so that for a considerable distance, a broad band of open land lined the river. In this cleared space the camp-fire of the Pawnees was burning, and they were grouped around it, with nearly as many warriors at varying distances in the wilderness beyond. When they looked, it was toward the nearest trees, from which they expected almost every moment to see some of their comrades emerge, escorting the prisoner.

Red Wolf seemed to glow with anger,

because the Shawanoe persisted in keeping out
of the hands of the Pawnees, who, it may be
said, surrounded him.   Removing his long-
stemmed pipe from between his teeth, he held
it poised in his left hand, while he gesticulated
with his right.

"Who are the bravest warriors that hunt
through the wilderness and over the prairies?"
he asked, launching out in that vain-glorious
boasting, so characteristic of his race: "who
drove all other red men before them? Whose
war-whoop makes the pale-faces run to their
cabins and hold their doors closed? Whose
shouts cause their enemies to tremble and call
on the Great Spirit to protect them? Who is
it that sweeps—"

A splintering crash broke in upon this series
of questions, and the bowl of Red Wolf's pipe
was shattered into a hundred fragments, the
atoms flying into the faces of the startled
Pawnees, who, accustomed to surprises, leaped
to their feet and glanced right and left to learn
the cause of the astounding occurrence.

At that instant something like the flitting of
a bird's wing twinkled in front of their eyes,

and the quick "chuck" which followed showed them an Indian arrow with its head buried in the ground fifty feet beyond, and the feathered point still a-tremble from the force with which it had been driven from the bow.

Like a flash they looked toward the opposite point, and that which met their gaze was perhaps the most alarming sight they had ever seen. Scarcely a hundred feet away, on the edge of the wood, stood Deerfoot the Shawanoe. He had already launched two arrows, and, when they caught sight of him, he was standing with a third drawn to the head, and apparently in the very act of letting fly at one of the terrified warriors.

The American Indian as a rule is not powerful, and his muscular development is moderate ; but his life accustoms him to quickness of movement, and he generally excels in running and leaping. Any one looking upon Lone Bear and Red Wolf at that moment would have set them down as the champions of their tribe. When they identified the archer and saw that he was on the point of discharging another missile, they made a break for shelter.

Red Wolf headed for the river, possibly because he didn't dare to lose the time it would take to turn partly on his feet. He ran as if he meant to make the effort to leap entirely across, or at least to outrun the arrow which he believed was chasing him.

He hadn't far to go, and it didn't take him long to travel it. A bound, a splash, and he vanished.

Lone Bear knew he was closer to the wood than to the water, and he was equally determined to attain shelter. In his tremendous effort, he seemed to think he could dodge the shafts that were whizzing through the air in quick succession after him. He bent his head so that he was crouching half way to the ground, and leaped from side to side, ducked and dodged and contorted himself in an indescribable fashion. When he bounded among the trees, he must have felt he had made the escape of his life.

But the third arrow did not leave the bow. Deerfoot had not sought to harm either of the Pawnees, but in obedience to that disposition to humor which he sometimes displayed, he took pains to fire as close as he could without hitting them. When he saw their dismay, he shook from head to foot with silent laughter.

But his mirth was brief. A slight noise caused him to turn his head. There stood two other Indians directly behind him, one with his gun levelled directly at his heart.

II

CHAPTER X.

WHEN Hay-uta, the ally of Deerfoot, parted with him so that the reconnoissance of the Pawnee camp could be made separately, he went down stream—that is, in the direction opposite to that taken by Deerfoot. He moved faster than the Shawanoe, and emerged from the river at the moment the other entered it.

Before this, he had taken another scrutiny of the two warriors, whom he had pointed out as members of the party that bought Otto Relstaub from the Sauks. He thought it unlikely that a mistake could have been made, and the second inspection proved he was right beyond all doubt.

Without any reason for such belief, Hay-uta concluded there were other Pawnees in the

vicinity. The appearance of the camp suggested in some way that several were missing.
He therefore conducted his movements as
though danger threatened him from all points.

Hay-uta was daring and skillful. He had
been engaged on more than one similar enterprise, with the difference that the camps where
he reconnoitered previously were those of bitter
enemies. Having met the Pawnees before, on
what may be considered neutral if not friendly
ground, he would have felt no great misgivings
while marching into their camp, without any
effort at concealment.

But, if discovered prowling through the
woods, the case would be different. It would
be hard to offer any explanation, and, therefore, it was the more necessary to avoid detection while thus employed.

The Sauk was as much puzzled as Deerfoot to
guess what had become of Otto. Two of the
warriors, if not all of them, were able to tell,
but Hay-uta could not expect to draw the information from them. Perhaps Deerfoot might
do so.

There was good ground to fear the poor lad

had been put out of the way forever, but the
Sauk was still more convinced that he was not
only alive and well, but was at no great distance from the camp of the Pawnees.

Instead of going directly toward the latter,
as did Deerfoot, the Sauk started out on what
may be described as a large circle, inclosing the
war party near the river. His action was based
on the somewhat curious theory that the
Pawnees which he had seen did not compose
the main body that would be found grouped
somewhere within the woods. It may as well
be said that he was mistaken in this supposition, though the reader has learned that a number of Indians were scattered at different
points, and it was their rapid convergence
which kept Deerfoot on the move.

Hay-uta had not gone far on the edge of the
semi-circle, when the shouts and sounds of firearms from that direction of the camp left no
doubt that trouble had broken out there.
Desirous of learning what it meant, he moved
toward the point, but before he went near
enough to discover any thing, he detected one
of the Pawnees doing the same thing.

The warrior was just far enough in advance for Hay-uta to catch a glimpse of his figure as it twinkled among the trees. He was going on a long, loping trot, which, if not very rapid, was sufficiently so to carry him beyond sight within a few seconds after the Sauk observed him.

The unexpected turn which events had taken led Hay-uta to stop and question himself as to the right course to follow. His intelligence told him that Deerfoot was fleeing through the woods, with an indefinite number of enemies in pursuit. The Sauk grimly smiled.

"The Pawnees will overtake the young Shawanoe when they outrun the eagle as he flies among the clouds. The arrow of his own bow is scarce faster than he."

The confidence of Hay-uta in the prowess of Deerfoot was warranted, as we can not help agreeing, but suspecting the truth, as the Sauk did, we can hardly understand how he believed he would succeed in extricating himself.

Making sure that no one was in the vicinity the Sauk stood for perhaps fifteen minutes, while he listened closely to the sounds which came from different points in the wood. He was able to form a pretty fair idea of what it all meant, though of necessity much was left to conjecture.

It was the training of Hay-uta, from his earliest youth, which led him to keep his glances flitting here and there in all directions, while using his ears to determine what was going on. Had he not done so, he would have failed to note a suspicious proceeding on his right.

Although looking toward a different point just then, he detected something which led him to believe that one of the strange warriors was trying to steal close to him. It seemed as if a Pawnee, having discovered the Sauk, was trying to get close enough to make the aim of his gun sure.

The first glance toward that point convinced Hay-uta that his enemy was making for the trunk of a tree, less than a hundred yards distant. Its diameter was so great that it would have sheltered two persons at the same time, and it exceeded to such an extent all the others near it, that it was natural for one to seek its protection.

The Sauk was sure that the warrior was several rods beyond this tree, toward which he was stealing, while striving to keep the trunk between him and Hay-uta. So long, therefore, as the Sauk remained motionless, the Pawnee would be protected, though there were other trees of less size behind which he could escape should it become necessary.

It is not to be supposed that the Sauk was stupid enough to stand like a wooden Indian, and allow his enemy every advantage he sought. There were plenty of trunks, also, which he could use as a screen while engaged in a characteristic duel with the other Indian; but, instead of doing so, he began striding off toward the right, keeping his gaze fixed on the larger trunk, and holding his rifle at full cock, so that it could be aimed and fired on an instant's call. At the same time, he swung his right arm about his head, and then struck the left hand over his heart. This was the sign of comity, and the moment it should catch the eye of the Pawnee, he would be sure to recognize it as such, though whether he would accept it remained to be seen.

The action of the Sauk was so prompt, and apparently so unexpected, that the crouching savage was caught unawares. He was uncovered with great cleverness, and indeed Hay-uta could have "winged" him had he chosen to do so. It was not from lack of inclination that he held his fire, but because prudence demanded it. As it was, he was confident of his ability to anticipate any hostile movement on the part of the other.

Flanked in this fashion, the Pawnee was equally prompt in reciprocating the gestures of good-will which greeted him. While in the act of straightening up, he imitated the salutations which, though somewhat different from those to which he was accustomed, were too plain in their meaning to be mistaken.

When two strangers open negotiations by declaring themselves friends, it is natural they should advance and shake hands (provided that manner of salutation is in vogue), and such was the next proceeding of the red men.

"The heart of Hay-uta bounds with joy when he looks upon the face of his brave brother of the unknown totem," said the Sauk.

" The Flying Deer, of the Pawnees, would weep till the Great Spirit in sorrow for him called him home, had he been made to wait for this brave warrior, who has journeyed so many suns that he may look upon his face," was the substantial response of the Pawnee.

All this was very fine, but one drawback remained—neither Indian understood a single syllable uttered by the other, but the beaming expressions scarcely needed literal interpreta- tion. Truth makes it necessary to add that, with all this effusiveness, the warriors distrusted each other.

Now began a conversation by means of signs, which it would be tedious to give in full. For- tunately for Hay-uta, he was so far removed from the scene of action in which Deerfoot and the others were playing such an active part, that he was quite secure against interruption, unless the fleeing Shawanoe should happen to take a turn in his flight which might bring the swarming pursuers in that direction.

It was impossible for Hay-uta to know the

real sentiments of the other, but, as a matter
of precaution, he sought to draw him further
away from the theater of action. The Pawnee
must have understood, from the signals which
had reached him, that an enemy was making a
great stir, and that his own presence was
desired.

Furthermore, as the Sauk was a stranger,
the natural supposition would be that he was
an ally of the enemy. This could not fail
to cause suspicion, but, having just vowed
eternal friendship, policy required him to conceal his real sentiments.

On the invitation of the Sauk, the other
accompanied him a few rods, during which
they conversed as well as they could in panto-
mime. While they managed to communicate
a great deal, yet the limit was speedily reached.
When Hay-uta tried to ask after the missing
Otto, the other did not comprehend him, or,
if he did, failed to make his sentences clear. In
that respect, therefore, the mission of the Sauk
was as barren of results as was that of Deerfoot.

The Pawnee had not gone far, when he

seemed to awake to the fact that he was doing an imprudent thing. He came to a halt and showed by his manner that he would go no further. Hay-uta could not urge him, and the two, therefore, stood face to face in the depth of the forest, while they talked to each other.

The Sauk asked himself more than once whether, in a hand to hand fight with the other, the struggle being fair on each side, he could vanquish him. The Pawnee was tall, well-formed, athletic, and the knife thrust in the skin-sheath at his girdle looked as if it was longer and keener than the one Hay-uta carried, without sheath at all. The Pawnee was certain to be a formidable antagonist in such a contest, but the Sauk would not have hesitated to assail him, except through fear that others would be brought to the spot.

No doubt the Pawnee took the measure of the stranger in the same manner, and it is reasonable to conclude that he felt no special fear of him. In fact, the two were like a couple of bull dogs, ready to fly at each other's throat, without once thinking of what the issue was likely to be.

But while they were holding their conversation, the Sauk carried out a singular thought. He asked himself whether he could not make a friend of the stranger—that is to say, a genuine friend, who would be held to him by gratitude.

As to the method by which this was to be attained, even the ingenious mind of the warrior was unable to determine. All he could do was to seek to keep him company until some way should be open. The coming of any of the Pawnees, who were trooping at the heels of the Shawanoe, would be liable to scatter all such plans to the wind.

The diplomats were doing their best to entertain each other, when a most unlooked-for interference took place.

From where they stood, they were able to locate the clearing by means of a thinness of the trees, a few more rays of daylight penetrating from that direction. Hay-uta happened to be looking toward that point, when he caught the outline of a figure stealing along the margin of the opening.

The sight was so unexpected that the manner

of the Sauk betrayed the discovery, the instance being one of those rare ones in which he was caught off his guard. He reproached himself, for the back of his companion was turned toward the other, who was moving as silently as the shadow over the face of a sun-dial.

The head of the Pawnee turned quickly, and he muttered a soft "—st!" At the same moment he began moving toward the other, with the absolute silence that the trained Indian shows when creeping into a hostile camp, where the rustling of a leaf brings discovery.

Hay-uta could not but admire the skill of the Indian. At the same time, the action of the Pawnee in moving away from the Sauk, while his eyes were turned from him, thus placing himself at the mercy of Hay-uta, was an appeal to the honor of the latter, which, of itself, was the strongest safeguard of the Pawnee.

Hay-uta fell in behind him, and the two advanced in their stealthy fashion among the trees for some twenty steps, when they gained full view of the third Indian, whose course was rather peculiar. He had stepped from the woods into the clearing, and was standing facing the other way, with his attention fixed on something too far off to be seen by the couple that were watching him.

Hay-uta was astounded almost into betraying himself again when he saw that the Indian was Deerfoot the Shawanoe. He was watching the two Pawnees near the camp-fire, and was in the act of discharging the first arrow which broke the pipe of Red Wolf and threw him and Lone Bear into such consternation.

It may have been because the youth carried a bow and arrow, instead of firearms, that the Pawnee thought he was a wanderer from beyond the Rocky Mountains, who had drifted into that section and was now making his way home. Certainly he could have had no suspicion of the prowess of the Shawanoe, nor could he have dreamed that he had been the sole cause of the hubbub that had reigned among the Pawnees, and even then was hardly ended. He appeared to believe, however, that he was one of a party who were their enemies, for he signed to Hay-uta that he meant that the stranger should not escape him.

CHAPTER XI.

THE situation was most peculiar for all three concerned. Despite the vigilance and woodcraft of Deerfoot the Shawanoe, he had allowed an enemy to creep up behind him and secure an advantage which could not be overcome. In the common parlance of the West, the Pawnee had the drop on the Shawanoe.

But Hay-uta the Sauk was too deeply attached to the matchless young warrior to permit harm to befall him. He learned from his companion that it was not his purpose to shoot Deerfoot, but simply to keep him covered with his gun until he surrendered. Hay-uta decided to permit this, because he believed no harm to his friend could result, and he saw the possibility of showing a chivalry toward the Pawnee which might win his friendship.

Having made sure the warrior did not mean to fire, Hay-uta kept a few paces in the background, while the two noiselessly advanced a half-dozen steps or more. It would have been the easiest thing in the world for the Sauk to apprise Deerfoot of his danger! a slight rustling of the leaves was all that was wanted. But it was not done, for, as I have said, Hay-uta was convinced that no immediate danger threatened his friend.

Sauk and Pawnee stood motionless until Deerfoot was seen to be shaking with silent laughter. The sight of the two warriors running for life from the camp-fire in the open space, satisfied the Pawnee that the youth had done his best to kill them, and was amused to see their fright at the moment when they were not in the slightest peril.

The Pawnee now purposely rustled the leaves with his moccasin. The Shawanoe faced about like a flash. As he did so, Hay-uta, standing just back of the captor, made a gesture to his friend. Deerfoot " caught on ", and dropped his hands to his side, to signify his surrender. He divined the situation, and, schooled as he was in self-control, it was hard for him to restrain a smile over the thought of the trick played on the Pawnee. Probably no man was ever "fooled" to a more astounding extent than he was at that moment.

The only thing feared by Deerfoot was that some of the other Pawnees would soon reach the spot and complicate matters, but, while the apparent conqueror was sanguine that he commanded the situation, Deerfoot knew he was master from the first.

Looking straight at the Pawnee, he slowly said :

"My brother the Sauk is wise ; his companion is a Pawnee ; let no harm befall him, for he has done no harm to us ; but other Pawnees may soon be here ; let Hay-uta point his rifle at the Pawnee so that he will turn his gun away from Deerfoot."

While speaking the Shawanoe kept his eyes fixed on those of the Pawnee, who, of course, supposed the words were addressed to him. He could not catch their meaning, but no doubt believed they referred to the completeness of the surrender just made. Had he been

I

an aboriginal linguist, how different would have been his feelings!

Having dropped his hands, and spoken his sentences, Deerfoot waited the action of Hay-uta.

The latter still held the hammer of his rifle at full cock, and he instantly leveled it at the Pawnee, harshly ordering him to lower his weapon.

The Pawnee was surprised. I am aware that this is stating it mildly, but so would it be if I used the strongest words at command. He seemed transfixed, and actually was unable to stir or even to lower his gun. But the action of his companion told the truth, and it must be believed that he was filled with biting chagrin because he was not acute enough to know that the aliens (one of whom seemed to come from the east and the other from the west) were allies.

However, the tables were turned and no choice was left him. Down came his gun, the hammer was lowered and the stock dropped spitefully to the ground. It was the Shawanoe and Sauk who now "had the drop" on the Pawnee.

By way of putting matters in a business-like shape, Deerfoot called to Hay-uta to keep his gun at a level, while he disarmed the prisoner. The Sauk obeyed, and Deerfoot walked quietly forward, and in the most matter-of-fact manner drew the knife of the Pawnee from its sheath at his girdle, extracted his tomahawk, and then gently removed the rifle from his nerveless grasp. Distributing the first two weapons about his person, the Shawanoe stepped back several paces, holding his bow in one hand and the gun in the other.

Supposing Hay-uta had not been present, what would have been the result?

I haven't a particle of doubt that the Pawnee would have been vanquished by Deerfoot. The former could not have stood forever with his gun aimed, and when he lowered it he would have presented an "opening" of which the Shawanoe would have availed himself with the quickness of the lighting stroke.

While Deerfoot was disarming the sinewy warrior, Hay-uta explained his wish to show him such consideration as to win his friendship. That being done, probably some way would open by which he could be used in tracing Otto Relstaub.

" My brother is wise," commented Deerfoot, who admired the cleverness of the Sauk, " but let him beware that the Pawnee does not betray him."

No one would have supposed from the deliberation of the Shawanoe that he was in fear of any thing, but, if it can be said that he was ever nervous over any thing, such was his condition now, through fear of irruption by a part or all of the Pawnee war-party. He felt that the danger increased every moment.

No time, therefore, was lost. The Pawnee was directed to move on, the course taken being directly away from the camp-fire, and close to the open space between the woods and river. No fault could be found with the promptness displayed by the captive, who strode off as though on his way to a marriage feast.

It was not necessary to keep a close watch over the prisoner, since the most he could do was to try to run away, and he was not likely to attempt that when two loaded guns almost touched him.

But the Pawnee did do something, which, under the circumstances, was a daring act.

The procession had proceeded for a hundred feet or so, when he gave utterance to a ringing whoop, which could have been heard a half mile. Deerfoot was astounded, and half raised the gun with the intention of shooting him, but he changed his mind before the weapon reached his shoulder.

But never did the Shawanoe display quicker readiness of resource than then. The Pawnee acted as though he believed his life would pay for what he had done, for, being a barbarian, he must have felt from the first that no mercy awaited him. Wheeling around, he folded his arms, straightened up and looked defiantly at the Shawanoe, saying plainly by his actions:

"I am ready; look and see a warrior die!"

But Deerfoot did a much wiser thing. Convinced that the whoop was a summons for help, he managed to impress the Pawnee with the fact, that the only way to save his life was to send a second signal, the import of which would be that he was in no need of help and had no news to give, but would be glad to receive any tidings his friends possessed.

It required some vigorous sign language on the part of Deerfoot to bring the Pawnee to his views. One of the most convincing arguments, however, was the thunder-cloud on the face of the Shawanoe, and the upraised tomahawk, poised and ready to be buried in the skull of the captive.

And so the desired message was sent from the throat of the frightened Pawnee. Deerfoot could not be certain that the cry conveyed the meaning he desired, but he noticed that the modulation of the voice was different and he was almost satisfied on the point.

As a matter of precaution, he now fell to the rear, directing Hay-uta to take care of the captive. He was at liberty to shoot him if he made a break for freedom, and there was little doubt that Hay-uta would do so.

As for the Shawanoe, he meant to keep watch for the other Pawnees, who were now all behind them. Even if their prisoner had countermanded his call for help, little time could elapse before Lone Bear and Red Wolf would make known how recently they had seen the dusky demon. Of course they would suppress the part they had played in the proceeding, but would be likely to send a large party after the Shawanoe, as soon as it could be brought together.

Deerfoot, therefore, dropped a hundred feet to the rear, still carrying the captured gun and his bow, and half disposed to make a compulsory trade with the Pawnee. He could hardly convince himself, however, that such a proceeding would be pleasing to the Great Spirit, and he put the temptation behind him.

He was on the lookout for the warriors who had shown themselves so plentiful only a short time before. His purpose was to apprise Hayuta the moment they appeared, when without a second's delay, the two would dash off, leaving their prisoner to return to his friends. In the event of such an issue, as it would be impossible to make a friend of their captive, the Sauk favored sending a bullet through him before parting ; but Deerfoot was so emphatic in protesting against such savagery, that Hayuta promised to obey him.

Succeeding events left no doubt that the prisoner did precisely as ordered by his captor; that is to say, he recalled his first signal and notified his comrades that he had no need of their presence.

When, some minutes later, several of the Pawnees straggled back to camp, they found Red Wolf and Lone Bear awaiting them. The former looked as if he had been put to soak for several days in the river, while Lone Bear was weak from the fright he had received. He did not blush, when he made the statement that the young demon had appeared but a few minutes before on the margin of the wood, accompanied by seven warriors, and that they instantly opened by launching arrow after arrow in the direction of the Pawnees.

Red Wolf said that he hastened to the river bank with a view of securing a spot from which to reconnoitre their enemies, but he caught his foot in a root and fell into the water; that accounted for his moist condition.

The warrior had hardly reached that point in his narrative, when he perceived that he had gone too far. Indian scouts, when stealing along the banks of a stream, are not apt to roll into it and under the surface, either accidentally or for the fun of the thing. The Pawnee, therefore, told the truth, except that he joined Lone Bear in declaring that their foe was accompanied by seven others, who seemed as eager as he to slay them.

It would seem that the fact that none of the other Pawnees had discovered any of the seven, would have discredited the statement of Red Wolf and Lone Bear ; but the two were so strenuous in their declaration that it produced the effect desired. Some of the listeners believed there was a large party of enemies at hand, and prudence demanded that their own warriors should be called together and precautions taken against surprise.

It was accordingly so done.

CHAPTER XII.

BY this time the sun had reached the rim of the horizon, and the shadows were deepening under the trees. Deerfoot dropped further behind the Sauk and Pawnee, the three still pushing westward, which was opposite the course that would have been taken to reach the camp-fire. The highly trained senses of the young Shawanoe could hear and see nothing to show that his enemies were near at hand.

Every minute now lessened the danger, for only a little more obscurity was required to prevent the keenest eyes of an American Indian from detecting the footprints in the forest. He concluded that, from some cause or other, the Pawnees had given over the pursuit.

So soon as Deerfoot was convinced on this point, he hastened to overtake Hay-uta, who

was walking almost on the heels of the captive.
The latter was not lacking in a certain dignity.
He did not shamble along, as though his
courage had been driven from his body. He
walked erect, with head high, scarcely deign-
ing to bend it to avoid an occasional interfer-
ing limb. He preferred to flank rather than
stoop to such an obstruction. His carriage was
so proud indeed that it looked as if he were a
conqueror, with his two slaves walking behind
him. Not once did he look about, or act as
though he suspected the presence of friend or
foe.

This curious procession lasted until the three
were nearly a half mile from camp. By that
time, night was closing in, and the gloom was
such that Deerfoot was persuaded he need give
no further thought to the Pawnee war party.

Hay-uta had acted the part of conductor,
without much thought as to the course they
were taking. Swerving to the right, they were
soon beyond sight of the open space, and for a
while the march was through the trackless
forest ; but, while the red men deviated very
little from the path, the river, like all streams,

took a winding course, and, just at the moment that Deerfoot joined the Sauk, the three debouched from the woods and (inasmuch as the open space had dwindled to a mere ribbon) found themselves close to the edge of the stream. There of necessity they halted.

The Pawnee now glanced over his shoulder and stopped, as if waiting for some command. Receiving none he started along the stream, but was checked by a word from Deerfoot, whose gesture explained what he meant. The warrior paused, and folding his arms confronted them with the same calm defiance as before.

There was something in his demeanor that compelled the admiration of his captors. It proved that whatever the Pawnee might be, he was not a coward, and it recalled to the young Shawanoe, the days when he wandered through the forests and cane brakes of Kentucky, like a raging cat o' mountain in his hatred of the pale-faces. There were depths in the nature of the youth which were rarely sounded ; but now and then he caught glimpses of the possibilities within himself which caused him to shrink

back, as if from the presence of a super-
naturally evil being.

For the last part of the march the same
thought occupied the minds of both Deerfoot
and Hay-uta : in what manner could they win
the friendship of the captive, and thus open
the way to a solution of the mystery respecting
Otto Relstaub?

Now that the journey was over for the present, the captors consulted together. When
Deerfoot called on Hay-uta for the method
that had presented itself to him, the Sauk
replied that the only thing of which he could
think was to make the Pawnee believe that he
had but a few moments to live—that there was
no possible escape ; and then, when that view
was impressed on the prisoner, they would
present him with his liberty.

Such was the plan also of Deerfoot, but
when Hay-uta proposed that the Pawnee
should be soused into the water and held
under the surface until on the point of drown-
ing, the Shawanoe shook his head.

Deerfoot showed a far-seeing mind in the
course which he adopted, and to which Hay-

uta assented without fathoming its full purpose. The youth felt that the circumstances were such that it was more important for the Sauk to figure as a merciful captor than for himself to play that part.

Deerfoot, it may be said, had proved his ability to take care of himself, where it was possible for a human being to do so. The Sauk was skillful, but in the perilous times close at hand, he was likely to stand in greater need of a friend "at court" than was the Shawanoe. It was this motive which actuated the latter in what he now did.

"Deerfoot will make ready to slay the Pawnee," said he, "and then Hay-uta will stay his hand."

The Sauk nodded to signify he understood the arrangement.

"Let my brother wait till all is ready ; let him stand still till the Pawnee has no hope : when Deerfoot raises his tomahawk, then shall my brother forbid."

There was something touching in the dignity of the Pawnee, when he felt that no hope remained to him. He had no blanket, and all

his weapons had been removed. He stood perhaps twenty feet, or slightly less, from Deerfoot, in plain sight, though the twilight had
given place to that of the moon, which was
partly full and shining from a sky in which
were a number of drifting clouds. He was only
a step or two from the woods, which it would
seem offered a temptation too great to be
resisted.

Doubtless some such thought entered his
mind, but the Shawanoe never turned his face,
and maintained such unremitting watch, that
the captive must have felt he was shut in on
every side.

Deerfoot had laid aside his bow and rifle and
grasped his tomahawk—that weapon which in
his hands was as unerring for a short distance
as was the arrow from his bow. On the first
motion of his captive toward flight, no matter
how quickly made, the tomahawk would split
the skull as if it were a rotten apple.

The Pawnee made no such attempt. He
remained with his fine figure drawn to its full
height. The weight of his body supported
mainly on his right foot, while the left rested

lightly a few inches in front, the posture similar to that which a trained athlete would
assume when about to leap over a slight
obstruction.

His arms were folded across his chest, his
shoulders thrown back, while his eyes were
fixed on the face of his captor a short distance
away. Once or twice they flitted to the gloomy
woods on his left, as though a faint hope fluttered in his heart that his friends would rush
to his relief ; but he knew that if such a thing
were possible, it would have been done long
before. Night and darkness had shut out all
help from them.

The words between Deerfoot and Hay-uta
were few, for the arrangements were so simple
that many were not required. Hay-uta
stepped back, and Deerfoot gathered himself
like a marksman about to fire at a target.

The slightest incident did not escape the
Pawnee. He saw that his last minute was at
hand. Without changing his posture or
unfolding his arms, he leaned forward and
bowed his head, so that the crown was presented to his master, and his eyes, had they

been open, would have looked directly on the ground. But they were closed, and his attitude was that of the devout worshipers in the congregation who, having risen to their feet and joined in the singing, bow their heads while the minister pronounces his benison.

The feet of Deerfoot were placed similarly to those of his victim, and his tomahawk was held idly in his left hand, the blade pressing the side of his knee. When necessary it would be raised over and back of his shoulder like a flash of light, and sent crashing into the brain of his victim.

The stillness became more impressive from a sound which blended with, rather than broke into it; a low monotone, like the sweeping of the wind over the strings of some rude instrument of music, issued from the lips of the Pawnee. It became broken, but at no time lost its distinctive character. It never rose to a high key, and from the beginning to the end, its variation in tone was no more than two notes of the musical scale. Had the volume been less, it would have called to mind the crooning of the housewife by her spinning

J

wheel or over the cradle of the infant she was lulling to sleep.

But there was a depth, and a certain sonorous resignation in the death-song of the Pawnee, which rendered it unlike any thing else. The Shawanoe and Sauk had heard it sung more than once, and, accustomed as they were to the most dreadful scenes, they were always relieved when it ended ; it was too much like a despairing refrain from the grave itself.

Gradually the volume of the Pawnee's death song deepened. For a time it was as if the voice were swaying from side to side in the struggle to free itself from some weight holding it down and smothering it. The weight was flung off, when, throwing up his head again, the Pawnee defiantly confronted the Shawanoe. The unspeakably dismal monotone sounded loud and clear as a trumpet blast borne on the wind, which, having blown at angles to the line of sound, suddenly becomes favorable, and throws the notes forward as if on eagles' wings.

The death song was ended ; the Pawnee had finished his preparation for the leap into the dark, and he calmly awaited the pleasure of his master.

Instead of whirling his tomahawk aloft, Deerfoot slowly brought it above his head, the blade making a gleaming circle, as it swung over and finally paused, the handle so held that it pointed upward and backward, at an angle of forty-five degrees. He seemed to be gathering his muscles for the supreme effort, which should extinguish life in the defiant Pawnee as quickly as if he were smitten by a bolt from heaven. But, before the missile could leave his hand, the Sauk uttered an exclamation, and, having laid aside his gun, strode forward with both hands raised in protest.

His first two steps were rapid, and then, making a great bound, he seized the left arm of Deerfoot with both of his hands. The Shawanoe seemed to struggle fiercely to free himself, and his voice sounded harsh and angry as he ordered the other to step aside and leave him alone. But the Sauk, with no abatement of earnestness, refused, and, for a second or two, the contest was so desperate that the wonder was the prisoner did not make a break for life.

Possibly he did not understand the nature of the struggle until it was over, or it may have been that, having made his preparations for death, he was loth to change the programme.

But the dispute ended as quickly as it began. The Sauk triumphed, as, judging from the size of the two, he was likely to do in such a wrangle. The hand of Deerfoot became nerveless and dropped to his side. He stood silent and sullen, as though he had no more interest in the matter.

Using mild language again, the Pawnee was surprised when the Sauk walked forward, and handed back the rifle, which Deerfoot had taken from him a short time before. The prisoner hesitated a moment as if in doubt, but the manner of Hay-uta was too plain to be mistaken. He accepted the weapon, giving utterance to what was probably meant as an expression of thanks.

Returning a few steps, the Sauk picked up the tomahawk and knife from the ground, and advancing once more in front of the Pawnee, presented them to him with the grace of the Crusader. His pleasure in giving was surely equal to that of the Pawnee in receiving them.

All this time Deerfoot remained like a statue of sullenness, glowering on the two, as though he would have been pleased to tomahawk both actors in the singular drama.

The Pawnee was quick to catch the purport of his friend in need. He shoved the blade of his knife into the skin-sheath at his girdle ; he thrust the handle of his tomahawk through the same support, but further to one side, as if to balance the other weapon. Then he grasped his gun near the flint, and was ready for the next step in the proceedings.

Placing his hand on the prisoner's shoulder, Hay-uta turned him partly around, so that he faced up stream and in the direction of the camp, where so many of his friends were gathered. Pushing him gently forward, he exclaimed in an undertone and in his own language :

"*Go!*"

The Pawnee obeyed, the same dignity marking his movement as when he stood in the presence of death. He strode forward until he reached the darkness of the wood, into which he seemed to blend as if a part of the gloom itself.

When within the shelter, however, he laid aside his courtliness, as it may be called, and used the utmost haste in placing himself beyond danger.

Having played a part so long, he seemed to "go all to pieces", and dashed under the limbs and among the trunks like a terrified deer.

This panic, however, was soon over, and he came to an abrupt stop when only a short distance away. Standing a second or two, as if in deep thought, he turned, and began stealing toward the narrow open space where he had stood a few minutes before, with bowed head, while he chanted his death song. His movement was noiseless, and he speedily peered from among the trees upon the forms of the Shawanoe and Sauk, who were in the act of moving off. They were in plain sight, and the swarthy countenance gleamed, as, carefully muffling the sound of the hammer, he drew it back and brought the rifle to his shoulder.

The distance was short and he could not mistake his aim. Though his life had just been spared by the couple, he fairly held his breath in his eagerness to take their lives. Could he have done so, he would have waited till they were in range, in order that he might bring both low.

But only a moment elapsed, after raising his rifle, when he pressed the trigger.

The dull click of the flint was followed by a whirring flash, as the powder vanished in a white puff, but there was no report. Deerfoot, while carrying the weapon, had quietly withdrawn the charge, leaving the priming, however, in the pan. He knew just how far it is safe to trust the average American Indian.

CHAPTER XIII.

S LIGHT as was the noise made by the flashing of the powder, Deerfoot not only heard it, but knew what it meant. He was so angered that he bounded back among the trees like a tiger leaping upon the hunter that has wounded him. He grasped his knife and sought the treacherous Pawnee, with a fierceness that seemed could not be denied.

Hay-uta stepped softly in the other direction, where he was under the shadow of the trees, and waited for events to develop before doing any thing further.

In the depth of the woods where the vegetation was dense, the darkness was impenetrable. Keen as were the eyes of the Shawanoe, they were not those of the owl or cat, and his enemy was wise enough to remain still. So long as he did so, he was in no danger.

Had Deerfoot been able to find the traitor, he would have made short work with him, but suspecting what he was doing, or rather what he was not doing, he did not tarry. He withdrew so cautiously that no straggling ray of moonlight could fall on his figure, as he moved among the trees. Rejoining the Sauk, they passed down stream.

They had not gone far when they stopped near the edge of the water. There was none of the band on the open space on which the Pawnee camp-fire had been kindled a half mile or so above, so they were covered by all the shelter they could wish.

From the moment of turning their backs for the last time on the Pawnee who had sought to shoot one of them, the Shawanoe and Sauk had not spoken a word. They understood each other too well to need conversation; but, remembering the click of the flint lock and the useless flash of the powder, they made sure that no chance was given for a second attempt.

The Pawnee, who understood why he failed to bring down one of them, was wise enough to withdraw and make his way back to the camp-fire, pondering on the road the explanation which he would add to the store of extraordinary narratives related by his comrades, who had been brought in contact with the young Shawanoe.

The sky was cloudy and the light of the moon treacherous and uncertain. Sometimes the surface of the swiftly flowing river in front was lighted up, and the shadowy line of wood on the other shore stood out clear, and again it seemed to recede, when the face of the moon was obscured.

It was not far to the other bank, and the Indian friends expected to swim across, as they had done scores of times under similar circumstances. Fully two hours had passed since they left young Jack Carleton. During that period not the slightest sign was received from him, and he might have been dead or a thousand miles distant, for all that indicated the contrary.

And yet, it is not to be supposed that either the Sauk or Shawanoe felt any concern for the lad. They had seen no hostiles on that side of the stream ; besides, the experience of Jack ought to have kept him from any possible harm.

But the understanding was that the three were to come together at nightfall, or as soon thereafter as possible. Consequently, Jack would be looking for them.

Deerfoot and Hay-uta stood by the margin of the wood, listening and looking. The soft murmur of the forest and the ripple of the current, as it twisted around some gnarled root along shore or struck against the dipping branch of a tree overhanging the water, were the sounds which first fell on their ears. But a moment later the wailing scream of a panther came from the depths of the wilderness, answered a moment after by a similar cry from a point a mile away.

As if the night was to be given no rest, a husky whistle, like that which a locomotive sends faintly through many miles of fog and damp, reached their ears. Deerfoot and Hay-uta recognized it as a signal from one of the Pawnees who were so numerous in the neigh-borhood. It came from a point near where

Deerfoot had caught his first sight of the group around the camp-fire.

But the friends were in a section where they had never been before, and were playing battledore and shuttlecock with a warlike tribe of whom they knew nothing. It was impossible, therefore, for them to understand the meaning of the signal, for whose response they listened with close attention.

They were astonished that no answer was returned. They would have heard it had there been any, but for several minutes the stillness was unbroken. It was as if one of the Pawnees had called to another who was too distant to be reached, and consequently no response could be sent.

But the next interruption was the report of a gun, sounding startlingly distinct on the quiet air. That, so far as could be judged, came from near the spot whither was sent the first signal.

The Sauk and Shawanoe waited further, but nothing was heard that threw the least light on the plans or doings of the warriors with whom Deerfoot had had such a sharp brush.

"My brother has learned naught of the pale-face?" remarked the Shawanoe, inquiringly, when his companion had related the experience through which he passed, after their separation during the afternoon.

"The lips of the Pawnees are shut to the Sauk," replied Hay-uta, alluding to the tongue of the red men, which was unintelligible to him.

Their lips are shut to Deerfoot, but Lone Bear speaks the words which Deerfoot can understand."

"What were his words to my brother!" asked Hay-uta.

"He says he and Red Wolf have never looked upon the pale face."

"Lone Bear and Red Wolf speak lies!" exclaimed the Sauk with more feeling than would be expected. "What does Deerfoot think?" he asked, as if his opinion was a matter of vital importance.

"Deerfoot believes the word of Hay-uta; he told Lone Bear, while looking in his eyes, that his tongue was double and his heart was full of lies; Lone Bear rushed upon

Deerfoot and sought to slay him for his words."

This reply was gratifying to Hay-uta, who held the young Shawanoe that had vanquished him with such brilliancy, in higher esteem than any one else in the world. He was silent, as if unable to express his feelings, and the Shawanoe continued :

" Hay-uta has talked with the Great Spirit; he has listened to the words of the kind Father who looks down from the moon behind the clouds; the whisperings of the Great Spirit have been sweet in his ears ; Hay-uta could not speak with a double tongue, when he thinks of his goodness."

As the Sauk replied, he looked upward at the sky. The ragged cloud which a moment before was passing across the face of the moon, glided off, and the soft light shone full upon the coppery countenance that glowed with a feeling, such as only a close communion with God stirs in the recesses of the heart.

" Hay-uta has heard the voice of the Great Spirit," said the Sauk, speaking in low tones, " but his words were whispers and Hay-uta did not hear them all, and sometimes he could not hear aright."

This confession that the mists had not cleared from before the Sauk's vision did not surprise Deerfoot, for his own gropings after light were too distinct for him ever to forget the winding path over which he trod.

"The Great Spirit never sleeps," replied Deerfoot, in a voice almost as low as his companion's; "he listens for the words of his children and his ear is always open; he will hear Hay-uta, if he calls upon him and speaks and acts so that when the Great Spirit looks down he will smile."

"Hay-uta will talk with the Great Spirit, so that the whispers which he now hears shall become so loud that Hay-uta can not mistake them."

Deerfoot added a few words of encouragement, and then, having paused long enough on the shore, they addressed themselves to the duty before them.

This was simply to cross to the other side, so as to rejoin Jack Carleton. As there was but the one means of passing over, it was idle to hesitate. The Shawanoe stepped carefully a few paces, when the water reached his armpits, and he began swimming. He did so, holding his bow above the surface with one hand, so as to protect the string from moisture. This was one of the disadvantages of that weapon, though the rifle was not free from a similar inconvenience ; but Hay-uta fastened it to his back, so that the muzzle projected above his head and the water could not run into the barrel. Sometimes he used a cork-like piece of wood to keep the load from wetting, and again he took no precautions, but drew the charge after leaving the stream. Even with all the care that could be taken, the clumsy hammer and flint let down in the pan often failed to protect the powder.

But both were splendid swimmers, and, though the current was powerful, they advanced with steady, even strokes until their feet touched bottom, when they walked out on the opposite side. There the shore was similar to the one just left, so that when their moccasins pressed dry land again, they stood in the shadow of the overhanging trees, millions of which, at that day, covered the vast western wilderness.

Their course had been such that (supposing Jack Carleton remained near the spot where the parting took place), it was now necessary to make their way for some distance up the stream. As there was reason to believe that the broad, swift current interposed between them and the hostiles, Deerfoot and Hay-uta looked back at the land just left behind.

The view was so similar to what has already been described, that no more words are needed. The clouds were still floating in front of the moon, and quaint shadows moved across the river, forest and openings, but the searching vision failed to show the twinkle of any camp-fire, nor could the keen eyes of the Shawanoe catch the faintest glimpse of any shadowy figures stealing along shore.

Though it was the mild season, the night was quite cool, and it will be remembered that neither carried his blanket with him. Most persons would have shivered with discomfort, but the American Indian is educated to the severest exposure and inured to sudden changes

K

of temperature. It would have been more pleasant had they been arrayed in dry clothing rather than in their clinging garments, yet neither acted as if he cared for the difference.

They were moving along the river bank in their usual guarded manner, when both came to an abrupt stop ; they had caught the twinkle of a camp-fire among the trees just ahead.

CHAPTER XIV.

WHEN Deerfoot and Hay-uta parted company with Jack Carleton, he feared he had several hours on his hands without any means of employing mind or body. The active operations of the campaign, so to speak, were in charge of the Sauk and Shawanoe division, while the young Kentuckian in reserve had little prospect of being called upon to take part in the engagement.

But Jack, it will be noted, was almost opposite the open ground, whereon burned the Pawnee camp-fire, and, by using care, he could hold it under inspection as long as he chose. He had his choice of peeping from the trees and undergrowth along shore, or of climbing the tree from whose top the Shawanoe and Sauk gained their first knowledge of the Pawnees. Nearly every one would have stayed on the ground, but in obedience to a whim, the lad climbed to the perch where his friends held themselves a short time before. He carried his gun with him, for though it would have been much more convenient to leave it below, the act would have been a piece of remissness unpardonable in his situation. When, however, he was half-way to the top, he carefully shelved it among some branches, where it could not fall. He continued to climb until the limbs bent with his weight. Cautious at all times, Jack then softly pushed aside the branches in front of his face and found he was looking directly across and down upon the Pawnee encampment.

At the moment of doing so, a slight incident caused him some uneasiness. Among the group on which he gazed with such interest, he observed a warrior standing on the other side of the fire, rifle in hand, with his face turned toward the young Kentuckian. Not only that, but he seemed to be watching Jack himself. So startling was his appearance, that the youth shrank back, allowing the vegetation to close in front of his face. This was done with a certain abruptness, which (if he was right in his suspicion), was unfortunate, since the action would be the more noticeable to the Pawnee. Then Jack stealthily parted the leaves and peered out again.

The warrior was motionless, the stock of his gun on the ground, while his right hand lightly clasped the barrel, his left thumb inserted at his girdle, close to the handle of his knife, much after the fashion of some of us who use the arm holes of our vests for that purpose.

The distance, slight as it was, prevented Jack Carleton from verifying or disproving his suspicion. The painted face was turned directly toward him and held stationary, as is often the case when a person is trying to identify some sound which faintly reaches his ear. Had he been gazing straight at the lad, he would have appeared just as he did when stealthily viewed by the youth.

"I wonder whether that rascal is looking at me," said Jack to himself, when he peeped timidly out the second time; "they're as sharp-eyed as owls, but he never could have thought of any one in this perch, if he hadn't accidentally looked at the spot. I'm afraid it would mix things for Hay-uta and Deerfoot, if any of them should get a sight of me."

He was reminded of the experience of himself and Otto Relstaub when, some weeks before, they were made captives by the Sauks, within a short distance of Martinsville. At that time, one or two of the warriors, while the boys were watching them, walked away from the camp in such an off-hand manner, that neither dreamed their real purpose was to pass to the rear of the prowlers and make them prisoners.

"I'll keep my eyes on him," was the wise conclusion of Jack, "and if he starts off in the woods, I'll slide down this tree and make a change of base in short order."

To the great relief of Jack the warrior did not maintain his impressive pose, nor did he do what was dreaded and half expected. One of the red men addressed him and he immediately gave attention.

"It was only an accident," was the conclusion of the youth ; "he couldn't have seen me —helloa!"

Jack had full warrant for his excitement, for, at that moment, who should walk into his field of vision but Deerfoot, the young Shawanoe.

He advanced from the wood as I have already described, and saluting the astonished Pawnees with a certain stateliness, opened the conversation. He was not long in discovering that Lone Bear was the only one with whom he could converse intelligently, and the two, as you remember, were soon seated beside each other. It was Lone Bear who, at the first glance, Jack Carleton thought was looking at him.

The dread that the boy felt, when first left alone, that time would hang heavily on his hands was gone. He knew the Shawanoe well enough to feel certain that he would keep things moving.

And so he did. I will not repeat the story of Deerfoot's experience, which partook more of a comedy than of a tragedy. The young Kentuckian held his breath when Lone Bear drew his knife and rushed upon the Shawanoe,

and his excitement was almost irrestrainable
as the latter began dancing backward with his
infuriated assailant plunging and striking at
him. When the Pawnee sprawled, with his
feet kicking the air, Jack forgot where he was
and laughed with delight.

"Hurrah for Deerfoot!" he called; "the
whole crowd ain't enough for you! you are
worth all of them!"

The Pawnees were on their feet hurrying
toward the combatants, and scarcely less ex-
cited than the young Kentuckian perched in the
tree-top. But, stirring as was the incident, it
was very brief. With the exceptions already
made known, the red men dashed into the
woods in hot pursuit of the fugitive.

"Deerfoot against the world!" exclaimed
Jack, jerking off his cap, as though he was
about to fling it toward the clouds, but he
restrained himself and the cheer which could not
be locked between his lips was so impeded in
its escape that it reached no ears on the other
side the river.

"Deerfoot beats the beaters," he added,
bringing his feelings under control; "I don't

believe there ever was such a fellow ; it must be that Providence intends him for some work, and like Washington he can not be killed until that work is done."

Jack had made a similar remark to his mother, when they were talking about the Shawanoe some weeks previous, and he now recalled with a shudder her comment, to the effect that the slightest of causes would bring death to him just as quickly as to any one else, and, sooner or later, he must succumb to the inevitable. It seemed not unlikely that the prowess of the young Shawanoe was an element of peril to him, since he relied too much upon it.

But the youth had eluded the hostiles, when they seemed about to overwhelm him, and Jack was confident now that he had the cover of the woods, where he was at home, that he could laugh his enemies to scorn. The reports of guns, however, which reached his ears, could not but produce a disquieting effect, which the lad felt for a long time afterward.

"I wonder whether any one could have heard me," he muttered some minutes later, when his nerves became calmer. "I forgot myself, as the Indians themselves did, but I guess no one noticed it."

That prudence which should never leave the frontiersman, suggested that he ought to descend the tree, and seek some other place of hiding. Unfortunately, he decided to stay for awhile where he was.

There was much to occupy his attention, and keep alive his interest; for the discomfited Lone Bear and his mock sympathizers were in plain sight, and the gesticulations were so clear that it seemed to Jack he could comprehend the words spoken.

But the most stirring scenes lose in time their interest, and, despite the situation of Jack Carleton, it was not long before his thoughts reverted to Otto Relstaub.

"Poor fellow," he muttered, "it does seem as if every thing went wrong with him; I have no father, but if I had, he could love me no more than mother. With Otto, however, it is a thousand fold worse, for he is treated as if he were an intruder in his own home. He has been abused, almost starved, and, to crown

all, sent into the woods to look for a horse
that was lost a long time before, and of which
there remains not the faintest footprint. I
wonder whether they will ever grieve for
Otto if we go back and tell them he is
dead ?"

When Jack pondered over the cause which
led his friend to leave home, he could not express
his feelings. To him there was something
incomprehensible in the brutality of the parents toward their only child. He was tempted
to believe it was all a great mistake.

But second thought showed there was no
error, and he asked himself whether there was
any ground to hope that the German lad was
alive, and, if so, whether he could be
restored to his friends.

The fact that Otto was not among the group
on the other side of the stream, added to the
misgiving. Hay-uta had made known that he
recognized members of the strange party of
Indians to whom the boy was sold. If they
had kept their captive, where else could he be
except with them ?

"Every thing points to his death," was the

sad conclusion of Jack ; "it isn't likely they would trade him off to some one else."

Indeed, to believe such a thing would be to give the captive an unreasonable value as a circulating medium ; it was far more likely that, finding his presence a burden, his captors had settled it in the most natural manner that presented itself.

A still darker side to the picture caused Jack to shudder. If the captors of Otto Relstaub had put him to death, was it by a quick taking off, or had he been subjected to torture ? Alas, that Jack Carleton was forced to answer the query as he most dreaded.

" But, if he *is* dead," he added, with a sigh, " he perished long ago, and it can make no difference *now* to him ; but I ain't ready to give up all hope and I won't do so, so long as Deerfoot holds on."

Forcing the distressing subject from his mind, the youth compelled himself to give attention to what could be seen on the other side of the river. Lone Bear and Red Wolf were seated by the camp-fire, talking together, as has been told elsewhere, but the rest of the hostiles

were out of sight. Jack naturally wondered
the cause of the sudden quarrel that had sprung
up between Deerfoot and the warrior who fig-
ured so ridiculously in it, but he could only
await the return of the Shawanoe to hear the
explanation.

The excitement of the lad boiled over again,
when, with eyes roaming up and down the
open space, he caught sight of his old friend,
standing, bow in hand, on the edge of the
wood. His pose showed he was making ready
to give attention to the unsuspicious hostiles.

"I wonder whether he means to send an
arrow through one, and follow it up with a
second through another, before he can get out
of their way. It may be that Deerfoot isn't as
chivalrous as he pretends to be ; give him a
chance, and, if he thinks no one sees him, he
will swing his tomahawk and use his knife
right and left."

But we know that Jack did his friend an
injustice, as speedily became apparent, when
none of the arrows which sped from the large
bow harmed either of the Pawnees. Their

frantic flight and the laughter of Deerfoot proved that he had done precisely what he set out to do ; he had given the couple a shock which they were not likely to forget for many a day.

The occurrence was so amusing that Jack parted the branches in front of his face and waved his hat to Deerfoot. If the latter saw the act of forgetfulness, he was so displeased that he paid no attention to it. When he vanished from sight in the wood behind him, he gave no responsive salute to that of his enthusiastic young friend.

CHAPTER XV.

THREE separate times Jack Carleton noticed a peculiar jar of the tree in which he was perched. He felt no alarm, but some curiosity to know the cause.

Peering downward between the limbs, he could see nothing to explain the occurrence. The first time he concluded it was imagination, but when it was repeated twice he knew there was "something in it". Still, as the most careful search failed to reveal the cause, he was at a loss to explain it. His first thought was that some animal might be chafing his body against the trunk, but that was unlikely, because no creature was visible. Then, when he noticed there was enough air stirring to cause a gentle swaying of the branches, he concluded that the disturbance was due to the friction of some of the limbs against others. The theory was more ingenious than reasonable, but was accepted in lieu of a better one, and once more the lad fixed his eyes on the open space across the stream.

The other Pawnees had not put in an appearance, and before they did so, the young gentleman in the tree-top found he had something on hand which required his whole attention.

A fourth time a jar went through the trunk from base to summit, and the disturbance was more marked than before.

"There must be some animal down there—"

Jack Carleton grasped a limb above him, leaned far over and peered among the branches below, but his examination was not finished when he saw the hand of an Indian warrior reach around the trunk, at a point half way between the top and the base, and grasp the rifle which the young Kentuckian had skewered between several supports. The stock caught slightly, and, while disengaging it, the savage brought his head into view.

He wore no scalp-lock, as was the fashion among many tribes, but the long, coarse hair dangled about his shoulders, and yellow, crimson and blue paint were mixed in that on his crown. There were no feathers, however, such as Deerfoot was fond of displaying, and the body was covered with a thin shirt of deerskin above the waist.

The Indian must have glanced aloft from the ground and taken in the situation at once. He had climbed with great care, and, when he stopped, was slightly below the point were rested the rifle of the youth. Had the latter taken the alarm, when he felt the first jar, he could have scrambled down and secured his gun ahead of the Indian. It would have been a stirring race between them, but as I have shown, the first knowledge of the truth came to Jack when he descried the extended arm and saw the coppery fingers in the very act of closing about his property.

Inasmuch as the dusky thief was forced to reach upward to seize the weapon, his face was lifted enough for the lad to gain a partial view of his countenance. It was similar to many he had seen among the Sauks and elsewhere. The forehead was broad at the base and nar-row at the top (which was close to the forehead) and very retreating. The protuberant temples, small eyes, heavy nose, wide mouth and retreating chin—the whole smeared with daubs of paint, such as soiled the horsehair-like covering of his head, rendered the features the most repulsive on which the lad had ever looked. He certainly had never beheld a more unwelcome visitor.

Having secured the property of the lad, the warrior now threw his head further back, and looked directly up at him. The face, ugly as it was, appeared the worse because of the grin that split it in twain and displayed the white teeth which gleamed like those of a ravenous beast. The expression and action said as plainly as could the words themselves :

"It's no use, young gentleman ; you may as well come down."

The Indian did not speak, and his frightful smile gradually relaxed until his mouth assumed its normal width. Then, holding the captured rifle in one hand, he began descending, Jack Carleton remained astride of the upper limb, watching the warrior, who went down with the nimbleness of a monkey.

Viewed from above, the sight was odd. He seemed to see nothing but a mass of dangling hair and an indefinite number of arms and legs which were sawing back and forth, and moving up and down, while the body to which they were attached, remained stationary. The illusion, however, was dispelled, when the Indian made a slight leap and landed on the ground.

Immediately he turned, and standing close to the trunk (the better to see among the limbs), fixed his eyes on Jack Carleton, and solemnly beckoned with his arm for him to descend.

"My gracious!" thought the latter, "I don't believe there's any help for it. Ah, if Deerfoot only knew!"

It occurred to the youth that possibly the Shawanoe could be reached by signal. He hastily drew aside the leaves and looked toward the spot where he saw him but a short time before. But the scene had changed. Deerfoot was gone, and the Pawnees were swarming back to camp, a number listening with rapt attention to the monumental yarns which Lone Bear and Red Wolf were pouring into the ears of their credulous listeners, whose experience having been what it was, prepared them to believe almost any thing.

"No help from *there*," concluded the youth with a sigh, as he let the leaves come together and shut out his view of the other shore; "I wonder what this warrior will do with me; I suppose he will run me over to the rest, and they'll even up matters by taking their vengeance on *me*—helloa! there's no need of *that!*"

Looking downward, Jack saw that his captor was no longer beckoning for him to descend. Like the old farmer, who, finding there was no virtue in grass, resorted to stones, the Indian had substituted the gun, and held it pointed at the youngster, who was slow in moving from his lofty perch.

There was no call to fire; the youth grasped the situation at once and began lowering himself with great promptness. While doing so, he occasionally took a peep between his feet, and each time saw the warrior standing erect and following his movements with the gun, as a hunter does when aiming at a gyrating bird.

JACK CARLETON AND THE INDIAN (*p.* 180).

"I hope I'm giving satisfaction," muttered Jack, who felt the cold perspiration breaking out all over his body ; "if he isn't satisfied, I'll let go and drop. I wish I could do it, so as to fall on his head and break his neck." When almost to the ground, Jack was relieved to observe the red man lower his weapon. He heard the click of the lock, as he let the flint down in place. It was a vast relief from suspense, but it may be doubted whether, after all, Jack's danger was any less than before. Whatever sinister thoughts were in the mind of the red man remained when the young Kentuckian stood before him an unresisting prisoner.

I need not say that while Jack Carleton was descending the tree he thought hard and fast. He was in a situation of the gravest peril, and there was no human arm on which he could rely for help. His hot Kentucky blood was aroused, and he resolved that if his captor offered him harm or indignity, he would give him the hottest fight of which he was capable. The youth still had his knife and he meant to keep it. While coming down the tree, he quietly shoved it inside of his coat where it could not be seen, but was available for instant use.

He feared the warrior had several comrades with him, but was relieved to find that such was not the case.

"He must have seen me from the other side," was the conclusion of the youth, "and slipped across without my noticing him, just as those Sauks got behind Otto and me when we never dreamed of danger. He ain't the Indian that was looking at me ; I suppose that one who tumbled over Deerfoot told this dog, and here he is."

Dropping the stock of the captured rifle on the ground, the red skin grasped the barrel near the muzzle, standing in an easy attitude, with the weight of his body resting on one foot, and looked into the eyes of Jack Carleton, as if trying to read the secrets of his breast.

The youth was almost as tall as his captor, and he returned the scrutiny. He did not assume any defiant manner, for he was far from wishing to exasperate him who was master of the situation.

"I think I could give him a pretty good tussle," was the conclusion of Jack, "and whenever he chooses to sail in, I am ready, but I wish things were nearer even between us."

It was noticeable that the only rifle in sight was the one belonging to the prisoner. It seemed incredible that the warrior should have left camp without the indispensable weapon, though, if he had brought it away, it was now invisible.

But, in addition to the stolen piece, he carried the tomahawk and knife at his girdle, and there could be no question that he was an adept in their use.

When Jack looked down from his place in the tree-top on the countenance of his captor, he perceived a curious distortion, which was now explained. At some time in his history the Indian had received a slash across the face, which clove the bone and cartilage of the nose and laid one of the cheeks open. The cicatrice, combined with the natural ugliness of the features, and the greasy ochre and paint, daubed and smeared over the skin, rendered the countenance of the warrior as frightful as can be conceived.

But Jack Carleton had met too many hideous Indians to be disturbed by their appearance. It was the *action* of this one in which he felt interest.

It was a noteworthy feature of the young Kentuckian's capture, that he was angered by the evidence that the Indian had brought no gun with him. Such a course implied that the youth was held in light regard, and not deemed the equal of a warrior in a hand-to-hand struggle.

"They think I am nothing but a boy," he thought, "and so they sent a warrior so horrible of face that they hope he will scare me out of my wits ; at any rate, they don't believe it worth while for him to bring a gun ; may be he'll regret that before he is through."

Having scrutinized the captive from head to foot, the captor seemed to be satisfied. Without attempting any words, he beckoned as before for Jack to follow him. The gesture was made at the moment the warrior turned and began walking over the course parallel to the river and leading toward its mouth.

The action placed Jack behind his master, instead of in front, and it could not but suggest several desperate expedients to him, who was resolved not to allow himself to be taken across the river. He had witnessed enough from his elevated lookout to convince him that the stream on his right was his Rubicon; if he once passed *that*, there would be no return.

CHAPTER XVI.

JACK CARLETON stealthily pressed his left hand against his breast; his knife was where he could whip it out when wanted.

Why couldn't he draw it, and leaping forward, bury it in the side of his captor before he could save himself?

"It will be a dreadful thing," he reflected, compressing his lips, "but it is the only chance I have; *I'll try it!*"

He began insinuating his hand under his coat, and groped for the only weapon on which he could now rely. In his eagerness he stepped more softly and slightly crouched, as one is apt to do at such a time.

It may have been that his captor took the lead for a short distance with a view of tempting him to make some such demonstration; but more than likely, the excessive caution of the lad betrayed him ; for, before he could draw his knife, the face was turned, and stepping aside, he motioned Jack to assume the leadership—that is, under his direction.

The captive did not think it wise to refuse, but moved promptly to the front and continued the march in the same direction they had followed from the first.

"I wonder whether he is deaf and dumb," said Jack to himself ; "he acts just as though he had no use of his tongue. Well, I don't know as it will make any difference, for I can't understand a word he says, and it isn't likely he knows any thing about English. But these redskins have a way of talking with their hands, heads and shoulders which almost any one can comprehend."

The change of positions caused Jack Carleton a new uneasiness. Having made ready for an attack on the Indian in front, it was only natural that he should suspect his captor would take the same course toward him. As indifferently as he could, the youth again slid his right hand under his coat, until it grasped the bone-handle of his hunting knife. He held it firmly, and listened closely for the first movement which would betray the other's intention.

But the youth erred as to the immediate purpose of the warrior. He strode along in his deliberate way, stepping in the footprints of his captive, so as neither to recede from nor approach him. Less than ten feet intervened between the two.

The couple were so near the river, that, when not able to catch a glimpse of its shining surface, it was located by the sparseness of the trees. Jack was so anxious to avoid the stream, that he began bearing to the left, hoping the individual behind him would not notice the deviation, but the lad was unwise to think such a thing possible.

The result of this weak piece of strategy was the proof that the red man was the owner of a voice.

" *Waoof!* "

The sound resembled the cough of a wild beast, and startled Jack. Glancing around, he saw the eyes of the warrior snapping, while his right arm was extended, and the finger pointing toward the river.

"All right," responded the lad, as though glad to be reminded of his forgetfulness ; "we won't quarrel over the matter."

Jack, however, was too prudent to make an abrupt turn, which would bring him to the shore before going more than several rods. His divergence was perceptible, though the angle was obtuse.

The prisoner was astonished and mystified by what followed, and it may be said that he never fully understood its meaning.

"The rascal has proven that he has the use of his tongue—that's certain. I don't like the idea of keeping in front of him and leading the way to the river's edge. When we reach that, he can call to the others and bring over all he wants to help him—that is, if he feels he needs the help, which isn't likely. I'll keep on till we are close to the river, and then I'll make a fight."

When only a few yards separated him from the river, the warrior emitted an exclamation precisely like that which first arrested the footsteps of the youth. He stopped, as before, and awaited the will of his captor. The latter advanced to the front, and, while the other stood still, the Indian made his way to the water's margin, parted the bushes and looked out.

The feature of the movement was its caution. The redskin acted as if his whole care was to escape being seen by any on the other side. Why he wished to do so was beyond the power of the youth to guess.

"They are his friends, and I should think he would want to let them know of his success."

The warrior stood fully two minutes leaning over the water, one hand grasping the gun and the other holding the undergrowth apart, while his eyes roved up and down, as if searching for that which he expected and yet dreaded to find. He was but a brief distance below the camp of the Pawnees, who were in sight. The sun had set and twilight was creeping through the wood and over the river. Soon objects would become indistinct; but, for a few minutes at least, it would be to the warrior as if the sun were in the sky.

The view was unsatisfactory, for he drew back, allowing the bushes to come together, and muttered some impatient expression.

Looking angrily at Jack, he extended his arm and finger so as to point away from the stream, and signified by gesture that the youth was to take that course.

"Nothing will suit me better," was the thought of the latter, as he obeyed ; "I don't understand what the mischief you are driving at, but I am glad to get as far as I can from the river."

As nearly as Jack could judge, this odd march lasted until he had tramped a hundred yards, when it was terminated by another emphatic " *Waoof!*"

They were in the woods, where the trees were close and there was little undergrowth. So far as could be seen, the nearest water was the river, but the captor showed that his purpose was to go into camp, as may be said, for a time at least. He broke off some dead limbs, threw them on the ground at the base of a large oak, and motioned to the captive to do the same. Jack's previous experience had taught him that the wisest course, under such circumstances, is promptly to obey, and he sprang to work with such vigor that it did not take him long to collect a large pile. As he always carried a flint and steel with him, he hoped to conciliate his captor to a slight extent by starting the fire, though the latter had also a stone in hand, from which, it is probable, he would have extracted fire with but little trouble. He stood still and watched the lad.

It was many years before such a thing as a lucifer match was known, and our ancestors acquired a deftness in igniting a flame from the simple contrivance named, which leads us to doubt whether they gained a great advantage when they threw it aside for the modern invention.

With the help of dried leaves, small dead twigs, and the swift blows of the steel across the face of the flint, a spark speedily darted to the combustible material and stuck there. Jack did not use the rag soaked in chemicals, which was common among the settlers, but caught the fire from the direct source, as it may be called. The tiny twist of flame was fanned and nursed by gently blowing until, in a brief space, a big fire was roaring, and scorching the shaggy bark of the oak.

It was impossible to tell from the looks of the Indian whether he was pleased or not. He stood a few paces off, watching the operation, and, when the fire was well under way, sat down cross-legged like a Turk, where he could feel the warmth, though, as I have stated in another place, the weather was not cold.

It was now growing dark. The shadows were on every hand, and the trunks of the trees looked grim and ghostly, as revealed by the fire, which Jack continually fed, until the circle of illumination was several rods in extent.

" I would give a good deal to know what he is thinking about," said the lad to himself, furtively watching the face on the other side of the fire ; " something seems to have gone wrong with him, though why he should want to keep his movements from his friends across the river is more than I can guess ; may be he has had a quarrel ; they have taken his gun and set him adrift."

This theory, however, did not sound reasonable, and the lad was unsatisfied ; whatever the cause of the redskin's erratic conduct, his captive could not explain it.

M

For a half hour the warrior was as mute and motionless as the oak against which the fire had been kindled. All that time, he sat six or eight feet from the flames and about the same distance from the captive. The fire, the Indian and the youth, each formed the corner of a triangle. He who was master of the situation retained his Turk-like pose, the captured gun between his arms and knees and his small eyes fixed on the flames, which the industry of the prisoner never allowed to grow less.

Strange musings must have stirred within the bronzed skull, but it is useless to speculate, since we have no more means of knowing their nature than had Jack Carleton, who wondered and guessed without satisfying himself.

But one thing was certain : whatever the thoughts of the warrior, they were of a disturbing nature. Jack could not mistake the scowl which wrinkled the brow, while now and then an evil light shone in the eyes.

" He doesn't think of supper, or, if he does, he knows there is no way of getting any thing to eat. He must make up his mind pretty soon what he intends to do with *me*. If he decides to stay here all night, I know I shan't close my eyes for a single second.''

But the test did not come, and it can not be known, therefore, what the result would have been. The Indian seemed to rouse all at once to a sense of the situation, probably concluding that he was wasting time by indulging in such musings. His awaking was characteristic. He sprang to his feet, threw his gun aside, and placed his hand on the knife at his girdle. As he did so, his countenance flamed with ferocity, and the meaning of the look he bent on Jack Carleton could not be misjudged.

"It has been decided that mine shall be the same fate as that of poor Otto," was the thought of Jack, who displayed genuine Kentucky pluck in facing the peril.

He was only a second or two behind the warrior in bounding to his feet, and as he came up he whipped out his hunting knife from under his coat, and confronted his foe. The latter probably was unaware until then that his captive had a weapon about him, for otherwise he would have deprived him of it at the muzzle of the rifle ; but surely it would seem he had no cause to fear the youth, who could not have been his equal in strength, activity or skill in handling such a weapon, though much his superior in courage.

Jack Carleton was as self-possessed as if he were awaiting a friendly wrestling bout with Otto Relstaub, though he knew that the assault meant death to one, and the chances were against himself.

"He will bound like a dog at me," was the thought of Jack, who, after the manner of a skillful boxer, kept his eye fixed on that of his foe, in the hope of reading his purpose; "and I will make believe I am bewildered by his style of attack (and may be I will be), but I'll jump to one side, as he comes, and, with the help of heaven, will show what a Kentucky boy can do when cornered."

Just then Jack Carleton smiled, and right good cause had he for doing so.

CHAPTER XVII.

THE Indian warrior was the picture of ferocity, as he crouched a few steps away, and, with his fingers griping the handle of his knife, slowly drew it from the skin sheath at his girdle. The end of his abstraction was the resolution to slay his captive then and there.

But, as the plucky youth faced the fierce red man and looked him in the eye, he saw another form rising to view in his field of vision. It was that of a warrior who slowly appeared behind the first, as if lifted upward from the ground, and peeped over his shoulder into the face of Jack Carleton. So perfect was the silence which marked the extraordinary manifestation, that it was like the shadow made by the firelight itself.

Just beyond and a little to one side of the second form, a third came to view, dimly revealed by the lesser firelight, but with a stillness of movement as absolute as that of the other. Had it been otherwise, the redskin would have discovered their approach.

The third Indian, indistinctly shown in the yellow glow, was recognized by Jack as the Sauk Hay-uta; the second was Deerfoot the Shawanoe. The latter smiled in his shadowy way, and shook one finger as a warning to his friend not to betray the presence of himself and companion.

Looking in the face of his foe, as though addressing him, the lad said:

"It's all right; the next time I wish you would not be so slow in getting here; if you'll keep still, I'll give this rascal a tussle that he don't expect."

The warrior must have thought it strange to be addressed in that fashion, and he must have noticed, too, the smile and flitting glances of his victim, but he could not have suspected the meaning of either, or he would have faced the other way.

With a partially suppressed shout, he

stooped, as if gathering his muscles, and then, like a lion on the edge of a chasm, he made a terrific bound at the captive.

But he didn't reach him. A quick blow of the upraised arm sent his knife spinning in the darkness, and a dexterous flirt of Deerfoot's moccasin in front of the foot of the Indian, flung him headlong, after the manner of a beginner taking a header from his bicycle. His discomfiture was more complete than that of Lone Bear while pursuing the Shawanoe, for not only was he thrown forward with great violence, but (as was the case with Hay-uta, when he attacked Deerfoot), the knife was knocked from his grasp, by a blow so cleverly given that it seemed to have fractured his forearm.

Using mild language again, it might be said that the warrior was surprised. Whatever the cause of his overthrow, he could not mistake its meaning ; it notified him that he ought to leave the spot without any tarrying. For- tunately, he had enough sense to do so. Despite the stinging pain in his arm, he scram- bled to his feet, glanced over his shoulder, and seeing two strange Indians, darted off like a deer, vanishing among the trees with a suddenness which, it is safe to say, he never equaled before or afterward.

"What a good fellow you would be to figure in a story!" exclaimed the delighted Jack Carleton, wringing the hand of Deerfoot, and feeling as though he would like to fling his arms around his neck and embrace him.

The Shawanoe evidently was in good spirits, for his even white teeth showed between his lips, and his handsome black eyes sparkled in the firelight. He enjoyed the figure the Indian cut when charging upon his captive.

"My brother speaks words which Deerfoot does not know."

"What I mean to say is, that you have such a way of turning up when you're wanted very bad, that you're just the scamp to figure in a lot of story books; I wonder whether some simpleton won't undertake to use you that way. The only trouble will be that if he invents yarns about you, he'll make a fizzle of it, and, if he tells the truth, he will hardly be believed; but," added the youth, as if the mantle of prophecy had fallen on him, "it will depend a good deal on who it is that writes your life. Like enough it will be some fellow who won't be credited, no matter what he says —so he will be apt to pile it on."

Although Deerfoot possessed a good knowledge of the English language, he failed to understand his young friend, and awaited his explanation.

Meanwhile Hay-uta came forward and shook hands with Jack, muttering a word or two in broken English, expressive of his pleasure over his good fortune.

"What I meant to say," added the lad, turning again to Deerfoot, "is, that you've got such a habit of dropping down on your friends when they are in trouble, that some day it will be put in a book, just as your Bible is printed."

"Put Deerfoot in a book!" repeated the young Shawanoe, blushing like a school-girl ; "he who will do that will be a fool!"

"Like enough," replied Jack, with a laugh ; "but all the same, he will come along one of these days, long after you and I are dead."

"How will he know any thing of Deerfoot?" asked the young warrior, with a dismay as great as that of other parties since then who, contemplating such a calamity, have burned their private letters and papers; "if Deerfoot is dead, who shall tell him any thing about him?"

"Why, my dear fellow," laughed his young friend; "don't you know that Ned Preston, Wild Blossom Brown, and all the folks over in Kentucky who know you, will tell their friends and children what you have done; and here on this side the river it will be the same; till some time it will all be gathered together and put in a book that will be read by hundreds and thousands of people not born?"

Deerfoot showed by his expression that he did not fully understand the meaning of his young friend, or, if he did, he believed he was jesting. The idea of him ever figuring on the printed page could not be credited. He smiled and shook his head, as though he wished to talk of something else.

The young Shawanoe, as a matter of course, was the director of all the movements of the little party, and he now said that it was best to leave the spot and spend the night somewhere else. The Indian to whom they had given such a scare might steal back, when he judged the three were asleep and take revenge.

"He hasn't any gun," remarked Jack, who had picked up his own weapon which the other left behind him, "so he can't shoot us."

"He has a tomahawk and knife—them he would use, though he had a rifle as good as Hay-uta's."

"How was it, Deerfoot, that that Indian was roaming through the woods on this side of the river, without a gun?"

The Shawanoe shook his head to signify he did not know : it was, to say the least, a curious incident.

"I thought possibly he was a stranger to the war party across the river ; he acted as though he was afraid they would see him."

"He is a Pawnee," observed Deerfoot, who had gained a view of him, "and is one of their best warriors."

"Why, then, should he act as he did? You must have some explanation even though you can't be sure."

"He was a passionate warrior; he may not have been right *there*," said Deerfoot, touching his finger to his forehead; "perhaps he was so evil the Great Spirit placed darkness where there was light."

"But when an Indian is unfortunate enough to be unbalanced in mind, the others become more kind to him than before; he would have no need to be afraid of them."

The Shawanoe reminded Jack that the stranger might hold the rest of his people in mortal fear, without having cause for doing so.

The Kentuckian was inclined to accept this explanation, and he told how curiously the other had acted from the beginning, and especially into what a reverie he sank while sitting near the fire.

But when Jack Carleton had convinced himself on this point, Deerfoot chose to express doubt. To him it seemed more probable that the Indian had had a quarrel with his tribe, or had committed some offense for which he was proscribed. It was not unlikely that one feature of his punishment was that he should go forth into the wilderness without firearms.

When he sat by the camp-fire, he was doubt-less meditating over the wrongs he had suf-fered, and when his passion flamed out, he sprang to his feet to kill the youth who had done him no wrong.

"I know one thing," said Jack, compressing his lips and shaking his head, "I wouldn't have stood still and allowed him to work his pleasure with his knife; I almost wish you had let him come on."

The Shawanoe gravely dissented.

"My brother is brave, but he could not pre-vail against the fierce Pawnee ; he might have saved his own life, but his wounds would have hurt ; *now* he has no wounds."

"May be you're right, Deerfoot ; you know more about the woods in one minute than I'll ever know in a lifetime ; so I'll drop the sub-ject."

Jack asked his friend about the experience of himself and Hay-uta on the other side the stream, and Deerfoot gave a summary of what had befallen them. When he recalled the overthrow of Lone Bear the first time, and afterward of him and Red Wolf, he laughed with a heartiness which brought a smile to the faces of Jack and Hay-uta. The sight of Red Wolf as he plunged into the river, his head down and feet pointed toward the sky seemed to delight the young warrior, who shook with silent laughter.

The Shawanoe never displayed his wood-craft in a more marked degree than at the moment he was telling his story and enjoying the picture he drew. While he seemed to be lost in mirth, Jack Carleton noticed, what he had seen before, his eyes flitted hither and thither, and occasionally behind him, and, between his words and laughter, he listened with an intentness that would have noted the falling of a leaf. Subtle would that foe have had to be in order to steal up to those who seemed to be thinking of every thing except personal danger.

Jack Carleton had learned that neither of his friends had gained any tidings of Otto Rel-staub. At the fount where the Shawanoe expected to receive knowledge, he was shut out as though by an iron door. Not a word, hint or look had given them so much as a glim-mer of light.

It was certain, however, that Deerfoot held some theory of his own to explain this phase of the difficulty which confronted them, and no one could travel so close to truth as he ; but when asked his opinion, he would not give it. He shook his head to signify that he preferred to hold his peace on the matter, and Jack knew him too well to press him.

Hay-uta was impatient to leave the place, for it was manifest he did not like the spot. Nothing seemed more likely than that the warrior whom they had used so ill would do his utmost to revenge himself. It is as much a part of Indian nature to "get even " with an enemy, as it is the rule and guide of multitudes of those around us, who see nothing inconsistent between the spirit of the Christianity they profess and the revengeful disposition shown toward those who, in some way or other, have given them offense.

CHAPTER XVIII.

THE spot fixed upon by the Shawanoe was fully a third of a mile from the camp-fire kindled by the strange Indian. It was in a hollow, through which ran a small stream of water, and where the undergrowth and vegetation were so dense that the flames which were started would not have attracted notice five rods away.

You will remember that it was just such a place as was a favorite with Deerfoot. It had attracted his notice during the day, while they were pushing westward, and it was an easy matter for him to lead the others back to it when the darkness among the trees was almost impenetrable.

Several facts, more or less pleasant, impressed Jack Carleton. One was that their camp was so secure from discovery that all three could sleep without misgiving. Their tramp through the wood had been conducted with such stealth that it was impossible for any one to have seen them, and of course it was beyond the power of an enemy to trail them except by the aid of daylight.

A fact less pleasant, was the absence of provisions. It was a goodly number of hours since they had eaten, and the Kentuckian possessed an appetite such as young gentlemen of his age, who spend much of their time out doors, invariably own. It must not be supposed that either the Sauk or Shawanoe were deficient in that respect, but they were used to privation, and seemed to feel no discomfort. Jack Carleton was sure that Deerfoot often went without food when he could have secured it, for no other purpose than that of retaining mastery over himself.

"I suppose it is a good way," muttered the discontented youth, stretching himself out for the night, "but it don't agree with my constitution. They needn't think they're going to make me whine," he added, with grim resolu-

N

tion. "I'll starve before I'll ask *them* for any thing to eat."

He became interested in his companions, however, and, as is the rule, when the usual hour for eating passed his hunger grew less.

Deerfoot leaned his long bow against the trunk of the nearest tree, his quiver lying at the base, and assumed an indolent attitude, his face toward the fire. The upper part of his body was supported on his left elbow, which held his Bible so that the firelight fell upon the printed page. The print was small, the light bad, and it came from the wrong direction, but the strong vision of the young Shawanoe read it as easily as if under the glare of the noonday sun.

Half way to the opposite side of the fire was stretched the Sauk, his posture precisely the same as that of Deerfoot, except that he rested on his right elbow. Their feet, therefore, were turned toward each other. His eyes were fixed on the face of the Shawanoe, who was reading the marvellous volume, and shaping its words into the tongue which Hay-uta could understand. Eliot, the Indian apostle, translated the whole Bible, and his work was one of the most striking ever done by man, but he put into the American tongue those truths into which he had been trained and with which he had been familiar for years—the character of the labor was immeasurably changed when the interpretation was made by an Indian to one of his own race.

Deerfoot, as he had done before, would read a verse or two in a low tone to himself, and then, looking across to his companion, explain as best he could their meaning. Now and then Hay-uta asked something, and occasionally Deerfoot faintly smiled as he answered.

The Kentuckian watched the Shawanoe with as much interest as did the Sauk, and, though his emotions were different, his wonder and admiration were fully as great.

" He is the most remarkable Indian that ever lived," was the thought which stirred the heart of Jack Carleton, as it had done many a time before ; " Hay-uta is in the prime of life, larger, stronger, and he has always been a fighter ; he did his best to kill Deerfoot, but he was vanquished as though he was only

a child. A short time ago they were
striking at each other like a couple of wild
cats, and now they are talking about the One
who taught men to forgive their enemies ; they
would die for each other. It's no use," added
Jack, shutting his lips tight and shaking his
head, as was his habit, when doubt was removed,

"there *is* something in that religion which can
tame a little fury like Deerfoot was, and make
savages as gentle as lambs."

By and by the senses of the youth began to
dull, and drowsiness crept over him. The last
recollection was the figures of the two Indians
stretched out in front of the camp-fire, one
reading and the other listening with rapt attention. The hum and murmur of voices was in
his ears when slumber gently closed his eye-
lids.

His awaking was pleasant. The sun was
above the horizon, the sky was clear and the
air was balmy. The warm season was at hand,
but it had not fully set in, and, under the shade
of the towering trees, the coolness was delight-
ful. Birds were singing and the brightness
and cheerfulness which pervaded nature every

where was like that which makes us fling our hats in air and shout for joy.

Jack appreciated all this, but there was something else which filled his being with more eager delight. The air was laden with the odor of broiling fish, and if there is any thing more fragrant to the senses of a hungry person, I have never been able to learn what it is.

Leaving the sleeper where he lay on his blanket by the fire, Hay-uta and Deerfoot had stolen out to the river, from which it required but a few minutes to coax a number of toothsome fish. These were cleaned, spitted, and broiled over the coals raked from the camp-fire.

The Shawanoe had travelled with the Kentuckian long enough to gauge his appetite accurately, and thus it came about that when Jack Carleton ceased eating, he had all that he wished, and in reply to the question of Deerfoot, said he was ready to go through the day without any thing more.

"Deerfoot," said the youth, placing his hand on his shoulder, and looking him earnestly in the eye, "where is Otto Relstaub?"

The Shawanoe gave him a reproving glance,
as he answered :

"Deerfoot does not know ; the Great Spirit
has not told him."

"I understand well enough that none knows
or can know where the poor fellow is, nor
whether he is alive or dead ; but you have done
a good deal of hunting, and, though you found
out nothing yesterday, yet you have formed
some theory ; what I want to know, therefore,
is your belief."

Deerfoot began examining his bow, as if to
assure himself it was ready for some use which
he seemed to think was close at hand. He
gave no answer to the question, and acted as
though he had not heard it. Determined that
he should not have such an excuse, Jack
repeated his inquiry with more directness
than before.

The young Shawanoe could not ignore him.
Pausing a moment in his inspection of his
weapon, he looked gravely at his young friend
and shook his head. Whether he meant to
imply that he knew nothing, had no theory, or
believed that Otto was beyond the reach of help,

was left to Jack himself to decide. The action of Deerfoot, however, proved that he had not yet despaired of the missing youth ; for, without any hesitancy, he announced that they would make their way to the river again, and crossing over, continue their search on the other shore.

"There's some comfort in *that*," was the conclusion of Jack ; "so long as he believes a chance remains, so long shall I not despair."

The fact that Deerfoot meant to take his friend with him, looked as though he had decided to push the search a long ways beyond the river. Jack succeeded at last in drawing from him his belief that Otto was not in the custody of the party with whom they had had the difficulty the day previous. That, however, was not an important admission, for the young Kentuckian had come to the same belief long before, and it did not help clear up the mystery as to the whereabouts of the missing boy. Deerfoot went somewhat further, and expressed the hope, rather than the belief, that Otto was alive. When Jack asked him whether it was not likely he had been transferred to the custody of other parties, the Shawanoe again shook his head, as he did when the same thing was said before.

There could be no doubt that he had a theory of his own which he did not make known even to Hay-uta. Jack could not extract the least hint, nor could he guess what it was, (and I can not forbear saying, just here, that, though the Shawanoe was far from knowing the whole truth, he suspected a part of it, as will appear all in due time).

The spot where the three had encamped was about a furlong from the river, and to the latter all three made their way without special care or haste. Jack Carleton felt compli mented that Deerfoot meant he should bear them company in the renewal of the effort to find Otto Relstaub.

But a disappointment was at hand. When they reached the stream, Deerfoot would not cross until after a careful reconnoissance. He had approached the river at a point above where the Pawnees held camp the evening before. He meant that if the passage was

effected, it should be without risk of discovery
from their enemies.

It must be admitted that the situation was a
peculiar one in more than one respect. First
of all, there was no reason to believe the Pawnees were aware that the two strange Indians
who created such a turmoil had recrossed the
river, nor was it known that the hostiles themselves were in the neighborhood. Besides, the
warrior who made Jack prisoner the evening
previous was playing a singular part in the
proceedings. There was no telling where he
was at that moment, nor when he would turn
up again. Added to this, was the absolute
ignorance about Otto Relstaub. If they could
have gained some inkling of the disposition
made of him (for there could be no doubt that
the warriors identified by the Sauk knew all
about it), the hunt could be forced to a conclusion, one way or the other, within a few hours.

Directing Hay-uta and Jack Carleton to
remain for the present where they were, the
Shawanoe said he would swim over and examine
the vicinity, before allowing his friends to join
him in the final search for the lad. This was

such a radical change of purpose that Jack
was impatient. He did not hesitate to ask for
an explanation ; but he quickly learned that
impatience. anger or dictation availed nothing
with the young Shawanoe. He was afraid of
no one, and if he chose to keep his thoughts
to himself, it mattered naught whether it gave
pleasure or offense to others.

Before attempting the passage, Deerfoot
ranged up and down the stream for a considerable distance, scrutinizing the belt of open land
on the other shore, and the woods beyond.
Not a vestige of the Pawnees was to be seen.
Then he climbed a tree, and from the top
looked off over the country for a space of
many miles. He hoped to detect the faint
stains left in the atmosphere by the camp-fire
of the hostiles, but he was disappointed in that
also. Had he not learned the contrary the
previous night, he could have believed that he
was the first human being whose feet had ever
pressed that solitude.

The Shawanoe was too subtle a woodman to
forget any point of the compass. It was not
impossible that the Pawnees, angered by the

indignities and the disappointments they had
suffered at the hands of the young warrior and
his companions, had tried to flank them. They
were not all cowards, and though some of
them looked upon the phenomenal youth as an
evil spirit, there were others who must have
known him as he was, and who were eager for
the chance to bring him low by means of their
rifles.

CHAPTER XIX.

DEERFOOT'S survey of the opposite shore was ended ; but whether it was satisfactory to himself or not, could be learned only by questioning him. Jack Carleton took good care not to do that. He had never seen the young Shawanoe so reserved, and having once been denied the knowledge he sought, he left his friend to work in his own way.

It looked to Jack as if the Shawanoe was seeking to wrap more mystery than usual around himself, for when he came back to his friends, he took off his quiver of arrows and placed it and his bow in their charge, thus showing his purpose to leave them behind in the business in which he was about to engage. It certainly was inconvenient to swim the river with them, and, in spite of the care and skill of the owner, it was impossible to reach land with bow and arrows in the best condition. Furthermore, they rendered him too conspicuous. No doubt some of the Pawnees were near at hand, even though no signs were discovered, and if the Shawanoe carried his weapons, his venture was likely to be defeated at the beginning.

" Let my brother open his eyes," said he, after a few words with the Sauk, which, of course, were not intelligible to Jack Carleton, " the Pawnees are not far."

"I will do my best to guard against surprise," replied the young Kentuckian, "and with Hay-uta as my friend, I am sure we shall take care of ourselves."

"Deerfoot can not say when he will come back," added the warrior, looking toward the river, as though expecting to catch sight of some clew among the leaves and branches, "but he hopes to be with his friend before the sun is overhead."

This was the only farewell uttered by the Shawanoe, who walked to the undergrowth which lined the shore and overhung the water. He entered the latter like a diving-bell, whose enormous weight causes it to sink silently and swiftly to the bottom.

"Hay-uta, let's watch him," said Jack, moving carefully to the margin of the river, from which they could peer out without detection. The Sauk could comprehend the action of the boy, though not his words, and I am warranted in saying that his curiosity was equal to that of his companion, when he gazed through the leafy interstices upon the river.

The Shawanoe now gave an example of his amazing skill in the water, such as Jack Carleton had never seen before. He remembered the dexterity which he displayed in towing the canoe across the Mississippi, with Jack and Otto in it, and with the Indians along shore blazing away with their rifles; he had seen the youth disport himself in a way that no one else could equal, but on none of these occasions were his achievements so extraordinary as when he let himself into the river, passed under the surface, and vanished from sight.

Jack Carleton had heard of his exploit in

sinking to the bottom of the Ohio in a large iron kettle let over the side of the flatboat, and of his swimming to shore behind the canoe in which sat Tecumseh, but it now looked to him as if he were passing the entire distance—more than a hundred yards—beneath the surface.

"That can not be," said the lad to himself, when he reflected on the time it must take to proceed that far; "no human being can hold his breath long enough to go more than half the distance, and I don't believe he can go even that far."

There was scarcely a zephyr stirring, so that the rapidly flowing river was without wavelet or disturbance. As none of us is amphibious, the most skillful swimmer must seek the air at brief intervals, and, knowing where the Shawanoe had entered, Jack fixed on the point in the river where he would be likely to rise. He knew that, of course, when he did so it would be only his nose which would appear. Any one on the shore would not suspect the meaning of such appearance unless previous knowledge had awakened expectation, but the closest scrutiny of Jack failed to see the slightest ripple, such as would have been made by the dropping of a pebble into the river. The lad was right, beyond all question, when he concluded that, wherever Deerfoot came up for air, it was a long ways from the spot on which he had fixed his attention.

Glancing at Hay-uta bending forward at his side, he observed that his scrutiny of the stream was as close as his own. He had, in fact, made the same guess as the pale-face youth, but with a more profound belief in the prodigious capacity of the Shawanoe, he fixed upon a point further down stream and closer to the other bank for his reappearance; but the seconds lengthened into minutes and nothing was seen. The wing of the flitting insect, had it glanced against the surface, would have caused a crinkle or two which the watchful eyes of the Sauk would have detected, but as it was, his vision, roaming back and forth, and here and there over the calm surface, saw no sign that any thing of the kind had taken place.

At the moment of greatest wonderment, both watchers were startled by the leap of a small fish, which sprang a foot or two into the air, flashing like silver in the sunlight, and then fell back. The first belief of the spectators was that this was their friend, but the truth was immediately apparent.

Jack Carleton was on the point of giving up, when the Sauk touched his arm and uttered an exclamation. He was pointing to the other shore, his extended finger indicating a tree which grew out almost horizontally over the river, for a distance of eight or ten feet and then curved upward like the runner of a sleigh.

As he looked he saw Deerfoot in the act of drawing himself out of the water. With one hand he raised himself upon the twisted trunk, along which he crept into the wood beyond, never making the least salutation to his friends, who he might have known were watching for him.

" By gracious ! " exclaimed Jack. " He swam the whole distance under water ! he can beat a fish ! "

It is not to be supposed that Deerfoot accomplished this feat, for it was beyond the range of

o

human attainment; but he did swim the distance with only a single rise—if such it may
be termed—when the tip of his nose gently
came up long enough to empty his lungs of
their hot air, and take in another draught of
the life-giving element. That he should do
this under the eyes, as may be said, of two
watchers, without their detection, was not the
least remarkable part of his performance.

Jack would have given much had he and
Hay-uta possessed the power of talking to each
other. The Indian was one of the best warriors of his tribe, and had formed a peculiar
affection for the young Shawanoe. More than
likely he held some well-founded suspicions of
the real reason which led Deerfoot to make his
curious trip across the river, and between the
two the truth might be brought out.

Deerfoot having disappeared, it was idle to
watch the river any longer, and the two withdrew a step or two and sat on the ground,
there to await the Shawanoe.

" I don't suppose I shall have time to teach
him the English language," thought Jack, surveying his companion, who lolled on the ground

as though he meant to put in an hour or two of sleep ; "and I'm sure he won't be able to make much headway with me. I spent some weeks visiting the Sauks (that is on their invitation), and never was able to get hold of more than a dozen or so of their outlandish words, but there isn't one of them that can be turned to account just now. So I'll wait till Deerfoot tells the story for himself."

Probably twenty minutes had gone by, when the stillness was broken by the report of a gun. It was from the other shore, and sounded so faint that it must have been fully half a mile inland. Hay-uta started up, and looking sharply at Jack, raised his hand for him to keep silent. No need of that, for the youth was listening as well as he. In the course of a few minutes Hay-uta rose and went to the river shore, where he stayed some time, peering out over the surface, but he came back without having seen any thing unusual, nor did the two hear another sound of a gun.

"It would be strange," thought Jack Carleton, "if that rifle killed Deerfoot ; the tiniest bullet, if rightly aimed, will do it, and great as is his skill it can not protect him against treachery. As mother says, his time will come sooner or later, but none of us can tell when, any more than we can name the hour appointed for us to die.''

Except for the slight disturbance named, the Sauk would have fallen into slumber, but all such disposition was now gone. Seating himself on the ground, he began examining the bow and arrows which had been left in their charge. Finding it somewhat awkward to do so while in the sitting position, he rose to his feet, and Jack placed himself at his side as if to give help, should it be needed.

Perhaps it should be said that Jack Carleton knew one or two interesting facts regarding Deerfoot not yet known to the reader. In the first place, the Shawanoe was the owner of at least two bows, nearly as long as himself and possessing tremendous power. That which the Sauk held in charge was of mountain ash, made in the usual fashion, the cord being composed of deer sinew, woven as fine and almost as strong as steel wire. The center-piece was round and had been polished hard and smooth by the friction of the Shawanoe's right hand, which had grasped it so many times. The entire bow had been stained a. dark cherry color, its proportions being so symmetrical that it would have been admired by any one.

When picked from the ground the bow was unstrung. Hay-uta carefully bent it over and slipped the noose in place on the notched end. Then, after examining one of the feather-tipped arrows, he fitted it in place and looked around for some target at which to discharge it.

Jack motioned to him to wait a moment while he furnished the mark desired. Running toward the most open part of the wood, he broke a branch and hung his cap on the stump, the distance being perhaps twenty yards. Jack would have made it greater, but for the interference of the vegetation.

The Sauk looked at the target a minute or two, then at the bow, and fitting the end of the arrow against the string, he slowly raised the weapon and took aim. Jack stepped back eight or ten feet, so as to be out of danger, and watched the result.

"I don't believe he can hit it, but like enough he will skewer my cap, which I ain't anxious to have done."

The Sauk held the bow slanting in front of him, just as he had seen the owner do, and he took long and careful aim. He formed a striking figure, his pose being graceful and correct. Unlike the Shawanoe, he was right-handed, as was Jack. His left foot was a little in advance of the right, the toe of the moccasin pointed in the same direction as the arrow, while the right foot was turned slightly outward. The left hand grasped the bow in the middle, while (as most beginners do) he clasped the end of the arrow against the string, between the thumb and forefinger. His body was erect and well-balanced, the head thrust a little forward, the left eye closed, and the right ranging along the line of the arrow as though it were the barrel of his rifle.

Slowly he drew back the string until his right hand was beside his cheek. He had seen Deerfoot many a time hold his right arm rigid, while the other pulled the string back of his head, but Hay-uta was surprised to find the tension so great that he could not draw it another inch. Holding it thus a second or two, he let fly.

CHAPTER XX.

JACK CARLETON fixed his eyes on his cap, wondering how near the Sauk could come to it. Feeling some misgiving, he took several more steps backward, until he was fully five yards from the pendant headgear.

Twang went the bow-string, and the next instant something flashed so close to the eyes of the youth that he winked and flirted his head backward. The arrow had missed his nose by less than an inch !

" Well, that's the greatest shooting I ever saw ! " exclaimed Jack, when he turned and saw where the missile, after clipping some leaves near at hand, had fallen to the ground. " Hold on ! " he called, with a gesture which the Sauk understood, " if you are going to try it again, aim at *me ;* then I'll be safe."

Hay-uta was as much astonished as he—so

much so, indeed, that he stood staring, neither smiling nor making any move to launch another shaft. Jack ran and picked up the arrow that had been discharged, for the quiver was not full and Deerfoot had none to throw away.

When the youth rejoined the warrior, the latter handed him the bow, as though glad to be relieved of it, but seeing he had done no harm, he made a successful attempt to grin.

"Hay-uta, you are not to be blamed because you ain't half as handsome nor smart as other folks; it is no fault of yours if nature made you a fool; you are entitled to pity; but if you want to learn something about handling a bow just study *my* style."

The reason Jack Carleton talked in this fashion was because he knew the one whom he addressed could not understand a word of what was said. Nevertheless, Hay-uta looked upon his actions with interest; for, feeling assured that the shot could not be as bad as his, the chances were that it would be much better.

Conscious of what was expected of him, the young Kentuckian (who could not repress a smile over the performance of the Sauk), did his utmost to make a shot which would command the admiration of the only spectator with whom he was favored.

"I'm in a peculiar situation," reflected the youth, as he fitted the same arrow to the string, "for I am to try to hit a target which I don't want to hit. I don't suppose there's much danger, but I would like to beat Hay-uta."

The latter walked to the stump of the limb on which hung the cap, but he showed his wisdom by dodging behind the trunk of a tree large enough to shield his body. Jack laughed when he observed him peeping timidly from behind this cover.

"I'll point a little to one side of my cap," reflected the youth, "and if I elevate my aim a little, as Deerfoot does, I ought to come pretty near it."

His manner of discharging the bow was similar to that of the Sauk. He slowly drew back his right hand, whose thumb and forefinger inclosed the arrow and string, until his strength was at the highest tension, when he let go.

The aim could not have been improved, for it was a "bull's eye". The flint-pointed shaft tore its way through the top of the cap, which was carried off its support and dropped to the ground with the feathered part of the missile sticking in the air.

Hay-uta ran from behind the tree, picked up the target with the head of the arrow tangled in it, and held up the two in view of the young Kentuckian, who viewed them with dismay.

"Great Cæsar!" he exclaimed, "I believe I've ruined my cap!"

But as that which had been done could not be undone, he put on the best face possible. He waved his hand and nodded his head, as though he was not unduly proud over his own success.

"That's the way I always manage those things," he said, loftily, "put it up again."

The Sauk saw what he meant and replaced the cap, from which he first drew the destructive arrow, with a good deal of recklessness as it seemed to the owner, who plainly caught the gleam of daylight through the top, when it slightly oscillated for a moment on its perch.

"I don't suppose another shot will hurt it much, so I'll send this one right in the track of

the first; then Hay-uta will know that my
skill is next to Deerfoot's, and it won't be necessary to do any more shooting with this plagued
bow."

The second missile was launched with more
care than the first, Jack doing his very best to
make a center shot ; but the result was astounding : the arrow impinged against the tree
behind which the Sauk had shrunk, chipped
away a piece of the bark, and skipped off at a
sharp angle, just as did the glancing missile
which slew the ancient king of England, when
hunting in the forest.

It looked to the amateur as if Hay-uta, when
he thrust his face from behind the trunk was
grinning to an extent that endangered his ears.
Nothing could have been more eloquent than
his gesture, when he pointed to the untouched
cap, then at the tree from which the bark had
been chipped, and then with a still more over-
whelming smile indicated the spot where the
erratic arrow lay at rest.

Jack Carleton flung the bow to the ground
(as if it were to blame for his miserable work),
but he could not help laughing when the Sauk

brought back cap and arrows, and gravely handed them to him.

"If there was any chance of my hitting the mark," said the youth to himself, "I might lead him to believe I missed it on purpose, but likely enough my third shot would be wilder than the second, so I'll resign my commission."

A brief examination of his cap showed that the shaft had inflicted a ragged rent, but when the strong material was pushed and doubled together, a good deal of the air was prevented from entering through the opening. The arrows were replaced in the quiver, the bow unstrung, and the two "shook themselves together", as the expression goes.

The forenoon was well along and the air promised to be warmer than on the previous day, though, where the shade was so abundant, it could not be oppressive.

It was not likely that any thing would be seen of Deerfoot until he chose to present himself to them, but, as if in obedience to the same impulse, the two moved toward the river bank, which was close at hand.

Jack allowed the Sauk to keep in advance,

for he did not mean to make any observation for himself. They were only a few paces apart when the lad caught the gleam of water among the trees in front and stopped, while the warrior stepped to the edge with the guarded step he always used at such times. While the surface of the river was partially visible when looking through the limbs, yet the undergrowth almost shut off the view if one stepped down the sloping bank. Just as he had done many times before, the Sauk reached his right hand forward and parted the vegetation, so as to clear the way in front.

A glance was enough ; near the middle of the river and almost opposite where they stood was an Indian canoe containing six Pawnees, two of whom were paddling the boat straight for the bank on which the Sauk and young Kentuckian had been practicing archery.

Jack Carleton saw that his friend had made some discovery, and he stepped quickly to his side. He did not heed the warning gesture of Hay-uta, and it took only a few seconds to learn the whole truth. Both moved back, allowing the leaves to close again. The Sauk then lay flat on his face and the lad did the same ; in that posture neither could be detected by any parties on the river.

It was noteworthy that, although the Pawnees were using no special caution in crossing the river, and though they were but a few rods distant, yet the swinging of their paddles and the advance of the canoe were so noiseless that Hay-uta and Jack only discovered them, as may be said, by accident.

Without taking time to consider the significance of the proceeding, the friends on shore must needs use great care to avoid a dangerous complication. If the Pawnees should learn where they were, the chances were ten to one that they would either kill or capture both.

There was good ground, however, to hope that delicate as was the situation of our friends they were likely to escape. Although nearly opposite to the Sauk, when he first saw the party, and heading as they were for the spot where he stood, yet the swift current carried the boat downward, so that it was sure to land a distance below. The footprints made by Jack Carleton, Hay-uta and Deerfoot did not lie in that direction, and, therefore, the peril was at its minimum, unless some impulse should lead the Pawnees to turn and move up stream. It remained to be seen whether that would be the case.

The two, therefore, lay still, listening and peering into the shrubbery and undergrowth which grew between them and the margin of the river. The straining ear was able to catch the faint sound of a ripple against the prow of the heavy laden canoe, and once or twice the dip of the paddle was heard. Then the Pawnee who was the leader said something in the guttural voice peculiar to his race, and one of his warriors answered.

All this was a relief to the couple, for it was proof that no one in the canoe suspected the truth, they had no thought that two of the parties whom, most probably, they were seeking, were anywhere near them.

The soft rippling sound which occasionally came to the watchers showed that the canoe was drifting with the current and that it would land at a point fully fifty feet below. Hay-uta and Jack ventured to raise their heads a few inches, and, as they did so, caught a glimpse of the boat and its occupants, as it ran sharply against the bank and the warriors began stepping out.

This was a critical moment, and lowering their heads, they pressed the ground as closely as they could. Jack half wished that some car of Juggernaut might roll over them, so as to flatten them still more.

The grunting of voices was plainly heard, while the Indians stood close to the boat and discussed some question. Had Jack and his companion raised their heads, as they did a few minutes before, they would have seen every one of them. The Sauk did elevate his nose, just enough to gain an indistinct view of the nearest Pawnee, but the youthful Kentuckian lay with his ear against the ground. Soft as were the footfalls of their enemies, the sound reached him through the better conducting medium of the earth.

" Suppose the Pawnees *do* come this way— what then ?"

This was the question which presented itself to the youth, and which, naturally enough,

p

caused him misgiving, for, beyond all doubt, the peril was critical. If the Pawnees moved up stream, nothing could save the two from discovery, and it then would be two against six—all brave and well armed. The former could make no stand before a force three times as strong as they, and their situation could scarcely be improved by flight. Grave as was the crisis, it was rendered still graver by the fact that Jack and Hay-uta could not talk to each other. At such a time, a perfect understanding must exist between the members of the weaker force, and I have shown that in the present instance, that was impossible.

"Ah, if Deerfoot were only here," was the prayer that trembled on Jack Carleton's lips more than once, while he lay on the ground listening to the grumble of voices so close at hand.

"It was queer on his part any way," added the youth, following the line of thought forced upon him ; "just when we need him the most he is gone ; the Sauk is a good fellow, but he can't compare with Deerfoot. Helloa ! " he muttered, noticing a movement on the part of Hay-uta, " something is up."

CHAPTER XXI.

JACK CARLETON thought himself warranted in imitating the action of Hay-uta, though he did not raise his head as high as he. The result was odd. He was able to look between the bases of the trunks and smaller bushes, so that he saw a number of moccasins, without being able to discern the bodies to which they belonged. He observed three or four pairs, and the fringes of the leggings to the knees. The Pawnees were walking, but their feet looked as if they were simply raised and put down again, without advancing or retreating. Inasmuch, however, as they soon disappeared, it was clear they were taking the right course—that is, for the best interests of our friends.

The Sauk, with the upper half of his body erect, watched the warriors, until they could be seen no longer, when he uttered an expression of relief, for both he and Jack realized that their escape—if it should prove to be such— was one of the narrowest possible. It is difficult to conceive how, in the event of discovery, they could have saved themselves from the Pawnees.

But the presence of the latter on that side of the river, was of importance to the Sauk and Jack Carleton, and was likely to complicate the situation. This would be especially true, if Deerfoot knew nothing about it. He having set out on some errand of his own, might have been led to a point which prevented him from discovering the canoe.

At any rate, the Sauk felt the necessity of keeping an eye on the hostiles. He motioned to the lad to stay where he was, retaining his own gun and Deerfoot's bow, while he looked after their enemies. Jack nodded his head, and the warrior moved away.

From his position, prone on the earth, the youth was able to follow him with his eyes for some distance. The sight was curious, as he dodged from tree to tree, his body bent over like a centenarian under the weight of his multitudinous years.

Nothing could have been done with more exquisite skill, and, when he too passed from sight, the one left behind knew that the Pawnees would steal no march upon them.

"Let me see," said he, his spirits rising as the situation improved, "I've got plenty of ammunition for my rifle, and besides that, here are Deerfoot's bow and arrows. If I had a fort, like that which sheltered Otto and me on the other side the Mississippi, I might stand a siege. There would be one good thing," he added, as he surveyed the aboriginal weapon ; "when I fired this off, none of the Indians would know which one it was to hit—it certainly wouldn't be the one I aimed at, and I couldn't guess for myself."

Rising to his feet, he scrutinized every part of the wood, but there were no signs of the Pawnees, who, it was more than probable, had passed down the river shore and away from the vicinity.

"Now we have done a good deal of tramping back and forth," reflected the youth, "and those redskins are so sharp that the chances are ten to one they will come upon our footprints. It won't do to sit here all day until some of them tumble over me."

It was clear to Jack that the hostiles had started out on what was likely to be an extended reconnoissance, and, therefore, were sure to be gone a considerable while. As the canoe lay only a short distance off, he passed through the wood and undergrowth until he reached the spot where it was drawn only a few inches up the bank.

He surveyed it with natural curiosity, though he had seen many similar ones further to the east. It was about fifteen feet long, made of bark, sewed together, and the cracks filled with gum. The ends were curved over, so there was no difference between them, and each was ornamented with paintings which composed a symphony in black, red and yellow.

Two long paddles lay lengthwise in the boat. They were double—that is, the handle was in the middle, the ends being dipped alternately by whomsoever was propelling the craft. Jack looked behind him several times, before resting his hand on the gunwale. Something else which lay at the further end interested him, but he could not make it out at once. Leaning forward, he reached it with his bow, and then observed that it was a scalp. The barbarous trophy, by some unusual accident, had dropped unnoticed from the belt of one of the Pawnees, for it is not to be believed that he would have left such a prized souvenir behind him, no matter on what duty engaged.

The ragged patch of skin that had been torn from the crown of some vanquished foe was three or four inches in diameter, and the tuft of hair was long, black and coarse. Whoever had succumbed and borne the outrage, one thing was certain—he was not a Caucasian, but belonged to the same race as his conqueror.

Jack, who had seen such trophies many times, raked this one still closer and picked it up. The dryness of the skin showed that several weeks had passed since it was taken. More than likely it was the accompaniment of some fight that took place while the Pawnees were pushing their explorations toward the Mississippi.

"Wouldn't that be a pretty thing for *me* to carry?" remarked the youth, placing the hand which held it against his waist, as though it were a watch charm which he was holding in place for the admiration of others. "If I should walk back to Martinsville, and stride up and down between the houses, wouldn't the folks open their eyes? and wouldn't mother conclude that her Jack was doing well?"

In order the better to examine the scalp, the lad had laid down his gun and the quiver and bow within the canoe, where they could be caught up if wanted. He was too prudent to hold his position, with the possibility of the Pawnees reappearing, without continually glancing around in quest of them. Aware, too, that his footprints were likely to be discovered, he would not have approached the canoe, had it not been for a well-formed purpose of turning the boat to his own advantage.

"The Pawnees have come over the river to raise the mischief with us, so it will only be

JACK CARLETON AND RED WOLF (*p.* 249).

fair if I do what I can to reciprocate. I'm sure that when they come back, this canoe will either be missing, or it will have to run into port for repairs."

A shiver as if from an electric shock darted from the crown of Jack's head to his feet, for at that instant, he heard a slight sound as if made by a person clearing his throat. Looking up, he saw one of the Pawnee warriors, twenty yards distant, walking toward him. He held his rifle in one hand, and was moving slowly with his eyes fixed on the ground just in front of him. His manner left no doubt that he was the owner of the scalp in the canoe, and that, having missed it, he was walking back over his own trail, while he searched every foot of ground for the trophy. He had not seen the young Kentuckian, and had no suspicion that he was in the vicinity. Discovery, however, must come within the next few seconds, for the nearest shelter was too far off to be of avail. The sight of the pale-face skurrying to cover, would be sure to bring a bullet from the Pawnee's gun, or he would summon his comrades to the spot, by one of those whoops which were heard so many times the previous day.

There was but one thing to do—shoot at the Pawnee and run. Jack bent over to pick up his gun, but in his panic grasped Deerfoot's bow by mistake. Fortunately, it was strung, and it took only a second or two to fit an arrow in place. Pointing it at the approaching Indian, he put forth his utmost strength to draw it to a head.

Before he could do so the Pawnee was within ten yards—close enough for him to discover some movement in his field of vision even though his gaze still rested on the ground. He stopped as if on the edge of a precipice, and looking up, saw a pale-face holding a formidable bow, with the arrow pointing at his breast.

This particular Pawnee was Red Wolf, who had been driven almost out of his senses when Deerfoot launched the shafts at him and Lone Bear, as they sat by the deserted fire. The figure on which he gazed was not the terrible Shawanoe, but the bow and the arm which slowly drew back the string and arrow were more than enough. He whirled like a flash and was off, bounding from right to left, as do the Digger Indians of the west when seeking to disconcert the aim of an enemy.

" Confound you ! " muttered the archer, " since you are so afraid, I'll give you cause to be ; I'll bury this arrow in your back, so that you may take it home in place of the scalp."

Whiz! went the shaft, with all the power he could throw into his arm, and with the best possible aim. It is enough to say that it did not come within ten feet of hitting the fugitive.

The incident showed that it would not be safe for the lad to stay where he was for another minute. Without stopping to consider the consequences, he shoved off the canoe, stepped into it, and, seizing the paddle, began guiding it down the stream. As he did so, he kept it as close as he could to the shore, where the likelihood of discovery was much less than further out in the stream.

Meanwhile, Red Wolf awoke to the fact that

he owned a good voice, and that one of the enemies for whom he and the rest of the Pawnees were hunting, was much nearer than was supposed. He emitted a screeching yell, enough to startle all who heard it, and, looking around and seeing nothing of the white archer, he stopped and again signalled for the rest to hasten while it was yet time.

The echoes were heard lingering among the arches of the woods, when a footfall fell on his ear. Turning his head, he observed another warrior, but the first glimpse revealed the startling fact that he belonged to a tribe not only different from that of the Shawanoe, but from the Pawnees. There could be no mistake as to his sentiments, for the moment he discerned Red Wolf, he brought his gun to his shoulder The Pawnee made an attempt to leap behind the nearest tree, but before he could do so, Hay-uta, the Sauk, pulled the trigger. There was no miss *that* time: the career of Red Wolf ended then and there.

"There's been too much mercy shown the Pawnees," probably thought Hay-uta, as he ran forward to tear the scalp from the head of his vanquished foe. Reaching the inanimate body, he caught the long hair, whipped out his knife, and was pressing the crown with the point, when he uttered an exclamation, dropped the horsehair-like locks, shoved his knife back in place, and ran from the spot.

That which upset Hay-uta's balance for the moment, was the sudden recollection that he was a *Christian* Indian instead of a heathen. One of the cardinal truths which Deerfoot had impressed on him, was that he should use no unnecessary cruelty toward his enemies ; that he should refrain from the barbarous practice of taking the scalp of a fallen foe.

The Sauk halted a few minutes until he could reload his gun, for, like all frontiersmen, he appreciated the need of having a loaded weapon always at command. Then he resumed his flight toward the point where he had left his young pale-face friend. This carried him so close to the canoe that he saw it in the act of moving from the shore, and recognized the figure of Jack within it. Suspecting what it meant, he hurried thither, and was observed by the lad at the moment he dipped the paddle in the current. He reversed the movement, and immediately after, the Sauk stepped within and took the second paddle.

The youth laid his down, saying:

"You understand this business better than I, and I won't mix things by trying to paddle in one direction while you work in another."

In turning over to Hay-uta the charge of the canoe, Jack did the wisest thing he could do, and he pleased his companion, on whom, it may be said, for the time the welfare of both rested.

CHAPTER XXII.

NO good reason could be thought of why Jack and the Sauk should remain in the canoe. In fact, they would have shown more prudence had they remained where they were when the Pawnees disembarked and walked out of sight in the woods; or, if they felt the need of changing their quarters, they ought to have gone as far as they could from their foes, instead of following them and inviting more peril.

The training of the American Indian makes him treacherous, subtle and full of resources. The desire to "get ahead" of, or to outwit a rival is natural to us all, and is one of the most characteristic traits of the red men. It was that prompting, more than any thing else, which led Hay-uta to leave the youth behind, while he trailed the Pawnees into the forest.

But the death-shriek of Red Wolf was sure to bring his comrades to the spot within the space of one or two minutes; they would quickly read the particulars of the story, and the footprints of the Sauk would be traced to the river's edge, where their arrival was inevitable within an almost equally brief space of time.

Should Hay-uta head for the opposite bank, and whirl the paddle with might and main, he and his companion would be riddled with bullets before they could pass beyond range of the Indians on shore. There really was but one thing to do, and that was done off-hand and without hesitation.

The canoe, under the silent but powerful strokes of the Sauk, and with its light load, skimmed over the surface like a swallow. Hay-uta ran as close in as he could, without allowing the overhanging limbs to obstruct his speed. Twenty rods were passed in this manner, when he turned the head of the boat toward shore, refraining, however, from letting it run against it. One bound carried him out, and Jack was at his heels. Then a gentle shove sent it beyond the dripping branches, where it was under full control of the current, and it resumed its downward flight, though in the bewildered fashion which showed it was under the control of no one.

It was fortunate for our friends that the margin of the stream was fringed with so much vegetation, as it afforded the best kind of a hiding place. Without entering the water, they crouched into the smallest possible space, Jack wondering whether their good fortune would still bear them company.

A wailing cry sounded a brief distance above, and the lad needed not the grimace and gesture of the Sauk to know that the Pawnees had discovered the body of Red Wolf and the theft of the boat. Within the following minute the tread of hurrying moccasins was heard, and they passed within a few feet of where the two lay, not daring even to look up. That was all well enough, but when another cry made known they had found the craft, the real peril of the two may be said to have begun.

Jack Carleton knew as well as if it had taken place under his own eyes, that one of

the Pawnees was making his way through the
water to the boat, whose gunwale was grasped,
and by which it was drawn back to land.   This
took place about as far below our friends as the
point from which they started the canoe was
above them.   If the Pawnees should retrace
the ground, carefully beating the bushes for
"game", they would be sure to drive it out.

Jack found the care of the bow of Deerfoot
quite a burden.   It was continually in his way,
and was of no help at all.   Seeing his embar-
rassment, the Sauk took it in charge, while the
youth suspended the quiver over his shoulder.

The Pawnees did not make the search that
was dreaded, and it is not difficult to guess the
reason.   They had just lost one of their number, and, though there seemed to be only two
foes near them, yet they must have suspected
there were more.   These strangers could do terrific fighting, as they had proven, and the five
Pawnees preferred to await the arrival of re-enforcements, which would soon come from the
other side.   In truth, a study of the events
which followed, as well of those which pre-
ceded, shows good reason to believe the curious

coincidence that the Pawnees were as ignorant of the reappearance of the Shawanoe on the other bank, as he was of the passage of the river by the half dozen hostiles in their canoe.

But the report of the rifle, the death-shriek, and the shouts of the Pawnees, had given Deerfoot an inkling of the truth, before he was able to learn all by investigation on his own part. Still it was a most annoying interference with a daring scheme he had set on foot, and which was in danger of being overthrown altogether. The brow of the youth wrinkled with impatience, for he knew that all this skirmishing could have been saved to his friends, had they used care ; but at the moment he was most discouraged, events took an unexpected turn in his favor.

Meanwhile Jack Carleton and Hay-uta did not stir for several minutes, but, as they listened, it seemed to the youth that their enemies required not to come very nigh, in order to locate them by the tumultuous throbbing of his heart. He was sure the brief silence which followed was occupied by the Pawnees in looking for them, but, as I have shown in another place, he erred. The rippling of water caused both to turn their heads, and, through the interlacing vegetation behind, they caught a glimpse of the canoe and its five occupants, heading toward the other side. The Sauk softly insinuated his hand between the leaves, so as to give a better view (though he ran much risk), and Jack ventured to peep forth.

The Pawnees, as our friends believed, had gone back for re-enforcements. Possibly a score, more or less, of warriors would be transferred to the shore they had left, and then the campaign would open in earnest.

Hay-uta could not close his ear to the whispering of prudence; clearly their duty was to leave the spot before their enemies could come back. Bravery, skill, and cunning, when allied to common sense, would permit no other course.

Throwing off, therefore, the extreme caution they had exercised, they rose to their feet, and the Sauk led the way to the river bank. They did not forget the care which a frontiersman always shows when treading the wilderness, but the tension of their nerves was relaxed, and Jack felt some of the jauntiness that was his during the first day he spent with Deerfoot in the hunt for Otto Relstaub.

It did not seem necessary to go far, and scarcely a furlong was passed when the Sauk selected a spot from which they could watch the river without exposing themselves to detection by any one on the further shore. If the Pawnees should return, as our friends were confident they would do, it was not likely they would delay long. It was an easy matter to summon all their warriors, and such as could not be accommodated in the canoe, could swim beside it.

At the moment that the Sauk secured a safe point from which to look out, Jack Carleton made the most important discovery that had come to the knowledge of any one of the three since starting on their journey.

Something on the ground just ahead and a little to one side of Hay-uta, caught his eye. The Sauk did not see it, and the boy did not suspect it was of any account. It was in obedience rather to a whim than to any reasoning impulse that he stepped aside and picked up the object.

"Great Cæsar!" he exclaimed. "It's Otto's cap!"

For a moment Jack stood transfixed, with the article held at arm's length, while the Sauk stared in turn, as if he thought the youth was beside himself.

But the lad was too familiar with that head-gear to be mistaken. He turned it over and over, held it close to his face and scrutinized every particle of it; it was the same peaked hat which poor Otto had worn so long, and it was on his head when he and Jack—both captives —parted company weeks before.

How long the hat had lain where it was picked up, could not be told. Its make was such that, while the owner had worn it several years, it was still good for an indefinite time longer. A day or a month of exposure would make little difference in its appearance.

When Jack had recovered from his amazement, he and Hay-uta examined the immediate vicinity. The action of the youth, and the emotion he displayed, told the story to the Sauk, who did not fail also to see the value of the clue that had fallen into their hands.

Ten feet from where the cap was found lay a small decayed tree. It had probably been blown down during some gale. The suggestion presented itself that Otto Relstaub was sitting on this support, when he either flung the hat from him, or some one else did so. That which the friends wished to find now was the footprints left by the lad when he went away : *they* would tell the story as nothing else could.

If the missing boy had gone within the preceding two or three days, the keen vision of the Sauk could see and follow the trail. Recognizing his immeasurably superior skill, Jack remained seated on the tree and nodded to Hay-uta to push his search.

The warrior did every thing he could, stepping as lightly as a fawn, his shoulders bending low, while he scrutinized the leaves with a minuteness which would have detected a pin lying on top of them. A faint trail leading through the wilderness is sometimes plainer a few steps distant than it is beneath one's own feet. The disturbance of the vegetation, the rumpling of the leaves resulting in the turning of the under side toward the sun, and those trifling disarrangements which you or I would never notice, can be identified by what may be called an off-hand scrutiny, possibly on the same principle that a careless glance at Pleiades will reveal each of the seven stars, when, if the gaze is fixed on the matchless group, one of them modestly shrinks from view.

There was no artifice known to the aboriginal brain which was not called into use by the Sauk warrior. He stepped with the utmost care, so as to disturb the leaves as little as possible. First of all, he gave his attention to the space between the log and the river. That was short, and its examination required but a brief time. Hay-uta seemed to suspect that the trail would be found to lead toward the stream, but he was disappointed, as not the slightest trace was discovered. I may as well say that though the scrutiny was continued for half an hour, and embraced a complete circle around the spot where the hat was found, it resulted in no success at all. The conclusion was inevitable—so long a time had passed since it was thrown to the ground, that every vestige of the footprints had been obliterated.

Finally Hay-uta straightened up, and, looking in the expectant face of Jack, shook his head. " I was afraid of it," said the boy, " so many days have passed since he lost it, that nothing is left but to guess how it all came about—and though I've done all the thinking I know how, I am done."

Such was the fact. How it was that Otto Relstaub had come to leave his hat lying there on the leaves was beyond the power of Jack Carleton to tell. It could hardly be that he had done so voluntarily, for it was impossible to conceive of a reason for it, and the probability that some one else was the cause, only intensified those misgivings which, in a greater or less degree, had tormented the young Kentuckian from the hour he started to hunt for his missing friend.

CHAPTER XXIII.

DURING the time occupied in the scrutiny of the surroundings, Jack Carleton forgot all about the river for which they had set out to watch for the returning Pawnees. Though the Sauk most likely kept it in mind, yet he was so occupied that he gave it no attention. Now, that he was relieved, however, he advanced the few yards required, and took a survey of the river as it swept past.

It so happened that he was just in time, for the canoe which had caused such a stir earlier in the day was returning. It was two hundred yards up stream, and was loaded to its utmost capacity with Indian warriors. There were fully a dozen, and the craft was sunk to its gunwales—so much so indeed that the two who were handling the paddles were forced to use care to escape swamping.

The Sauk thought that probably other Indians were swimming alongside or behind the craft, but a brief study of the water convinced him that such was not the case : all the Pawnees who were coming over to push the campaign were in the boat. It would seem that a dozen brave and well armed warriors were sufficient to combat the force on the other side.

Hay-uta stood watching the river with such quietness that Jack, who was still sitting on the prostrate tree, never suspected he had discovered any thing, until he turned about and signified by signs that the craft and its occupants had landed some distance above.

I need not say that all this time the lad was longing for the return of Deerfoot, the Shawanoe. If any one could penetrate the mystery which shut them in at every step, he was the one to do it. None could have attained a point nearer perfection than he, so far as woodcraft was concerned.

"But what can we do ?" was the question which presented itself to the youth ; "if the faintest footprints showed on the ground, the

Sauk would have discovered them, and if they ain't there, Deerfoot can tell no more than we know.

"I wonder what in the name of all that's sensible he meant by crossing the river, and leaving his bow and arrows in my charge. If I owned such an arrangement the first thing I would do would be to fling it into the river. Whatever plan he had in mind when he swam over, must have been a blunder which is likely to upset every thing."

The knowledge that the Pawnees had landed on the same shore where were the Sauk and Jack Carleton required attention on their part, for if their enemies decided to search for the marauders who, after slaying Red Wolf, had run off with their canoe, it would not do for the parties to remain idle.

In making their way to the spot where they were now resting, our friends had taken much pains to hide their footprints, and it would be a hard matter for the Pawnees to trace them. In fact, Hay-uta felt little fear of it.

While he and Jack busied themselves in the manner described, Deerfoot had not been idle.

He swam the river, as you have been told, and reached the other shore, without awakening suspicion on the part of the Pawnees. After emerging from the water, he set about locating the war party, for the first step in his scheme required that to be done. His expectation was that the company were gathered near some point not far removed from the camp-fire of the night before.

A scout through the woods, however, showed he was mistaken. He found what seemed to be half the party grouped around a new fire, where there was evidence that most of the previous night had been spent. Breakfast was over, and a number were smoking pipes. The experienced eye of the Shawanoe told him there was no purpose just then of moving away. The Pawnee villages were still far to the north-west, but the warriors were in the comfortable condition of those travellers who are at liberty to spend as much time as they choose on the road. It mattered little to them whether they were a week early or a month late.

Had any one observed the countenance of

the young Shawanoe while he was studying
the group around the camp-fire, he would have
seen that he was deeply interested in one
warrior, who was standing with arms folded,
and leaning lazily against a tree, smoking a
long-stemmed pipe. It was his old acquaintance Lone Bear, and it was clear that, whatever the plan of the Shawanoe, it assigned a
prominent place in it to that individual.

Without affecting any secrecy in the matter,
I may as well say that the scheme of Deerfoot
was as simple as difficult. He could converse
readily with the Pawnee, Lone Bear ; the latter
knew the fate of Otto Relstaub ; he had lied
when asked for information ; Deerfoot resolved
to compel him, if possible, to tell the truth.

The project at first seems absurd, for it may
well be asked by what possible means could
Deerfoot hope to extract reliable information
from the rogue. It would never do to venture
among the war party for that purpose, for the
previous experience of the Shawanoe showed
how he was hated, and the situation had not
improved since then.

Deerfoot hoped to separate Lone Bear from

the rest of the company, so as to have him
alone to "operate" upon; but that would
require strategy more delicate and skillful than
that by which the hunter detaches a choice bull
from a herd of bison, until he has him where
he wants him.

Enough has been told to show in what terror
the Shawanoe was held by Lone Bear, who
believed he was under the special patronage of
the Evil One. Should he encounter the dreaded
warrior alone in the woods, more than likely
he would succumb without a blow.

But the Pawnee was among his own people,
and it looked as if he meant to stay there for
an indefinite time to come. As nothing could
be done so long as he had company, the one
and all important problem which faced Deerfoot at the beginning, was how he was to draw
the warrior away to a safe point in the
wood.

There really was no means of doing so. Deerfoot could conjure up no strategy which, when
launched against a party of Indians, would
produce the desired effect upon a single member, leaving the others unaware of what was

going on. He had asked the Great Spirit to open the way, and he was prepared to wait, with the stoical patience of his race, for the "moving of the waters".

Lone Bear smoked his pipe with the placid enjoyment of an ancient Hollander, while the Shawanoe surveyed his painted and sodden features with peculiar interest. Red Wolf and several warriors, with whom he had become familiar, were missing, but the presence of one party caused surprise. The redskin who had held Jack Carleton prisoner for a short time the evening before was among the group, also smoking his pipe with as much pleasure as Lone Bear himself. He did not seem to attract any attention, and was as much at home as any of them.

His case was a singular one, but Deerfoot concluded that he had had some quarrel with the members of the company. He had probably killed his antagonist, and had fled without stopping to catch up his gun. After his experience on the other side of the stream, he had opened negotiations at long range with the company, and, finding them ready to receive him, had passed over and joined them.

Suddenly Lone Bear stood upright, like a man who recalls a forgotten engagement. He took his pipe from his mouth and stared around in the woods, as if looking for some one. Deerfoot's heart fluttered with the hope that he meant to start off alone.

At this moment, the battle on the other side of the river opened. The whoops, report of a gun and cries caused much excitement among the Pawnees. All of them sprang to their feet and looked toward the river (too far off to be seen), as if they expected to learn by observation the meaning of the hubbub.

The Shawanoe frowned with impatience, for, as has been stated, it looked as if the imprudence of his friends across the stream would destroy the purpose which had brought him to the vicinity of the Pawnee camp. The probabilities indicated great danger, so far as Hayuta and Jack were concerned, and Deerfoot was on the point of rejoining them, when he decided to wait. Whatever their peril, the end was likely to come before he could reach them.

R

The sound of the turmoil borne to the war party in camp soon ceased, and a long silence followed. Two of them walked toward the river, and a third sauntered in another direction—all apparently in pursuit of information. Deerfoot's eyes sparkled. Ah, if that third man had only been Lone Bear!

The warrior on whom the young Indian had his attention fixed, however, seemed to be partial to his former attitude, and, still puffing his pipe, he leaned once more against the tree, as if lost in meditation.

By and by the red men from the other side came over in the canoe, and, as may be supposed, they had a stirring story to tell. Deerfoot watched them from his concealment, but heard nothing from which he could gain any information.

Among the dozen selected to make the return in the canoe was Lone Bear. Suspecting their intention, Deerfoot kept his eye on them until the craft left the shore.

It was then he "grasped the situation". The Sauk and his young companion had taken care of themselves in spite of the large party

of enemies ; they had stirred the wrath of the
Pawnees to that point that they had secured
re-enforcements to go back and crush the
daring foes.

All this proved that it would not do for
Deerfoot to linger after the departure of the
party, especially as the one in which he was
particularly interested was in the canoe.

The boat, laden so deeply with painted valor,
reached the shore only a few minutes in
advance of the Shawanoe, who, with his usual
skill, avoided detection by friend or foe.   The
point where he landed was above that which
the canoe touched, for he tried to approach as
nearly as he could the spot where he had left
his two friends.   He quickly learned they were
not there, and then moved down the stream
parallel to its course, keeping near enough to
observe it all the way.

It will be noticed that this took him close to
the Pawnees, who were also searching for Hay-
uta and Jack Carleton.   In one sense, the
larger body was between two fires, but in no
danger.   The shape of affairs was singular.
The Pawnees were hunting for the Sauk and

his companion, while Deerfoot, their friend, was also looking for them, but doing it in the wake of their enemies. The difficulty of Deerfoot was increased by the fact that whatever signal he sent to his friends, would have to be thrown over the heads of their enemies.

But the Shawanoe addressed himself to the task with his usual coolness and confidence. When he caught sight of the warriors, moving along the bank of the river in no particular order, he fell in, and "joined the procession," as may be said. It is not to be supposed that the Pawnees had struck at once the trail of those who took so much pains to keep out of their way, but the loose manner in which they were following them indicated that they suspected, rather than knew, the course taken by the fugitives.

When this had continued some minutes, the Shawanoe appeared to feel the necessity of reaching some understanding with his friends, despite the great risk incurred. He therefore emitted the soft, bird-like signal, which he knew would be recognized if it reached them.

Indeed, there could be no mistake in that

respect. The trouble lay in the fact that it would also be heard by enemies, who, if they did not know, would be quite sure to suspect its purport.

CHAPTER XXIV.

THE ear of the American Indian, like his eye, is trained to wonderful fineness, and the faint, tremulous note, which seemed to float from among the tree tops, stirred the suspicions of the Pawnees. They stopped in their straggling pursuit, and showed such interest that Deerfoot was compelled, for safety's sake, to steal further to the rear. If they should locate the point whence the call was sent, it would be advisable for him to move still further away.

But the result of the signal, if disappointing in one or two respects (for it brought no response from his friends), was gratifying from another point of view. It was apparent that the call of the Shawanoe produced uneasiness among the Pawnees. It showed that, while they were hunting for their enemies in one direction, one of them, at least, was in another place. It must have deepened the old fear that a large number of foes was in the neighborhood, maneuvering on the outer part of the circle which inclosed the Pawnees. Enormous advantage was thus placed at the command of the strangers, and the situation of the warriors bore a suggestive similarity to that of the hunter who, while hunting the tiger, discovered that the tiger was hunting him.

Deerfoot did not withdraw so far that he lost his surveillance of the Pawnees. He smiled in his faint way, when he noticed their glances toward different points of the compass, and saw them gather for consultation.

They stood thus only a few moments, when a singular movement followed. Three of the Pawnees took each a different direction through the wood, while the main body continued its advance in a more stealthy manner than before. Their line was along the river and close to it, which looked as if they were following the trail of the Sauk and Jack Carleton. Whether or not such was the fact could not be determined

by Deerfoot, since the footprints of the Pawnees, covering the same course, hid those of
the two in advance.

In fact Deerfoot did not care, for, if the
Sauk and Jack Carleton knew no better than to
allow a party of hostiles to overhaul them in
the wilderness, they deserved the consequences ;
but cool and collected as was the young Shawanoe, his heart gave a quick throb when he
noticed the other movements which I have
named.

One of the dusky scouts took a south-west-
erly course, another went almost due south,
while the third faced the south-east, the paths
of the three diverging like so many spokes of a
wheel. The course of the last named, if persisted in, would take him within a hundred
feet of the tree behind which the Shawanoe
screened himself.

What rendered this prospect more gratifying was the fact that this Pawnee was Lone
Bear, the very warrior whom the Shawanoe
was so eager to detach from the main party,
so as to gain the chance to "operate" on him ;
the opportunity he sought was thrust into his

hands so unexpectedly that he believed it was in answer to his prayer.

It would seem that Deerfoot ought not to have found any difficulty in manipulating matters to suit himself, but his situation was exceptionally delicate ; for, above every thing else, it was necessary that he should not be discovered, or have his presence suspected. It would seem, however, that the signal should have given the clue.

Lone Bear had started on a scout, and, recalling his experience on the other side of the river, he was sure to put forth all the cunning of his nature to escape any surprise from his enemies. He was alert, and glanced from side to side, and indeed in all directions, while advancing on a slow, loping trot. It was easy enough to avoid discovery from him, but, in moving round the trunk of the tree (so as to interpose it as a guard), there came a time when the Shawanoe was likely to be seen by the main party, which was not only close, but showed no hurry to move on.

This danger was avoided by Deerfoot with characteristic deftness. He lay flat on his face,

in which posture he could not be detected by
any one a dozen yards away, and skillfully
shifted his position until the back of Lone
Bear was toward him. Peering around the
trunk, he kept his eyes on the Pawnee until the
intervening trees and vegetation shut him from
sight. Then Deerfoot rose to his feet, and took
his trail like a blood-hound.

The Shawanoe felt the battle was won. There
could be no doubt that Lone Bear had started
on the same errand as the other two—that of
scouting through the neighborhood for the
main party of Pawnees. Deerfoot might have
wondered that he should do so, after the wild
panic into which he had been thrown by him,
but like enough he felt the need of some such
action in order to repair his damaged reputation.
It was not impossible that he volunteered for
the perilous duty.

But having taken such a step, it must not be
supposed that Lone Bear forgot the perils to
which he would be exposed. His vigilance was
unremitting, and it need not be said that he
looked well to the rear.

In a few minutes the pursuer and his unconscious fugitive were beyond danger of discovery from the main party, and there was little fear of Lone Bear escaping Deerfoot. He had his trail and was sure to run him down.

The Pawnee scout followed an almost direct course for twenty rods, when he stopped, and, standing erect, slowly turned his head and body, using eyes, and ears for all they were worth. He seemed to be satisfied with what he failed to discover, and advanced at a slower gait in the direction of the river, displaying the same vigilance shown from the first.

The distance between Lone Bear and his friends was great enough to suit the purpose of Deerfoot, who now began to manœuvre with a view of getting near his man without the latter suspecting it. Great as were the cunning and woodcraft of the Shawanoe, it is difficult to believe such an exploit possible, in view of the watchfulness of the Pawnee. He was scouting against his enemies, and to suppose he would permit one to approach him unobserved is to declare him a stupid Indian—which he was far from being.

But a guarded pursuit and study of his

actions, made it clear what his line of conduct was to be, and like the most successful of wood-men, Deerfoot in adopting a certain policy anticipated the action of his adversary.

The latter had not proceeded far in the direction of the river when he again stopped, and, standing motionless, looked and listened, just as he had done many a time when stealing through the country of an enemy, and just as he did years before when fleeing for so many miles through the wilderness to escape the Shawanoes.

For aught that he saw, the Pawnee might have been the only living person within a thousand miles of the lonely spot. Looking aloft at the arching trunks, the branching boughs, and the spread of the leafy roof, he saw no sign of life, except a gray squirrel, which, running lightly along the shaggy bark of a huge limb, whisked out of sight in the wealth of vegetation beyond. Here and there patches of blue sky could be detected, with the white flecks of clouds drifting past, but neither the ground nor the trees nor the air showed aught else. Not even a bird, sailing high overhead, flitted to sight, and the leaves below were rustled by no step of bear or deer or smaller animal.

But such might be the case, with a score of red men prowling near at hand. They would flit hither and thither like so many phantoms, and all the acuteness the Pawnee possessed was needed to elude the traps they were likely to set for his feet. He seemed to believe he was alone, and, resuming his noiseless advance, he did not stop until the listening ear detected the soft flow of the stream, and the daylight between the trees showed the river close at hand.

Again, having satisfied himself, he moved forward until he caught the gleam of water. The same form of scrutiny which has been described was repeated, after which Lone Bear faced down stream and hurried toward the main party fully a half mile distant.

The course of the Pawnee may be described as similar to that of starting from the hub of a wheel, following one of the spokes to the tire, and after travelling some distance along that, returning to the hub by another spoke. Lone Bear had gone to the limit of his tramp, and as the other scouts had taken the same course through different portions of the wood, it will be seen that the neighborhood was sure to be thoroughly examined.

Lone Bear must have concluded that, wherever their enemies had located, they were not within his bailiwick, for, having faced to the westward, he dropped into his loping trot, which, in the case of many Indians, appeared to be more natural than the ordinary walking gait.

It is not impossible that when the dark eyes of the warrior rested on the large trunk of a white oak almost in his path, he reflected what a capital armor it would make against an enemy. At any rate, whether he thought of it or not, he made the discovery in the most astounding manner.

Less than a dozen steps intervened between him and the dark, corrugated bark of the towering wood king, and he was surveying it with a curious expression, when Deerfoot, the Shawanoe, stepped from behind it, and with his tomahawk raised over his head, faced the Pawnee.

" Let Lone Bear stand still and make no outcry, and Deerfoot will not harm him ; let him
disobey, and the Shawanoe shall split the skull
of the Pawnee before he can utter a cry."

The previous experience of Lone Bear had
taught him that it was lost time to argue the
question ; indeed, no choice remained but to
accept the situation, and he did so with a certain meekness which was not without its effect
on the Shawanoe. .

" Deerfoot is the greatest hunter of the Shawanoes, and the Pawnee bows his head before
him."

As he spoke, Lone Bear surprised the other
by the completeness of his submission, doing
that which was unexpected to his conqueror.
The rifle which he was holding in his right
hand, when summoned to surrender, was thrown
on the ground ; then the tomahawk was flung
from the girdle, the knife from the sheath, and
all three lay beside each other on the leaves.
Not only that, but Lone Bear moved three
steps backward and signified to the Shawanoe
that he was at liberty to come forward and take
them without molestation from him.

"Let my brother, Lone Bear, listen," said Deerfoot, lowering the left hand which held the tomahawk aloft and resting it against his hip, where it could be used the instant needed; "let the words of Deerfoot be heeded, and it shall be well with Lone Bear; his rifle and tomahawk and knife shall be given to him, and his brothers, the Pawnees, shall never know he was vanquished by Deerfoot."

This was promising a great deal, and the Pawnee looked questioningly at the other, though it could be seen that he placed much reliance on his pledges.

"The ears of Lone Bear are open; he hears the words of the great Deerfoot; his words reach his heart; what is it my brother, the mighty Shawanoe, would say to him?"

It must have been that Lone Bear had some suspicion of the business of Deerfoot, though it was impossible for him to know his full purpose before Deerfoot made it known.

"My brother will be wise if he heeds the words of Deerfoot; he will please the Great Spirit, for Deerfoot asks him to speak only with a single tongue."

" Lone Bear will speak with a single tongue."

" Then," said Deerfoot, " he will make known the truth of the pale-faced boy for whom the heart of Deerfoot mourns."

CHAPTER XXV.

WITHOUT hesitating a moment, the Pawnee made answer:

"Lone Bear speaks with a single tongue; he can not tell where the pale-faced warrior is."

It might have been supposed that the Indian was trying to mislead Deerfoot, but the latter saw his meaning and understood that it was his anxiety to tell the truth which caused him to make answer as he did.

"How many suns ago did the Pawnee part with the pale-face?"

Lone Bear showed he was thinking. His brow wrinkled and he seemed to be looking at something a mile behind the Shawanoe. Then he began counting on his fingers, like a child solving some problem in addition. Seeing that Deerfoot was watching him, he held up his left hand, with his fingers spread apart, and touched them one after the other with the fore-finger of the right, until he had checked off four, thereby indicating that four days or suns had elapsed since he had seen Otto Rel-staub.

"What tribe bought him from the Paw-nees?"

"The pale-face went with no warriors."

"With whom did he go?"

"The pale-face was in the woods alone."

This was astonishing information, for it implied that Otto, like Jack, had managed to escape from his captors ; such, however, was not the case.

Deerfoot repressed all sign of deep interest as he plied Lone Bear with questions.

"Did the pale-face run away when the skies were dark, or was it when the sun was in the sky?"

"The sun was so high that when Lone Bear walked in the clearing it cast no shadow," replied the Pawnee, thereby signifying that Otto Relstaub disappeared at high noon. As it was clear that even the acute Deerfoot did

not grasp the full story, Lone Bear attested
his sincerity by adding :

"The youth whose face was pale became
ill ; he could not walk ; the Pawnees lingered
hours, hunting and fishing ; but his face was
white like the snow ; he tried to rise, but fell
down like a pappoose when its eyes first look
on the day. Red Wolf raised his tomahawk
to slay him, but Lone Bear stayed his arm.
The Pawnees marched on and the pale-face lay
on the leaves, white and ready to die."

There at last was the practical solution of the
mystery. The Pawnees had not bartered off
Otto with any other tribe, but were journeying
homeward with him when he fell ill. His captors had tarried near him for a time, but instead
of recovering he had grown weaker, until one
of the Indians proposed to end the trouble by
sinking his tomahawk in his brain. He had
been prevented from doing so, and then the
warriors had quietly moved on, leaving the
poor youth to die alone unattended in the wilderness.

But had he in reality perished ? That was
the question which was to be answered, but in

order to do so, it was necessary for Deerfoot to gain all the information he could from Lone Bear, who, in fact, was the only one that could give it. He therefore plied him with questions, until nothing more was left to tell. His revelation was pitiful indeed.

Without any sense of the pathetic side of the narrative, Lone Bear repeated his account of how, while they were moving at a leisurely pace, Otto fell ill. It happened to be late in the afternoon, and as the spot was favorable, the company went into camp. The poor fellow lay ill all night, and on the morrow was so pale and weak, that his captors believed he could not live many hours. Still they stayed in the neighborhood until noon, when they abandoned him to his fate. Believing he would not survive more than a few hours, Lone Bear and another warrior placed his gun beside him, covered most of his body with leaves, laid his hat over his face, and composed his limbs, as if for the grave. Otto seemed about to die, and showed no interest in the last sad rites, his eyes being closed when they departed.

Having obtained these particulars, Deerfoot

learned another surprising fact—the point where Otto was abandoned to die, instead of being a long distance to the east, was full three days' journey in the opposite direction. That is to say, the Pawnees, after parting with the lad, had doubled on their own trail and were now the distance named from where it was supposed he had died.

The cause for this retrogression was the love of migratory life which is characteristic of the American race. The Pawnee villages, as I have stated, lay a long ways to the north-west, but among the party that had been on the long tramp, was a strong minority in favor of moving their town to the neighborhood of the river across which we have seen friends and foes pass so frequently. It abounded with game, had plenty of water, numerous fish, and its surface was undulating enough to suit their fancy. All this, no doubt, could be found in other places nearer home, but the stretch of open land which followed one side of the stream for a considerable distance, it may be said, was the deciding inducement. It was the ideal of a site for an aboriginal metropolis, for there was just enough land to put under cultivation to meet their simple wants.

The attractions of the locality formed the principal theme of discussion, until, when three days' journey from the river, the minority had become the majority, and it was decided to return and make a more thorough examination of the neighborhood. They were thus engaged, in their lazy fashion, when Deerfoot, Hay-uta and Jack Carleton overtook them, and the incidents already told followed.

By the time all this became known, the young Shawanoe felt that Lone Bear had nothing more to tell him. Otto Relstaub, if alive, was to be searched for many miles further toward the Rocky Mountains, though, if he was as ill as was represented, he must have succumbed long before.

While Deerfoot had no thought of breaking his pledge to the Pawnee, he was too prudent to trust him. Should he hand him back his weapons he might not attempt to injure the youth, but he would tell his comrades enough to lead them to do their utmost to thwart the purpose of Deerfoot and his friends.

"Let my brother listen," said the Shawanoe, stepping closer to him, as if to make his words more impressive. "When the sun is yonder," pointing to the horizon, "Lone Bear will come to this tree ; he will look on the ground, and will draw the leaves aside ; when he does so he will find his rifle, his knife and his tomahawk ; his brothers shall never know they have been touched by Deerfoot ! "

There was a certain chivalry in this proceeding, for it gave to Lone Bear the means of rejoining his friends without the humiliating confession he would be obliged to make if he appeared unarmed ; for he could invent no fiction that would wholly conceal the truth. All that remained to do was to keep out of sight until sunset, when he could make his way to the spot, recover his weapons and go back with a story of the long reconnoissance that had held him away much longer than was anticipated.

Lone Bear thanked his conqueror for the regard shown him, and the Shawanoe strode off toward the main body of hostiles. He made no change in the route, until beyond sight of the Pawnee. Then he turned to the left, his course being part of the circumference of a large circle, until it brought him to the westward, or, as may be expressed, to the rear of the single enemy. He now approached the large tree which had served him so well. As he expected, Lone Bear was not in sight.

Deerfoot smiled as he stepped to the spot, and, bending over, laid the captured weapons on the ground and covered them with leaves, so as not to attract the notice of any one passing near. That done, he withdrew, the faint smile still playing around his mouth.

Having promised Lone Bear that his weapons should be given back to him in payment for his story (which the Shawanoe was satisfied was true), the conscientious young warrior would not allow any thing to prevent the fulfillment of his pledge ; but he expected that when sunset came he would be many miles away, and it would be a grievous inconvenience to return. Much, therefore, was to be gained by this course. Again, Lone Bear, having no thought that his property would be given up by the Shawanoe before the time he had set, would not be likely to go near the tree until the close of the day. Then, when he was armed again, it would be too late for him to work Deerfoot ill. Possibly, however, he might take it into his head to return earlier; but the Shawanoe cared very little if he did, for even then he felt there was little, if any, cause for fear.

That which Deerfoot now wished to do was to proceed westward with all speed. He had learned from Lone Bear a description of the camp where Otto was left, so that he was confident he could find it with little trouble. Although considerable time had passed, yet when such a party moved through the wilderness they left a trail which could be followed a long time. Deerfoot was confident he and his friends could reach the spot in a couple of days, but his plan was that he should press on alone, leaving Hay-uta and Jack Carleton to follow at a pace more suitable to them. By putting forth his amazing speed, he knew that the three days' journey of the Pawnees could be covered between the rising and setting of a single sun.

Had he been alone, he would have crossed the river at once, and by the time night was closing in would have been many miles on his way ; but the first step was to rejoin the Sauk and his young friend. A perfect understanding must exist between him and them, and that could be done only by an interview.

Furthermore, though a quiet seemed to hang over wood and river, it could not be doubted that Hay-uta and Jack were in much personal danger. They were on the same side of the stream with the hostiles who were hunting for them, and it would be no trifling matter to extricate themselves.

And again, Lone Bear would be sure to give a "pointer" to the rest of the warriors, by which they would suspect that the purpose of the little party was to push on and hunt for the boy that had been left alone to die in the woods. Thus, while Hay-uta and Jack were following their friend, the Pawnees would be trailing them and another curious complication of affairs was likely to result.

Deerfoot had seen enough, while along the

river, to satisfy him that his friends were
further down the stream than the hostiles
whom they were seeking to avoid. His first
step, therefore, was to circle to the left, so as
to pass around the spot where he had seen
them gather near their canoe. On his way, he
discovered one of the scouts prowling through
the wood; he easily avoided him and took
care that his own presence was not suspected.

At the proper moment he emitted the signal,
which in case the Sauk was listening, would be
understood by him. It required great care,
for more than likely some shrewd Pawnee
would catch it up and turn it to account, as has
been done times innumerable under similar circumstances.

There was no response, and Deerfoot did not
repeat it until he had gone some distance
further. Then the whistle was emitted in the
same guarded manner, and almost immediately
brought its reply. Fearful that the latter came
from a foe, Deerfoot kept his position, and,
with all his senses alert, indulged in some
variations which were answered as only

Hay-uta could answer them. All doubt being gone, Deerfoot now advanced unhesitatingly, and a minute or two later was with his friends.

CHAPTER XXVI.

THE faces of the Sauk and Jack Carleton lightened up, when Deerfoot appeared, and warningly raised his finger for them to remain quiet. That he did not mean they were in imminent peril was shown when he said, as he took each hand in turn :

"Deerfoot is glad to look upon his brothers."

"And we needn't tell you how glad we are to see you, old fellow," responded Jack, modulating his voice to the same low key as that of the Shawanoe ; "you were gone so long that we began to think we would have to hunt you up. Here, take these blamed things," he added, passing the bow and quiver to their owner ; "I never was so glad so get rid of any thing."

The lad had shoved the hat of Otto Relstaub

under his coat, where he meant to keep it from the sight of the Shawanoe until after hearing his story. The young warrior, convinced that no Indians were near, and that it would require an hour and probably more for the Pawnees to trace the little party, conversed freely.

The narrative, as may well be supposed, was one of transcendent interest to Jack Carleton, for it was the first definite knowledge obtained of his missing friend. The heart of the listener was filled with pitying sorrow when he learned how Otto had been left to die alone in the wilderness. Tears filled his eyes, his voice trembled, and he said:

"We know now that he was living a few days ago, but what hope is there that he has lasted this long? I am afraid that the most we can do is to give him burial—and we haven't the means to do even that very well."

The three seated themselves on the fallen tree near which the hat was found, and talked as freely as though no hostile was within a hundred leagues of them. The Sauk had little to say, a few words between him and Deerfoot being sufficient. Then, as if to allow them to talk unreservedly (though, of course, he could not understand any thing said), he walked a short distance away. He was just far enough removed to be visible to the two friends. His purpose was to mount guard while they conversed, though there was little need, for Deerfoot could never forget his vigilance.

When the touching story was ended, Jack looked at his friend and asked:

"Do you think he is dead?"

The young Shawanoe nodded his head.

"The Pawnees saw he was very ill; his face was like snow; he was weak; they laid his gun beside him and covered him with leaves."

"Why didn't they take the gun? It was worth a good deal, and the Indians hold such things in high value."

"When the Pawnees bury a warrior, they bury his weapons with him; they were afraid to take the gun; they covered his face with his hat——"

"Are you sure of that?" broke in Jack.

"Such were the words of Lone Bear, who spoke with a single tongue."

"If they left Otto three days' journey away,

with his hat lying on his face, I should like to know how it comes to be *here.*"

And Jack drew the article from under his coat, and handed it to Deerfoot. The latter did not conceal his astonishment, for he identified Otto's property at once. He asked his friend for the particulars, and received them.

Deerfoot's theory was overturned by this discovery, and it was beyond his power to explain the presence of the hat so far away from where the owner had been abandoned. It would be supposed that the discovery would throw discredit on the story told by Lone Bear, inasmuch as the two seemed irreconcilable; but such was not the case. Deerfoot did not doubt Lone Bear's words, and I make free to say just here, that subsequent discoveries proved that the vanquished Pawnee had not deviated from the truth in the first particular.

The active brain of the young Shawanoe grappled with the puzzling problem, and he was still unable to solve it, when the faint report of a gun was borne to the ears of himself and friends. It was so faint, indeed, that

T

Jack Carleton just caught the sound, but it was as distinct to the warrior as if fired within a hundred yards.

I am aware that it sounds incredible when I state that the single report of the rifle, far away in the wilderness, as it was softly borne through the miles of intervening space, told the whole story to Deerfoot the Shawanoe; it solved the mystery; it made clear that which was hidden; he no longer saw through a glass darkly; the history of Otto Relstaub was as plain as if it had fallen from his own lips.

I repeat that it will seem incredible to the reader that such a thing could be true, but I shall soon make plain how it all came about.

The sound of the gun was from a point due south. Deerfoot having fixed it clearly in his mind, said something in a low voice to the Sauk, who had turned his head and was looking as if he expected some summons. Then, rising to his feet, he addressed Jack:

"The night will soon come; we must make haste."

"Ain't you going to search the ground for Otto's trail?" asked Jack, who had hoped that the powerful eyes of Deerfoot would reveal to him that which was hidden from the Sauk.

"There is no trail here," replied the Shawanoe, glancing at the ground, and walking away with a stride which seemed reckless, when it is remembered that the Pawnees were not far off. In fact, the course of the three took them close to the war party who were so clamorous for their scalps; but the task of flanking a company of hostiles was not difficult to Deerfoot. He let his friends know when the situation was delicate, and each used the utmost circumspection; but the young leader deviated so far to one side that he soon placed them in the rear.

Nearly half the day remained, and there was time to cover a great deal of ground. Deerfoot did not break into that loping trot which he could maintain from sunrise to sunset, but his strides were so long and rapid that Jack was on the point more than once of being forced into a run.

The Shawanoe so shaped his course that he passed the tree near which he had placed the

rifle, tomahawk, and knife of Lone Bear. A
glance showed him they were still there, and
he smiled in his shadowy way, but held his
peace. He did not tell his friends the story,
knowing the panic-stricken Pawnee would not
reclaim his weapons until the hour fixed—sunset.

Jack Carleton was well aware, from the
manner of Deerfoot, that he was carrying out
some theory of his own, though the boy failed
to connect it with that far-away report of a
rifle. He was far from suspecting the surprising truth. Nothing would have pleased him
more than to have had the Shawanoe explain
what line of policy he had adopted, but I have
shown long ago that Deerfoot was inclined to
keep such matters to himself until their truth
or falsity was established. Jack knew better
than to seek to draw any thing from him, and,
since he was equally reserved toward Hay-uta,
the young Kentuckian could not feel that he
had any ground for impatience.

As they advanced, the ground became
broken and rocky. Travelling was difficult—
that is, to Jack Carleton—who bruised himself

several times in his efforts to hold his own. He was on the point of protesting, when Deerfoot halted.

Hay-uta showed some signs of the severe strain to which he had been subjected. His chest rose and sank faster than usual, and his dusky countenance was slightly flushed. Jack's face was aglow; he breathed hard and fast, and felt as though he would like to sit down and rest a few hours. But Deerfoot was as unruffled as if he had walked only a mile or two at a leisurely pace.

And yet a crisis was at hand. There was something in the eyes and face of the Shawanoe which showed a consciousness that they were near the end: within the following few hours it would come.

Deerfoot pointed to a ridge a short distance to the south. The top was rocky and precipitous, and the trees and vegetation were so scarce that the rugged baldness could be seen a long ways through the woods.

"The Sauk will hunt from *there to there*," said the Shawanoe, indicating a spot a quarter of a mile to the south, and pointing by the sweep of his arm to another almost opposite where they stood. "Deerfoot will hunt from *there to there*," he added, marking out a similar, though more extensive field, in the other direction.

"And what am *I* to do?" asked Jack, half amused and just a little provoked at what he knew was coming.

"My brother's legs are weary; they want rest; let him sit down and wait till Deerfoot and Hay-uta come back to him."

"The same old dodge!" exclaimed the lad. "I would give a good deal if some one would explain why in the mischief I was brought along with this party anyhow."

"My brother is gentle-hearted; his voice is soft as that of the pappoose when it laughs in its mother's eyes; his face is beautiful; the hearts of Hay-uta and Deerfoot are sad, but when they look into the face of their brother their hearts become light and they feel strong."

This was the most extensive joke in the way of a remark that Deerfoot had ever been known to originate. Jack Carleton saw his slight smile and the twinkle of his black eyes, and knew he was quizzing him. Assuming a seriousness which deceived no one, the doughty Kentuckian deliberately leaned his gun against the nearest tree, pretended to roll up his sleeves, spat on his hands, rubbed them together and clenched them and advanced threateningly upon the Shawanoe. The latter feigned alarm, and, ducking his head, as if to dodge the threatened blow, ran away so swiftly that before Jack could take more than half a dozen steps in pursuit, he was out of sight.

Hay-uta could not be considered handsome, but the smile which lighted up his features made them interesting, to say the least. When he grinned, he did so to the extent of his ability, which was considerable in that direction.

But the Sauk had been assigned to an important duty, and the Shawanoe having departed, he did not linger. He waved a parting salute to Jack Carleton, who, a few minutes later, found himself alone, much the same as he had been left when Shawanoe and Sauk crossed the river to reconnoitre the Pawnee camp.

"There's one thing certain," he said to him-self, recalling the parallelism, "whatever hap-pens, I won't be caught as I was then; I'm not going to climb a tree, and I mean to hold fast to my gun ; but we have come so far from the river that we must be a long way from that party of Pawnees, unless," he reflected, glancing to the rear, "they have struck our trail and have followed hard after us."

The possibility of such danger was not great, but Jack Carleton changed his position to one where he could keep a better lookout, with less danger of discovery. He was sure his friends would not be absent a long time, and he meant to avoid embarrassing their action.

"It was the sound of that gun which led Deerfoot to come all this way. I wonder what it can mean."

Jack had got this far in his meditation, when he heard a footfall near him, and, just as he turned his head, a familiar voice called out :

"*Helloa, Shack, ish dot you?*"

CHAPTER XXVII.

A STRANGE STORY.

THE amazement of Jack Carleton, when he recognized the figure before him, was beyond description. It was Otto Relstaub— the same honest German lad from whom he parted weeks previous when the two were captives in the hands of the wandering Sauks, the divisions of which took such different directions. It was the same lad—the only noticeable difference being that he was bareheaded and his garments were much frayed and torn. He held his gun in his right hand, the stock resting on the ground, while he looked with a half-inquiring expression, as if doubting the identity of the young Kentuckian who had come such a distance to help restore him to his friends. But a second stare satisfied both, and rushing toward each other, they shook hands, laughed and cried for very joy, their expressions disjointed and only clear in their evidence of the delight which overflowed in their hearts.

"Oh, I forgot!" exclaimed Jack, drawing Otto's hat from under his coat and slapping it on the yellow crown of his friend; "here's something which belongs to you."

"Vere did you got him?" asked Otto, taking it from his head and inspecting it. "I never dinks I would sees him agin."

Jack gave the particulars which the reader learned long ago, adding an account of the efforts made by Deerfoot and the Sauk to trace him, and of the despair all felt when they were told the captive had been left to die alone in the woods.

"I never expected to meet you again," said Jack, "and I couldn't understand why it was Deerfoot had any hope."

"'Cause he *knowed*," was the truthful remark.

"But what was the matter with you? You must have got well in a hurry."

Otto threw back his head and laughed in his old-fashioned, hearty style, adding:

" Do you dinks I vos *very* sick ? "

And then the lad told his strange story, which perhaps you would prefer to hear in a little better accent than that of the narrator.

The statement made to Deerfoot by Lone Bear only a few hours before was shown to be accurate in every particular by the narrative of Otto himself, but it had a phase which neither Lone Bear nor any of his comrades suspected.

The Sauks who wandered away from their fellows, taking Otto along as their prisoner, met the Pawnees, who, as the reader well knows, were a long ways from home. Otto was bartered to them, and his captors continued toward their village, many days' journey to the north and west. They went at a moderate pace, stopping and hunting by the way and making themselves familiar with the country, with a view of removing their lodges thither, provided they could find a satisfactory place.

They were many hours on this dismal tramp when Otto asked himself whether it would not be as well to give up all thought of returning home, and of becoming one of the people into whose hands he had fallen. The hardship imposed by his parents impelled him to such a course, and, more than once, he decided not to make any effort to leave the Pawnees, even if a good opportunity offered. Had it not been for Jack Carleton and his kind mother he probably would have become an adopted Pawnee.

But, as the distance between him and his humble cabin in far away Martinsville increased, a feeling of homesickness crept over him until he was utterly miserable. He finally reached the resolve that he would never rest until he was back again in the log cabin near the banks of the Mississippi; no matter how oppressive his lot, it was *home*, and that was preferable to a gilded palace.

The prisoner in the dungeon finds no difficulty in making up his mind to leave; the insurmountable task is to carry out his intention; and the days and nights passed without the first glimmer of hope appearing in the sky of Otto Relstaub.

Several times he saw chances which he believed would enable him to get away, but he feared the inevitable pursuit. He was so many

miles from home that the most laborious tramping would be required for many days, even if
able to proceed in a direct line.

It was this dread which prevented such an
attempt on the part of Otto, while his homesickness increased until his appetite vanished
and his looks were woe-begone. While in this
pitiful condition the poor fellow asked himself
whether he could not feign illness to such a
degree that his captors would abandon him to
die.

The probabilities pointed the other way. In
the first place the Pawnees were quite certain
to perceive the sham, and, in case they were
deceived, they were likely to tomahawk Otto
so as to end the annoyance. These two considerations kept him plodding along with the
party, which, fortunately for him, progressed
slowly.

But while the youth's physical condition was
not bad enough to deceive the Indians, he
became desperate, and determined to take the
first opportunity that presented itself. Within
an hour he found a chance to pilfer some
tobacco belonging to Lone Bear. He did so

with such care that he was not suspected. Straightway he swallowed it, and I need not say that it was unnecessary for Otto to pretend he was ill ; he was never in such a state of collapse in his life.

His deathly paleness convinced the Pawnees that their captive was at death's door. They urged him to walk, but he could not, and they stayed in camp longer than was intended, in the hope that the patient would rally.

Otto showed a good deal of pluck when, finding himself recovering, he resolutely swallowed some more of the poisonous weed and soon became so prostrated that he really believed his last hour was at hand. He was in great danger, for the nicotine threatened the seat of life, and Otto lost interest in every thing, feeling that it would be a relief to perish and end his misery.

This was his condition when the Pawnees formed the opinion that he could not live more than an hour or two at the most. Accordingly, they covered him with leaves, laid his hat over his face, and, placing his gun beside him, went off. The youth lay hovering, as it seemed,

between life and death. While in that condition, he detected a footfall near him. He was
able to turn his head, but could not move
his body. He recognized Red Wolf, who was
standing a few steps away, knife in hand. He
had returned to take the scalp of the dying
lad, and would have done so, had not Lone
Bear, coming from another direction, interfered. By some argument he led the other to
change his mind, and both walked away.

From that moment reaction set in, and Otto
rallied fast. It was beginning to grow dark,
and he was soon shut in by impenetrable gloom.
Fearful that Red Wolf or some one else would
steal upon him in the night, he crept deeper
into the wood, where he knew he could not be
found when the sun was not shining.

Although his rugged system rapidly threw
off the nicotine poisoning, he was weak and
dizzy. He gained a few hours sleep before
morning, but was awake at the earliest streak-
ings of light and started on his return.

Otto Relstaub's previous experience in the
woods now served him well. He discovered
that the war party, instead of continuing west-

ward, were retrograding and doubling on their own trail. He suspected the true reason—they were prospecting for a new site for their villages. He had judged from their actions that something of the kind was in their thoughts.

As the course of the lad lay in the same direction, he wisely chose to deviate until he was far off their trail, so as to avoid any risk of them.

Otto's deliverance from captivity was singular indeed, but he was too wise to consider it complete until certain that such was the case. He feared that Red Wolf or some of his comrades would return to the spot where he had been abandoned; and, discovering the trick, instantly pursue him.

He therefore devoted many hours to elaborate efforts to obliterate his own trail, or to shape it so that even a bloodhound could not track him. He crossed all the streams he could, wading long distances through the water where the depth was too great to permit his footprints to be seen. When he finally emerged, he often did so on the same side which he entered, perhaps repeating his manœuvre once or twice before leaving the stream by the opposite bank.

This played havoc with Otto's garments, which were torn and injured until it looked doubtful whether they would last him through his journey. Sometimes, while walking where the water was only a little above his knees, he would abruptly step into that which was six or eight feet deep, but he always reached bottom.

During the first day, when the vigorous system of the fugitive demanded food, and he saw the chance of bringing down a wild turkey which trotted swiftly across his path, he refrained through fear that the report of his gun would betray him. He ate a few berries that seemed to have lived over from the preceding winter (the season being rather early for any thing of the kind to have grown since), chewed some tender buds, and lying down at night, thanked heaven he felt so well.

Reaching the bank of the river across which his friends had passed several times, he felt the opportunity for which he longed had come.

With much labor, he succeeded in con-

r

structing a raft sufficiently buoyant to float him without resting any part of his body in the water. Pushing this out into the stream, he drifted fully three miles, gradually working the support toward the further shore.

"Dere," he exclaimed, when he stepped out on land, "dey won't find my tracks if dey don't look all summer."

This was the fact, so far as trailing the fugitive from the spot where he was abandoned, but it so happened that the course of the raft down stream carried him into the very section where his late captors were hunting back and forth. The wonder was that he was not discovered, for there must have been times when his enemies were on each side the river, and he was floating directly between them—and that, too, when the sun was shining.

He was so tired that he lay down beside a fallen tree and slept until near nightfall. Even then he was aroused by the report of a gun so near him that he started up and rushed off in such haste that he left his hat behind him. Soon another rifle was discharged so close that he believed he was surrounded by foes. He had missed his hat, but dared not go back after it, the last gun seeming to have been fired from a point near it. All he strove to do was to get as far from the spot as he could in the least time possible. A strong wind, accompanied by some rain, followed and hastened his footsteps.

It certainly was remarkable that the fugitive's presence so near a number of the hostiles was not discovered, but there is no reason to believe that any such suspicion entered their minds, or that they dreamed of the trick played on them by the captive when he seemed to be lying at the point of death.

Otto pressed on, until once more he felt he had the best ground for believing he would elude his enemies; but he was famishing for food, and when in the moment of temptation, a dozen wild turkeys trotted by him in the woods, he fell and let fly at the plumpest, which also fell.

CHAPTER XXVIII.

A STARTLING INTERRUPTION.

WHEN Deerfoot, the Shawanoe, first saw the recovered hat of Otto Relstaub, and tried hard to guess how it came to be left where Jack Carleton found it, he recalled the words of Lone Bear to the effect that it was placed over the face of the boy who was deserted three days' journey away in the woods. The conclusion was natural that the hat had been carried the intervening distance by the boy himself, who must have recovered from the severe illness that brought him low.

At the very moment the young warrior was beginning to suspect the truth about the youth's illness, the faint report of a rifle came to his ears. Necessarily there could be nothing in the sound of the gun which could identify it, but Deerfoot was sure it was fired by Otto, who was either defending himself against some danger or was after his dinner.

Whatever the immediate cause, the Shawanoe felt that haste was necessary to reach the fugitive, who was likely to be sought by the Pawnees, who also must have heard the report of his rifle. He therefore started on the pursuit, as it may be called, with the Sauk and Jack Carleton at his heels.

That marvelous delicacy of hearing, which was one of the characteristics of Deerfoot, enabled him not only to assure himself of the precise direction of the sound, but to fix the point whence it came. Gaining sight of the ridge, he was convinced that the lad who fired it was in that vicinity. He therefore pointed out the portion which was to be examined by the Sauk, while he reserved a similar area to be gone over by himself—the difference being that he was confident of finding Otto, provided he had not moved far from the spot where he stood when he discharged his gun.

On the way thither, the Shawanoe glanced right and left in search of the trail, but as an intervening storm had obliterated it, and Deerfoot went in a direct line, he of course failed to find it.

Otto Relstaub's woodcraft enabled him to travel intelligently through the wilderness. The second storm overtook him just before reaching the rocky ridge, and he was fortunate to find shelter in a slight cave from the driving rain. Despite the peril from which he had just escaped, he determined to stay where he was until, so to speak, he could recruit. The wild turkeys, of which I have spoken, were abundant in the neighborhood, and he had no difficulty in killing one when he wanted it. He did so, on first reaching the vicinity, and the last one was brought down at the moment Deerfoot was studying the vexing problem as to what had become of their young German friend.

The Shawanoe was approaching the truth when, as I have said, the report solved the mystery, and, while hurrying through the woods with Jack and the Sauk, he was almost positive that they would find the lad for whom they had sought so long in vain. He did not believe, of course, that Otto had entirely feigned the sickness which was the means of saving his life, for the story of Lone Bear forbade that. He did suspect, however, that the captive had been taken ill and probably made it appear worse than was the case, and that, when left alone, he rapidly recovered and took advantage of the surprising chance thus given him in perfect innocence by the Pawnees. What struck Deerfoot as singular was that the Indians should have been so deceived, and that none of them returned afterward—excepting Red Wolf and Lone Bear—to learn whether he had perished. Most likely they went over their trail once more on their homeward journey. That of necessity must have been so long after the abandonment of the lad, that (leaving out of account the doing of Otto's friends) the Pawnees would not make the effort to hunt again for the fugitive whose long start put him beyond danger of recapture.

When Otto Relstaub had finished his story, Jack's eyes sparkled and he again grasped the hand of his friend.

" It is the most wonderful experience of which I have ever heard. I thought my escape from the Sauks was remarkable, and so it was, but it can't compare with yours. I never knew of the Indians being fooled in that manner; but show me where you have spent the last day or two."

"It ishn't as fine as your cabin dot is home in Martinsville, but it ish de best dot I can find."

"You're mighty lucky to find any thing," was the remark of Jack Carleton, following his young friend toward the rocky ridge which had attracted the notice of the Shawanoe some time before.

"I wonder whether Deerfoot will find it?" said he, musing over the strange experience of his friend; "I suppose you have left plenty of footprints which he is likely to see and which will guide him to the right spot."

"I vos going to leave dis place to-nights or to-morrow mornings," said Otto, quite proud of the part he was acting as guide of his old friend, "but dinks dot I stays till I feels like being better."

Before Otto Relstaub could finish his remark, the crack of two rifles cut short his words. At the same moment the whistling bullets and the war whoops left no doubt of the explanation.

Several Pawnees had been prowling along their trail, when the sight of the boys moving away led them to believe they had taken the alarm and were trying to escape. Firing hastily, they broke into a run, with less than a hundred yards separating pursuer and pursued.

"Fly, Otto!" called his companion; "if you can run, now is the time; they're on our heels!"

As the German lad knew the right course, he was obliged to take the lead, while Jack Carleton was behind him. The latter was much the fleeter of foot, and it made him desperate to observe what seemed the sluggish movements of his guide.

"Hurry!" he added, pushing him forward; "they will be on us in a minute and then it's all up!"

"Yaw; I ish doing petter as nefer I couldn't does," replied Otto, who in his excitement dropped back into his crooked words and sentences.

"You ain't half trying, I've seen you do twice as well."

"Yaw; but I dinks—"

The catastrophe came. Like the immortal John Smith, Otto was so busy with his eyes that he had no opportunity to watch where his feet led him. He sprawled forward on his hands and knees, and Jack Carleton narrowly missed going headlong over him. The situation was too critical to laugh, and Otto, thoroughly scared, was up again in an instant, plunging forward with unabated ardor.

The Pawnees lost no time, and the peril was of the most imminent nature. But having regained his feet, Otto dashed forward with the utmost speed he could command, so that the frightened Jack could not find fault with his tardiness.

The leader was following no beaten path or clearly marked trail, but was heading toward a point half way up the ridge, where a mass of rocks rose higher than any others near them, and among which the boy had found a refuge from the storm that drove him thither—a storm which it may be necessary to say, was so local in its character, that Deerfoot and his friends, who were not far off, saw nothing of the elemental disturbance.

The Pawnees, who were seeking to surround the boys at the moment they started, came from different points, all converging so as to shut in the fugitives, as they would have done had a little more time been given them. As it was, when Jack and Otto faced the rocks, their enemies in their rear, one or two were uncomfortably close.

Indeed, there was one fierce warrior nigh enough to interpose across the path of the fugitives. Otto had taken a dozen steps or so after climbing to his feet, when the savage, brandishing his tomahawk in one hand while he grasped his gun in the other, shouted continually some exclamation which was clearly a command to halt, but which, it need not be said, was disobeyed.

Quick to see that he was wasting his breath the red man, with a couple of bounds, placed himself so directly in front of Otto that the latter could not pass him without turning to one side.

"There's no use of fooling with that fellow," was the conclusion of Jack Carleton, raising the hammer of his gun, without slackening his speed ; but before he could bring the weapon to his shoulder, Otto stopped short, throwing up his gun at the same moment, and let drive at the warrior, who could not have had any suspicion that he was in danger until the red tongue shot from the muzzle almost in his face, and then scarce time was given him to know what was coming when his interest in earthly things ceased.

With an ear-splitting screech, he flung up both arms, the gun and tomahawk flying several feet in the air from the spasmodic movement, and he went forward on his face, head and shoulders being thrown so far back that his chest struck the ground first, chin and forehead following like the rockers of a chair.

"Well done!" called out Jack. "Push ahead and we shall be safe."

Suddenly Otto slackened and turned about with a blanched face.

"Mein gracious ! I dinks I hef got de wrong road !"

Jack was in despair ; then he was angered.

"Go on ; go *somewhere ;* don't stop here ! " he said.

And he almost shoved him off his feet in his desperate impatience.

"Vosn't dot fooney?" said Otto, breaking into another desperate run; "it is the road arter all."

Not only at that moment, but for some time previous, it must have been in the power of the Pawnees to bring down both boys by shots from their guns. The intervening space was so brief, that all could not have missed, and when Otto made his last dash for safety, Jack Carleton was in such a direct line behind him, that a single well-aimed bullet would have laid both low; but the Indians, confident there was no escape for the boys, determined to make both prisoners.

Deerfoot, the Shawanoe, always referred to the action of the red men at that time as almost unexplainable. They must have known that the youths had friends close by, and that one of them was the young warrior whom they believed to be in league with the Evil One. The footprints which had guided them through the forest told that fact. There were only four Pawnees (one of whom was the warrior whom

Deerfoot and Hay-uta held a prisoner the night before, and then allowed to go), and as the number of fugitives, if such they may be called, was the same, the advantage certainly could not be claimed by the hostiles. What common sense directed was for them to shoot the boys, and then withdraw, at least until re-enforcements arrived. Their failure to do so was a piece of shortsightedness which neither the Shawanoe nor Sauk understood.

The respite gained by the quick shot of Otto Relstaub was provident ; it threw every one of their pursuers behind them, and the redoubled efforts of the lads carried them swiftly over the remaining space.

"Here we ish !" exclaimed the panting Otto, almost falling again.

"Where ?" demanded the terrified friend ; "I don't see any thing like the cave you told me about."

"It ish de pest dot we have," replied the German lad, noticing the disappointment of his companion.

CHAPTER XXIX.

A FIGHT AND A RETREAT.

THAT which Otto had called a cave proved really no cave at all. Up the winding ascent the fugitives sped, until opposite a lip or shelf, which projected from the rocks on their left. It extended forward three or four feet, rudely sloping away like the forepiece of a cap, but the concavity below was less than half that depth. Jack expected to find a retreat ten or fifteen feet deep. As it was, there was barely room to screen themselves from the flying bullets, and had the rain been driven from the opposite direction when Otto first sought refuge there it would have given no protection at all.

Jack was half disposed to continue his flight over the ridge, but fearful of the greater peril to which they would be exposed, and alarmed by the knowledge that their enemies were almost on their heels, he darted to the left, and stood with his back against the rocky wall, grasping his loaded and cocked rifle, ready to fire on appearance of the pursuers. Otto did the same, and, taking a position beside him, began reloading his weapon.

The hostiles did not stop, but hastened up the rough gorge, and in a twinkling the foremost dashed into sight. Quick as Jack was in bringing his gun to his shoulder, some one else anticipated him. The red man bounded high in air, with the inevitable death shriek, and went over backward, his body pierced clean through with an arrow driven with resistless force from the bow of Deerfoot, the Shawanoe.

This checked the rush of the other two, who found, what they ought to have known before, that the "Evil One" was on hand. They turned and ran at break-neck speed down the slope, vanishing with a swiftness that rendered it almost impossible for Deerfoot to bring down either of them had he been so disposed. Rapid as was their charge up the slope, their descent was a great deal more rapid.

Directly behind the arrow came Deerfoot, landing in the presence of the youths with such suddenness that Jack half raised his gun under the belief that he was an enemy.

Otto was so startled that he spilled the powder he was pouring into the barrel of his rifle, and the young Shawanoe smiled and said:

"My brother is not glad to see Deerfoot."

"I ishn't! you shust waits till I gots dis gun loaded."

Working rapidly, he soon had the charge rammed home and the weapon primed for action. Then, leaning it against the wall, he impulsively threw his arms around the neck of the Shawanoe and kissed him on the cheek.

Jack Carleton was horrified, supposing the young warrior would be offended, but he smiled in a way which showed he was pleased with the honest fellow, who was not ashamed to show the affection he felt.

During the brief moments spent in pleasant interchange, Deerfoot was never quiet. His eyes were continually flitting hither and thither, and he glanced right and left, as though expecting some person or the occurrence of some event. The fact was, that, although the Indians who made the rash attack had fled, the Shawanoe was by no means satisfied. He reflected, that while only the four warriors had been seen, it was more than likely that others were within call.

There was no good reason for tarrying on the slope, and, as soon as Otto had finished loading his gun, Deerfoot signified they were to leave. For a brief spell nothing was to be feared from the panic-smitten Indians, but the Shawanoe glanced furtively down the gorge before leaving the partial shelter of the excavation in the rocks. Then they moved hastily to the top of the ridge, where a stop was made until all could take a survey of the surrounding country. This was an important matter, and Deerfoot did it in his usual thorough fashion, his eyes taking in the whole horizon.

The elevation of the ridge, and the sparse vegetation on the crest, gave the Shawanoe the best kind of an observatory, and he gained an extensive knowledge of the vast expanse of surrounding country.

Looking toward the south-east, the three saw a somewhat similar ridge, though less in extent. It seemed more than ten miles distant, and the attention with which Deerfoot regarded it showed that he was meditating some scheme in connection with it. It took him but a minute or two to form a conclusion. Then he scrutinized the territory in the opposite direction. Toward that point he was looking for enemies : it was there the Pawnee party was in camp or hunting back and forth.

Deerfoot was able to trace the river, on the other shore of which had been kindled the camp-fire of the Pawnees, but he could discover nothing of the warriors themselves. More than likely some of them identified the little party on the slope, and took good care to keep themselves out of sight.

Both Jack and Otto wondered at the absence of Hay-uta, the Sauk. He had been absent much longer than Deerfoot, and the report of guns and shouts of the Pawnees must have told him the same story which brought the Shawanoe in such haste to the spot.

Once more Deerfoot faced the distant ridge

in the south-east. Pointing toward it, he said :

"Let my brothers make haste thither, and wait for the coming of Deerfoot."

"What's the matter now?" asked Jack; "why don't you go with us?"

"The Pawnees are on our trail; they will follow fast; my brothers must make haste while Hay-uta and Deerfoot tarry."

A few words made clear the plan of Deerfoot. The Pawnees, like all their race, were extremely revengeful in their disposition, and they would never consent that the four intruders should be allowed to go back without punishment. They had slain several of their warriors, without receiving any injury in return. What though the Evil One, in the guise of a young Shawanoe, had charge of the little party, neither he nor they were invulnerable, and the well-aimed bullet must be more effective than the arrow of the matchless archer Deerfoot.

An additional incentive to pursuit lay in the fact that the Pawnees had learned of the trick that Otto Relstaub played on them. His pres-

ence in his own flesh and blood was evidence
that could not be disputed. These and other
considerations, which it is not necessary to give
in detail, convinced Deerfoot that a sharp pursuit would be made by the hostiles. Such a
pursuit would be pushed at a pace which
neither of the pale-faced youths could equal ;
they were certain to be overtaken unless skillful strategy was employed.

The Shawanoe, therefore, directed the boys
to make for the ridge which he pointed out in
the south-east. He told them to use all haste
and reach it at the earliest possible moment.
It was probable they could not do so before
dark, but he impressed upon them the duty of
making no halt until their arrival there. If
darkness overtook them while several miles
away in the woods, they must push on. Both,
and especially the young Kentuckian, had had
enough experience to know how to maintain a
straight course when the sun was not shining.

Deerfoot expected to join them before daylight, but in the event of his failing to do so,
they were forbidden to wait for him. At the
earliest dawn, they were to press their flight,

and keep it up to the utmost limit until night-fall. If by that time no further molestation resulted, they might consider all danger ended, so far as that particular party of Pawnees was concerned.

Deerfoot instructed the two friends to resort to every expedient to hide their trail. When they reached a stream, they were never to cross it by a direct line, but, if possible, wade a considerable distance before stepping out on the other bank. If they should find their path crossed by any thing in the nature of a river, they were to make a raft and float a long distance with the current, before resting their feet again on dry land.

It followed, as a matter of course, that all this strategy designed to throw the hostiles off the trail, ought to be equally effective against Sauk and Shawanoe; but the latter made necessary provisions against going astray. He had a clear understanding with Jack as to the distance he was to follow a small stream before leaving it on the other side, and, in case a river was reached, it was agreed that the youths were to drift downward a half mile. Then, when they emerged, a sign was to be left in the shape of a broken limb, dipping in the current. Such evidence would be detected at once by the Shawanoe from the opposite side of the bank —that is, if he had the daylight to assist him, and he could easily arrange *that*.

The sagacity of Deerfoot enabled him to provide against almost every contingency, and the time which he took in making such provision was but a fraction of that which I have consumed in the telling. Within three minutes after he directed them what they were to do, they were traveling down the slope, with their faces toward the distant ridge, and their feet carrying them rapidly in that direction.

Each of the boys understood the scheme of Deerfoot, and lost no time in speculating over its final issue. In fact the rule of invariable success seemed to apply so forcibly to every thing which he undertook that I am warranted in saying that neither felt any fear when he left the ridge and plunged into the forest stretching so many miles beyond.

"You have never seen Hay-uta," said Jack,

after they had walked some ways, the Kentuckian taking the lead.

"No," replied Otto, walking faster than was his custom.

"He is a Sauk, and one of the five who went off with you when we parted from each other."

"Den I dinks I seen him," was the natural remark of the grinning German.

"Of course you have seen him very often, as he has seen you, but you never heard his name Hay-uta, and won't recognize him from any description I give you."

"Why not?" queried his companion.

"It seems to me," replied Jack with a laugh, "that all negro babies and all Indian warriors look so much alike that no one can describe the difference. I have seen a great many Sauks, but it was hard work to tell them apart when they were a little ways off. Some of them were so hideous that they could be identified by their appearance, as others could by the scars on their features or the particular style they had of painting their faces."

Otto naturally wanted to know how it was that a Sauk had come to be the ally of a

Shawanoe, and why, when Hay-uta was any thing but a friend of Otto, he should travel so far and run into so much danger for the sake of rescuing him.

You and I know the explanation, and so it is not required that I should repeat the story of Hay-uta's encounter with Deerfoot in the depths of the wilderness, when the Shawanoe vanquished the warrior, overcoming not only his physical prowess but his hatred, and how the words fitly spoken at that time had proven to be seed sowed on good ground which was already springing up and bearing fruit.

The boys became so interested in the subject that they involuntarily slackened their gait, while they discussed the incident and recalled the gentle reproofs which Deerfoot had given them more than once. It is at such times that we feel the prickings of conscience, and both Otto and Jack asked themselves the question : If this American Indian, born and nursed as a heathen, was so quick to grasp the Word, what excuse shall we offer in the last day when God shall demand of us why, with a hundred fold more light, we persisted in rejecting him ?

CHAPTER XXX.

"WHAT do you suppose Deerfoot once asked me?" said Jack Carleton, stopping short and staring in the face of his friend, who answered with native innocence,

"If you vasn't ashamed mit yourself, 'cause you didn't know more apout de woods?"

"He handed me some cold water in a cup which he made of oak leaves, and when I thanked him he smiled in that way of his which shows his beautiful teeth, and asked me whether I always thanked *every body* who handed me any thing like that, or who did me a favor; I told him that I would consider myself rude if I failed to do so. Then smiling a little more, he came for me! 'Who gives you the sunlight?' he asked; 'who makes the moon and stars to light your feet at night? who gave you your good mother, your health, your food and drink, your clothes, your life?

Do you thank Him when you lie down at night, and when you rise in the morning, and through the day ? '

" I tell you, Otto," continued Jack, " I stood dumb ; he has reproved us both and made us feel thoughtful, but I never had any thing that went home like *that*. I have thought of it a hundred times since then, and that night when I lay down I prayed harder than ever before, and something told me that my prayers went higher, and that He who never turns away His ear was pleased. I didn't say any thing to Deer-foot, but you know, young as we are, that in running back as far as our memories will carry us there are some words and little occurrences that stick by us forever. It is so with that question which was asked me by an American Indian in the deep woods just as night was closing in about us ; his questions will cling to me if I live a hundred years."

" I nefer heard him speak just dot way," said Otto, who was in as serious a mood as his companion, " but he said a good many dings to me and sometimes to both of us which I forgets nefer—nefer—nefer ! When he left me and the

Injins was as cruel almost as fader and moder, I dinks a good deal apouts dem; when I was a layin' by de fire and not knowin' weder dey wouldn't kill me, den I dinks apout dem again and prays hard; when I swallers de tobacco and feels as if I was dead, den I prays agin to Him and He makes me well and prings me owet all right; arter this I nefer forgets to prays to Him."

There could be no misjudging the sincerity of Otto. Jack heard nothing in his quaint accent which could cause him to smile. In truth he was equally thoughtful.

"Most people are willing to call on God when they are in trouble or they think death is close," was the truthful remark of the young Kentuckian, "but it seems to me He must despise a person who forgets all about Him when the danger goes by. I think if I was ashamed to profess Him before others, He *ought* to be ashamed of me when I came to die and called out in my distress."

The conversation continued in this vein, until both awoke to the fact that they were violating the orders of Deerfoot, by loitering on the road ; they had allowed valuable time to pass unimproved—that is according to one view, but in another sense it could not have been better used.

As if to make amends for their forgetfulness, it was agreed they should cease talking for the time, and break into a moderate trot, which both could maintain for half an hour or more without much fatigue. Jack took the lead, and keeping the right direction, he struck the pace which resembled that of Deerfoot, though it was not so rapid nor could he maintain it for a tenth of the time the Shawanoe could run without becoming tired.

The wood as a general thing was favorable, though the occasional undergrowth cropping out of boulders and rocks compelled some deviation and delayed their advance. No water appeared until they had gone several miles. Then it was that they found themselves alongside a stream of crystalline clearness. It was not very broad nor swift, though quite deep. Standing on one shore, the bottom could be distinctly seen clean to the other side. The bed was mainly a reddish clay, and here and there a few pebbles and large stones, but there was no difficulty in following with the eye the beautiful concave until the deepest portion in the middle was reached, and with the same line of beauty it arose to the land beyond.

"Otto, let's have a swim!" called out Jack Carleton, after admiring the stream for several minutes.

What youngster could withstand such temptation? The afternoon was warm, and though rather early in the season, the water itself could not have been more inviting. The only answer Otto Relstaub made was to begin disrobing as fast as he could. Then it became a race between him and Jack as to who should be the first. The Kentuckian was only a few seconds in advance, and both frolicked and disported themselves like a couple of urchins who know they are doing something which they should not do.

Deerfoot had ordered them to push on and not to rest until they reached the ridge many miles beyond, where he hoped to join them. He would not be pleased if he should learn in

what manner his wishes had been disre-
garded.

The boys dived and swam hither and thither,
splashing each other and reveling in the very
luxury of enjoyment. It will be understood
how a couple of persons so placed as were
they found such a bath not only a luxury but
a necessity. Men who spend days and weeks
in tramping through the woods, without a
change of clothing, can not preserve the most
presentable toilet, and the washing of clothing,
which at other times was done by those at
home, was looked after to a greater or less
degree by him who was many miles away.

But, on the other hand, the garments worn
by woodmen were far different from the fashion
of to-day. They were tough and enduring,
and the coarse texture next to the skin pre-
served its good appearance much longer than
does the finer linen we wear. Often Jack
Carleton had washed his, and frolicked in the
water or lolled on the bank until it was given
time to dry in the sun. He and Otto did not
do so now, because their consciences would not
permit them to linger long enough. As any

wading they might do would leave their foot-prints in plain sight on the bed of the stream, they tried to satisfy their sense of duty by placing their garments and weapons on a light raft, and swimming behind it while it floated down stream. In this way they left no trace of whither they had gone, and a bloodhound would have been baffled in attemptingpursuit.

The only mishap of this novel voyage was that while making it, the gun of Otto rolled off and went like a stone to the bottom, but the clearness of the current revealed where it lay, ten feet deep, and it was easy to dive and recover it.

When at last they emerged, a long distance below the point of entrance, a branch was bent and broken as Deerfoot had told them to do in case they crossed a river, and donning their garments, they turned the light raft adrift, and resumed their journey toward the ridge which still lay a long distance away.

By this time the sun was well down in the sky, and it was clear that if the elevation was to be reached before going into camp, several miles would have to be travelled by night, when the moon would give them scant light indeed; but both had done a good deal of that kind of traveling, and the prospect caused no uneasiness. The sight of some game or any thing which could be utilized as food would have been most welcome to the hungry lads.

Lest it may strike my reader that both were showing a degree of recklessness inconsistent with their training and character, it should be said that they kept their ears open for sounds from the rear. It was not considered possible for the Pawnees to press the pursuit with any vigor without the discharge of more than one firearm. The instant such report reached the youths, such tardiness would end.

That report came just before the sun sank from sight. Faint but distant as it floated to them from across the miles of wilderness, it told (like the sound of Otto's gun when heard by Deerfoot) an important truth; the Pawnees were on the southern side of the further ridge, and were pushing the pursuit of the boys with a persistency that left no doubt of their earnestness.

"I dinks we petter goes fast," said Otto,
W

breaking into a trot, which Jack imitated in order to prevent himself from falling behind. They kept it up until the gathering darkness forced them to moderate their pace. A couple of miles still remained to be passed over, but their training rendered that an easy matter, and, but for the craving hunger, there would have been little choice between that and stopping short where they were.

The boys were relieved over one fact: they had come upon no broad stream or river. Indeed, they had seen but the one stream which proved such a means of enjoyment to them, and the configuration of the country rendered it unlikely that they would meet anything of the kind, until after passing the ridge where they expected to go into camp.

Another source of relief was the certainty that their long swim down the stream would be an obstacle to pursuit by their enemies. They would be compelled to make search before the trail could be recovered, and that would take till the rising of the morrow's sun.

And thus it was that, while hurrying on, they were shut in by darkness, and progress became difficult. Even had the moon been at its full, the dense shadows under the trees would have rendered the sense of touch more useful than that of sight, but, as it was, they were making good progress when Jack, who still kept a slight lead, exclaimed in an under-tone :

"By gracious, Otto, there's a light ahead ! What can it mean ? "

" It means dot some wood ish burning, I dinks."

Of one thing the boys were convinced— whoever had kindled the camp-fire was not a Pawnee. None of them could have reached such a position in advance of the fugitives, and the villages of the tribe were so far to the north-west that no other beside the main party were in the neighborhood.

" Deerfoot told us that we must not camp this side of that ridge," added Jack, " so we'll keep on until we find out who our neighbors are."

This was an easy matter, since no effort had been made to hide the light of the fire, which was visible a long distance away. As is the case at such times, it appeared to be closer than it was, both the lads expressing disappointment that it seemed to recede, like the *ignis fatuus*, as they walked toward it.

But when at last our friends halted within a few rods, they were amazed to see but a single warrior in camp. It required some manœuvring to make certain on the point, but the fact was not only demonstrated, but the equally astonishing truth was established that the warrior belonged to the Sauk nation.

Both lads were so familiar with that people that it was scarcely possible to err. In spite of what Jack Carleton had said about the similarity in appearance of all Indian warriors, there were peculiarities of dress and looks which identified them. More than that, the young Kentuckian recalled this one, whom he had seen during his own captivity among that people. He was one of the wildest revellers at the feast described in "Campfire and Wigwam", though generally he was reserved. What drew Jack toward him was the recollection that no one in the village showed more consideration toward him than did he who sat

on the blanket smoking his pipe and looking
into the fire, as if in deep reverie. He had
interfered several times when the prisoner was
threatened with violence, and was so consistent,
indeed, in his chivalry, that when Jack had
assured himself the Sauk was alone, he walked
forward with Otto at his heels, and offered his
hand.

The red man showed no surprise, though he
must have been astonished to meet the white
youths so many miles from their own home.
He rose to his feet, without any appearance of
haste, shook hands with both, muttering something which was doubtless meant as a welcome. Jack managed to speak a few words
in the Sauk language, but, for practical
purposes, they might as well have remained
unspoken.

But several facts were extracted from the
Indian which added to the pleasure of the
visitors. The Sauk was alone, he had not
seen any Indians for several days, and he had
some meat left from that which he had rudely
broiled for his own meal. When I say he
placed this at the disposal of the guests, it

need not be added that in a short time there was none of it left.

The reason why the Sauk had fixed on that spot for his camp was that a tiny spring bubbled from under some rocks near at hand. The bowl-like cavity, in which it collected before rippling away among the gnarled roots of the trees, held enough to afford all they could wish. The added moisture of this spring, as is often the case, nourished a vigorous growth of succulent green grass, which was also turned to good account.

Just as the boys finished eating, they were startled by the whinney and stamp of a horse near them. They looked inquiringly at the Sauk, who smiled and nodded in a fashion which showed that the animal belonged to him. Instead of travelling the long distance on foot, as did our friends, he had ridden a horse, which had been cropping the grass close at hand when the boys came up. The latter's reconnoissance of the camp before presenting themselves failed to show the presence of the animal.

Observing the interest of the boys, the Sauk

picked up a brand from the camp-fire, swung it over his head until it was fanned into a vigorous flame, and then motioned them to follow him, while he showed his steed, of which he was very proud.

The horse snuffed and displayed some timidity when the flame was brought near him, but a few words from his master quieted him, and he stood still while the three walked around and admired his points. The boys said nothing until they were through. Then Jack, with the firelight lighting up his face, looked at Otto, who laughed and nodded his head.

The two had discovered the fact that the horse before them belonged to Otto Relstaub, and was the one for which the poor lad had hunted in vain so long and which, therefore, was the cause of all the misfortunes that had befallen him and Jack Carleton.

CHAPTER XXXI.

A FATAL FAILURE.

DEERFOOT the Shawanoe made known only a few of the thoughts which troubled him, when he hurried Jack Carleton and Otto Relstaub forward with orders to make no tarrying (except to cover their footprints), until they should reach the distant ridge, where, as I have stated, he hoped to join them.

But the conviction had come upon him that afternoon, that the crisis of the long hunt was at hand, and that success or failure, absolute and entire, was near. It will be admitted that they had been in situations of apparently much greater danger, but there was "something in the air" which foretold stirring events.

While he said nothing of the absence of

Hay-uta the Sauk, he was uneasy over it. His own delay was meant to be as much in his interest as in that of the boys. If it should prove that the Sauk needed the help of Deer-foot, the latter wished to be free to give it, and that could not be done so long as the care of the boys was on his hands. When they were out of the way, nothing could interfere with the marvelous woodcraft of the young Shawanoe.

The first point which Deerfoot established, so far as it was possible to do so, was that the four Pawnees, with whom they had come in collision, were the only ones who had reached the neighborhood. The others were near the river, where they were first seen by our friends. The Shawanoe interpreted the reason of this state of affairs to be that, brave as the Paw-nees were, the majority were unwilling to pur-sue their enemies further. They had eagerly crossed the river to engage in the fight, but, learning that the Evil One and two com-panions were moving toward their distant hunting grounds, as though indifferent to pur-suit, they came to the conclusion that they had had enough of the business, and refused to go further.

But among the party were four, who either were braver, or were impelled by a more rancorous hatred, for, as we have learned, they pressed toward the ridge, overtook the fugitives, and paid the penalty of their rashness by losing two of their number. The other couple fled in wild haste down the slope, and one of them never paused until he rejoined his comrades, to whom he told his terrifying tale. The fourth stopped when he had run a short distance, and, after a brief rest, began making his way back to the ridge again.

It probably occurred to him that, since their enemies would not believe it possible for any of the Pawnees to return so soon, then was the opportunity to do effective work, and to get safely away. Accordingly he made his way with great care through the woods to the ridge, from which he had just fled in such mortal fear.

The return of this Pawnee (who was the one held captive by Deerfoot and Hay-uta the night before), was executed with such skill,

that the Shawanoe learned nothing of it. He
believed none of the hostiles was near, though
he acted as though he suspected the contrary.

Deerfoot now devoted himself to finding
Hay-uta. He emitted several signals, such as
the two were accustomed to use, and he was
disturbed because they brought no reply.
Knowing the territory given his friend, he
decided to make search through it. Possibly
some accident had befallen him and he needed
help.

Fortunately Deerfoot had not hunted long
when he was more successful than he expected
to be. He caught sight of Hay uta, who was
sitting on the ground with his back against a
rock, his arms folded, and his gaze fixed on the
western horizon, toward which the sun was
sinking. His fine rifle was leaning against the
rock beside him, and his other weapons were
in place.

The position of Deerfoot was such that he
had a view of the face of the Sauk, and it took
him but a moment to understand the meaning
of the action, or, rather, want of action on the
part of his dusky friend. Many days before

Deerfoot had spoken strange words to the Sauk whom he vanquished; they were words that lingered in his memory, and finally sent him in quest of the youth, that he might learn more of their wondrous meaning. He had sought and had obtained that knowledge, and its length and breadth and depth were so infinite, that at times it mastered the warrior, who gave himself up to meditation until he lost consciousness of every thing else.

Deerfoot was half tempted to smile when he reflected that the vigilant Sauk, while engaged on a delicate duty, had forgotten all about it, even to the personal danger involved. Reflecting on the new and divine revelation, he had sat down where he believed he was not likely to be disturbed, and given himself wholly up to the sacred joy of the hour.

While he sat thus guns were fired, shouts were uttered, and signals were sent out that were intended for his ear alone, but he was no more conscious of them, than if he had been wrapped in slumber a hundred miles distant. No statue in bronze could have been more immovable than he.

Viewing the countenance of the Sauk, Deerfoot noticed the radiant light which seemed to glow through every feature, and which told of the great peace that was brooding in his heart.

O blessed hope! as free to the beggar at the gate as to the master within the palace ; to the sinking mariner, as to the sceptered king ; to the savage in the depths of his own solitudes, as to those who listen to the silver chimes of magnificent churches ; thou art free to every man, woman and child, and to the uttermost islands of the sea ! Beneficent Father ! thine ear is ever open, and thine hand is ever stretched forth to save the perishing everywhere !

Deerfoot stood lower down the slope, where he instinctively screened himself behind a tree. He was watching the face of his friend, when he became aware that another individual was similarly employed.

Still lower down the slope, and about the same distance from Hay-uta as was Deerfoot, a Pawnee warrior, who was creeping along noiselessly, rose to the upright position. He was bent so low at first that Deerfoot failed to see him; but when he straightened up behind the trunk of a tree, the Shawanoe shrank back a few inches, so as to hide himself. Then he watched the Pawnee, who was less than a hundred feet distant.

The first sight showed Deerfoot that he was the warrior whom he and Hay-uta captured the night before, and who was given his liberty by them. More properly it was given to him by Hay-uta, who, you remember, played the part of Pocahontas to Captain John Smith. The whole thing was a scheme of the Sauk, who hoped thereby to make a "friend at court", and to secure an ally who would give them help in their quest for Otto Relstaub.

The Pawnee, therefore, saw before him the party who, he must have believed, saved his life, when the captive was in such despair that he sang his death-song, and bowed his head to receive the crashing blow of the upraised tomahawk. Common gratitude would have bound the Pawnee to his preserver for life.

The red man must have been puzzled when he observed the abstraction of the warrior, but without losing time in studying the question, he cocked his rifle and slowly brought it to his shoulder, keeping his eyes fixed on the warrior up the ridge, whose arms were still folded, and who was gazing vacantly in the direction of the setting sun. There could be no mistake about it : the Pawnee meant to slay the Sauk.

But while the treacherous wretch was making his preparations, Deerfoot, with silent dexterity, fitted an arrow to the string of his bow. The Pawnee was within easy range, and, before the latter could bring his gun to a level, the Shawanoe with his unerring left hand drew back the string of his weapon. The sight of the hostile seeking the life of the Sauk who had befriended him, stirred the heart of Deerfoot to a fury which he rarely felt. He had seen ingratitude before, but rarely was he moved as by the sight before him.

Confident of his aim, he meant to drive the shaft with such force, that, unless stopped by some bone, it would pass clean through and beyond the body of the Pawnee, who, unconscious of his own peril, made his preparations with a deliberation which showed an almost inconceivable depth of hatred.

"Dog of the Pawnee!" muttered the Shawanoe; "you shall have no time to chant your death song this time!"

The arrow was drawn almost to a head, but in his anger Deerfoot give it a quick pull, as expressive of the fierceness of his wrath. As he did so, a sharp, splitting sound was heard, and the center of his closed palm felt as if pierced by a hundred needles.

The bow which had never failed him before had splintered in the middle, and the poised arrow dropped to the ground, its nerveless point falling between the moccasins of the astounded Deerfoot, who realized the full effect of the awful accident.

CHAPTER XXXII.

DEERFOOT knew the extent of the mishap the instant it took place. There was no means at command for repairing it, but, in the hope of arousing Hay-uta and disconcerting the aim of the Pawnee, he bounded from the tree, giving utterance to the most terrific shout of which he was capable, and dashed toward the traitor. He had flung aside his useless bow and held his tomahawk in his left hand.

He failed in both his intentions, though possibly he might have succeeded had a few seconds more been at his service. The frightful cry did arouse the Sauk, but it hardly passed the lips of the Shawanoe when the gun of their enemy was fired, and Hay-uta, leaping half way to his feet, fell back mortally wounded.

X

The Pawnee saw the raging Shawanoe rushing toward him like a flaming meteor. Knowing what it meant he dropped his gun and grasped his tomahawk, ready to fight the man who threatened his life only a short time before. The weapon was drawn but half way from his girdle, when, without checking his speed, Deerfoot sent his hatchet as though fired from the mouth of a cannon. The Pawnee could not have seen it coming when his skull was cloven in twain, and, with a half-suppressed shriek, he went to the earth, every spark of life driven from his body.

Deerfoot stood for a moment, panting and glaring at the miscreant whom he had brought low. Then without speaking or seeking to recover his tomahawk, he turned and walked toward the Sauk, knowing it was too late to help him.

A long time before when the rifle on which the young warrior relied flashed in the pan, he flung the weapon into the Ohio, and returned to his loved bow and arrow ; but the failure in the former case could not be compared with that of the present; the bow had given out in the most disastrous manner that can be imagined.

Deerfoot never shrank from any duty, no matter how trying to his feelings. He supposed that Hay-uta was dead, but when he looked at him, he saw that he was sitting as before with his back against the rock, his arms folded, while he was gazing at the western sky as if lost in pleasant meditation ; but the deathly pallor visible through his paint, showed he had but a short time to live.

Deerfoot hastened his steps, and Hay-uta turned his eyes with a smile and feebly extended his hand. The Shawanoe eagerly took it and kneeled on one knee.

"Why does my brother the brave Hay-uta smile?" he asked, in a voice as low as that of a mother.

" Hay-uta was looking at the clouds in the sky and he saw the face of the Great Spirit that Deerfoot told him about."

" Was the Great Spirit pleased ? "

"He smiled and showed he loved Hay-uta, —who sees him again," added the dying war-rior, turning his gaze toward the billowy clouds, tinted with gold in the rays of the declining sun. " He smiles and is waiting for me."

A divine joy suffused the heart of the Shawanoe, when he not only heard these words, but noted the expression which illuminated the countenance of the Sauk, who had but a few more minutes to live.

And while stirred by such emotions, there were other matters which Deerfoot could not forget. True, he had slain the only Pawnee near, but he could not feel sure that all danger from that source was gone. Others might be drawn to the spot, within a brief period, and he cast a searching glance on his surroundings, to make certain he was not taken unawares. Had a half dozen hostiles burst upon the scene, the Shawanoe would not have deserted Hay-uta, so long as breath remained in his body.

There was hope for a moment on the part of Deerfoot that his friend might not be mortally hurt, but such hope vanished almost as soon as it came. The wound was in the breast; it bled slightly, but the eye of the Shawanoe (aside from the appearance of the Sauk), showed the poor fellow was beyond the power of human help.

"The heart of Deerfoot is glad," said the Shawanoe, still resting on one knee, and holding the hand of Hay-uta, while he looked kindly into his face. "Deerfoot had drawn his bow, and would have driven his arrow through the heart of the dog of a Pawnee, but the bow broke and the arrow fell at the feet of Deer-foot."

This statement seemed to recall Hay-uta to his situation ; he compressed his thin lips, as if forcing back a moan, and his free hand groped at his side in feeble quest of something. Before Deerfoot could divine his purpose, he grasped his handsome gun, leaning against the rock, and made as if to pass it to Deerfoot. The latter was obliged to help him, and resting the stock on the ground, he leaned the muzzle toward the other, and awaited his words.

"Had that been in the hand of Deerfoot, then Hay-uta had not died."

"My brother speaks with a single tongue, as he always did," replied the Shawanoe, in a sad voice ; "the bow is broken."

"Let my brother use it no more; let him take the rifle which he now grasps."

"It shall be done as my brother wishes."

"The heart of Hay-uta rejoices; let my brother take the powder-horn and bullet-pouch of Hay-uta."

With great gentleness, Deerfoot slipped the string of the Sauk's powder-horn over his neck, unfastened the bullet-pouch, and placed them and the proffered tomahawk about his own person. Before doing so, he detached his quiver and flung it from him. The Sauk watched his actions with more interest than would be supposed, and his pale face showed that he was pleased with the change.

"My brother was given skill with the bow, but his skill is as great with the gun, and it will not fail him when he points it at the deer or at his enemy."

"It is the Great Spirit who guides the arrow and bullet," was the response of the Shawanoe. "Deerfoot will use the bow no more; he will keep the rifle and tomahawk his brother Hay-uta gave him. He will think of Hay-uta and the gun will be better in the hands than the bow."

"Then Deerfoot will be greater than any hunter in the west," was the remark of his friend, and that he was a true prophet will be shown by the incidents in which the Shawanoe was soon called to take part.

The young warrior had no wish to hear the deserved compliments at such a time, for he saw that only a few more words could fall from the lips of the Sauk. Still holding the hand tenderly in his own, he asked in a gentler voice :

"Does my brother see the face of the Great Spirit now?"

The eyes that were growing dull, brightened again, and were fixed on the tinted horizon as though he saw the countenance of his Heavenly Father (and who dare say he did not?), with as much distinctness as he discerned that of the Shawanoe kneeling before him.

"I see Him. He stands now with His side toward me; one foot is forward, and He is leaning over as if He is about to take a step. He reaches His hand toward me ; He is only waiting till I place my hand in His." Then, fixing with an effort his gaze on the Shawanoe, Hay-uta, whose mind began to wander, said :

"The Great Spirit looks toward Deerfoot; He waits to hear him speak."

The Sauk became silent, and Deerfoot prayed for a few minutes with the touching faith of childhood. When he was nearly done, he unconsciously dropped into his own tongue.

"The prayer of Deerfoot to the Great Spirit is that He will take the hand of Hay-uta, which reaches upward to Him and lead him into the hunting grounds, beyond the clouds and sun and stars. The prayer of Hay-uta is the prayer of Deerfoot."

Having finished, the Shawanoe ceased and looked into the face of the Sauk, awaiting what further request he might make. The calm, triumphant expression which lit up the features, led him to expect a movement of the lips, but it needed only a second glance to discover that Hay-uta the Sauk was dead.

Deerfoot looked closely at him, and then, rising to his feet, scanned the surrounding solitude. While Hay-uta had seated himself where he gained an unobstructed view of the sky, he

was not at the top of the ridge, nor was he liable to be discovered by any enemies at a distance. It was a fatal mischance which brought the treacherous Pawnee that way.

From where Deerfoot stood, he could see the feet and leggings of the fallen Pawnee, who lay flat on his back as though looking at the sky ; but no living person was in sight.

The Shawanoe waited a brief while, debating with himself as to his duty toward his dead friend. While he was without the means of burying him, he could place the body in some less conspicuous position, yet he took a different course.

Before the limbs of the dead warrior were given time to stiffen, Deerfoot adjusted them as they were when he first discovered him sunk in meditation. The body was made to sit erect, the back supported by the rock behind it ; the feet were extended in a natural position, and the arms folded across the massive chest. The partly-open eyes seemed still to rest on the western horizon, behind which the sun had set. Though Indian superstition would have caused the body to face the other way, to greet

the rising sun, Deerfoot had no wish to change
the posture; for Hay-uta died not as dies the
heathen, but as passes away the Christian.

It would have been hard for any one ventur-
ing from the woods, and catching sight of the
body for the first time, to believe the spark of
life had fled.

The Shawanoe viewed the striking figure, and
felt that he had done the most fitting thing.
Looking up at the darkened sky he asked the
Great Spirit to protect the body from molestation by wild man or beast, and then, with a
faint sigh, he turned away, and passing over
the ridge, hastened toward the rendezvous,
where Jack Carleton and Otto Relstaub had
been told to await his coming.

Months afterward, a party of trappers
penetrating further than usual to the westward,
came upon the skeleton of an Indian warrior,
seated on the ground with his arms folded, and
back resting against a rock behind him. They
supposed he had been killed and then placed in
that posture, but we know they were not
altogether right in their belief.

Having turned his back for the last time on

Hay-uta, the Shawanoe hurried toward the ridge where he expected to rejoin his friends. It was too dark to follow any trail, and indeed there was no call to do so. Had nothing interfered, he knew the neighborhood of the spot where he would find the boys, and he hastened toward it. Even if he went somewhat astray, it would be no difficult matter to open communication with them.

The stream in which Jack and Otto had such rare sport scarcely checked the progress of the Shawanoe, but when a short while after, he caught the glimpse of a camp-fire on the slope of the ridge, he was displeased; for it showed a degree of recklessness in them that he could not excuse. If they chose to encamp there, they ought to have known better than to turn it into a beacon light to guide the hostiles for miles around.

With an expresson of displeasure, Deerfoot hastened his footsteps, and reached camp sooner than he or his young friends anticipated. It can be understood that the surprise was great on the part of all.

CHAPTER XXXIII.

IT was a surprising discovery for Jack Carleton and Otto Relstaub when they learned that the solitary Sauk warrior who welcomed them to his camp, had in his possession the horse belonging to the German lad, for which they had sought so long in vain.

"Mine gracious!" exclaimed Otto, when they seated themselves again by the fire; "if we gots him, won't it be shust too good!"

"Then I suppose your father and mother will be satisfied."

"Yaw—but holds on!" he added, looking down at his clothing; "I have torn my trowsers shust a little, and dot will gif dem de oxcuse to whip me."

"No; they will be too glad to get the colt back to mind such a small thing as that; but isn't it one of the strangest things in the world

that this Sauk should find and bring him all
the way through the woods and across streams
and prairies to this point, and then that we
should come upon him."

"It peats everydings," replied Otto; "but
he can't told us how he didn't do it."

"No; we shall have to wait till Deerfoot
comes; he can talk the Sauk tongue and it
won't take him long to find out the whole
story."

The boys felt so little misgiving about entrust-
ing themselves to the care of the stranger, that
when they began to feel drowsy they stretched
out on the blanket, with their backs against
each other, and went to sleep.

An hour later, just as the Sauk was on the
point of also turning in for the night, Deerfoot made his appearance. His coming was a
surprise to the warrior, and at first caused
him some alarm, but, so soon as he learned
who he was, his feelings underwent a change,
for, truth to tell, the Shawanoe was the very
one whom the Sauk had come so many miles
to meet.

The story of the Sauk was impressive. He

was the brother of Hay-uta, and on the return of the latter to his home, he told of his encounter with Deerfoot, and dwelt on the extraordinary words of his conqueror. He, too, had heard something similar from the missionaries, whom he had seen at different posts in the West, but like most of his people he was indifferent to their arguments.

But the "sermon" preached by Deerfoot, through his kindred, got hold of the Sauk, and would not let go. He affected to despise the words, but he could not drive them from him. Some time afterward Hay-uta told his brother he must hunt up the friendly Shawanoe, and learn more of the Great Spirit whom he told him about. He asked him to bear him company, but the Sauk declined, just as all of us are prone to rebel against the better promptings of our nature.

The time soon came however when he started to hunt, not only for Hay-uta, but for Deerfoot also. Of necessity his search for awhile was a blind one, but while threading his way through the woods he found the horse of Otto Relstaub cropping the grass on a slight stretch of prairie.

Some curious fortune had given him his liberty and led him into that section.

The brother was so prompt in following Hayuta, that he kept to his trail long after the latter had found Deerfoot and Jack Carleton, but a peculiar shame-facedness held him back from joining them. Once or twice he resolved· to overtake them, but each time he shrank back, and finally lingered so long that he lost the trail altogether.

But that restless longing for the great light, of which he had only the dim glimmerings, kept his face turned westward, while he hoped and yet dreaded to meet the young Shawanoe, who, unsuspected by himself, was the cause of his strange discontent.

The meeting took place in the manner already told. It was Deerfoot who found the Sauk instead of the Sauk who found him. In a tender, sympathetic voice the Shawanoe gave the other the particulars of his brother's death, making clear to him that when he crossed the dark river it was to enter the hunting grounds of the true Great Spirit, who beckoned him thither. The Sauk showed no grief over the loss of his kindred, though he mourned him with an emotion that was a singular mixture of sadness and pleasure. He seemed more interested in the story which Deerfoot told him about the One who died that all men might live, and whose approving smile could be won by whomsoever would do His will.

The two warriors lay a long time by the camp-fire, which was replenished several times, while the Shawanoe read from his Bible and discoursed of the momentous truths contained therein, and the listener questioned and answered, and appropriated the revelations thus made to him. Deerfoot, the Shawanoe, sowed good seed on that evening a long time ago ; but the full fruitage thereof shall never be known until the last great day, for which all others were made.

When the Sauk learned that the horse which he had found astray in the wilderness belonged to one of the sleeping boys, he said it should be returned to him on the morrow. Deerfoot encouraged him by replying that such action would always please the Great Spirit, who knew the thoughts, words and deeds of every person that lived.

While the boys were sleeping, and when the gray light of morning was creeping over the forest, Deerfoot scouted through the country surrounding them. As he anticipated, he found no sign of enemies. The Pawnees had been handled so roughly that they made no further attempt to molest the little party that seemed to them to be under the special care of the Evil One.

Jack Carleton and Otto Relstaub were permitted to sleep until breakfast was ready; then, when aroused, they were in high spirits over the prospect before them. The young Kentuckian, however, was saddened by the tidings of the death of Hay-uta, the brother of the Sauk who had befriended him.

Otto was informed that the lost colt was his property again, and all that he had to do was to prevent him from wandering beyond his reach, since no such good fortune was likely to repeat itself.

Three days later the Sauk bade them good-by, his course to his village rendering a

Y

divergence necessary. When in sight of the humble cabins of Martinsville, Deerfoot parted from Jack and Otto, expressing the hope that he would soon meet them again ; when urged to visit his friends in the settlement he shook his head, making a reply which was not fully understood.

"Deerfoot must hasten ; he is wanted by others ; he has no time to lose."

Then flirting the gun given him by Hay-uta over his head, he added with a smile :

"Deerfoot uses the bow and arrows no more ; the rifle is his weapon."

Waving them farewell again, he soon vanished from sight in the forest, and they saw him no more.

I need not tell you of the welcome Jack Carleton received from his mother and friends. He promised his anxious parent that he would never leave her again, and his pledge was not broken.

Perhaps the long absence of Otto softened his father and mother's hearts, or it may have been the return of the lost colt moved them to greater kindness. Be that as it may, henceforward all went smoothly in the Relstaub household, and the hardships and sufferings of Otto, so far as his parents were concerned, were ended forever.

THE END.

Printed by CASSELL & COMPANY, LIMITED, La Belle Sauvage, London, E.C.

𝕴𝖑𝖑𝖚𝖘𝖙𝖗𝖆𝖙𝖊𝖉, 𝕱𝖎𝖓𝖊-𝕬𝖗𝖙, 𝖆𝖓𝖉 𝖔𝖙𝖍𝖊𝖗 𝖁𝖔𝖑𝖚𝖒𝖊𝖘.

Art, The Magazine of. Yearly Volume. With 500 choice Engravings. 16s.

After London ; or, Wild England. By RICHARD JEFFERIES. 3s. 6d.

Along Alaska's Great River. By F. SCHWATKA. Illustrated. 12s. 6d.

Artist, Education of the. By E. CHESNEAU. Translated by CLARA BELL. 5s.

Bimetallism, The Theory of. By D. BARBOUR. 6s.

Bismarck, Prince. By CHARLES LOWE, M.A. Two Vols. 24s.

Bright, John, Life and Times of. By W. ROBERTSON. 7s. 6d.

British Ballads. With 275 Original Illustrations. Two Vols. 7s. 6d. each.

British Battles on Land and Sea. By JAMES GRANT. With about 600 Illustrations Three Vols., 4to, £1 7s. ; Library Edition, £1 10s.

British Battles, Recent. Illustrated. 4to, 9s. ; Library Edition, 10s.

Browning, An Introduction to the Study of. By ARTHUR SYMONDS. 2s. 6d.

Butterflies and Moths, European. By W. F. KIRBY. With 61 Coloured Plates. Demy 4to, 35s.

Canaries and Cage-Birds, The Illustrated Book of. By W. A. BLAKSTON, W. SWAYSLAND, and A. F. WIENER. With 56 Fac-simile Coloured Plates, 35s. Half-morocco, £2 5s.

Cassell's Family Magazine. Yearly Vol. Illustrated. 9s.

Cathedral Churches of England and Wales. Illustrated. 21s.

Choice Poems by H. W. Longfellow. Illustrated from Paintings by his Son, ERNEST W. LONGFELLOW. Small 4to, cloth, 6s.

Choice Dishes at Small Cost. By A. G. PAYNE. 1s.

Cities of the World : their Origin, Progress, and Present Aspect. Three Vols. Illustrated. 7s. 6d. each.

Civil Service, Guide to Employment in the. 3s. 6d.

Civil Service.—Guide to Female Employment in Government Offices. 1s.

Clinical Manuals for Practitioners and Students of Medicine. A List of Volumes forwarded post free on application to the Publishers.

Clothing, The Influence of, on Health. By FREDERICK TREVES, F.R.C.S. 2s.

Colonies and India, Our, How we Got Them, and Why we Keep Them. By Prof. C. RANSOME. 1s.

Columbus, Christopher, The Life and Voyages of. By WASHINGTON IRVING. Three Vols. 7s. 6d.

Cookery, Cassell's Dictionary of. Containing about Nine Thousand Recipes. 7s. 6d. ; Roxburgh, 10s. 6d.

Co-operators, Working Men : What they have Done, and What they are Doing. By A. H DYKE-ACLAND, M.P., and B. JONES. 1s.

Cookery, A Year's. By PHYLLIS BROWNE. 3s. 6d.

Cook Book, Catherine Owen's New. 4s.

Countries of the World, The. By ROBERT BROWN, M.A., Ph.D., &c. Complete in Six Vols., with about 750 Illustrations. 4to, 7s. 6d. each.

Cromwell, Oliver: The Man and his Mission. By J. ALLANSON PICTON, M.P. Cloth, 7s. 6d. ; morocco, cloth sides, 9s.

Cyclopædia, Cassell's Concise. With 12,000 subjects, brought down to the latest date. With about 600 Illustrations. 15s. ; Roxburgh, 18s.

Dairy Farming. By Prof. J. P. SHELDON. With 25 Fac-simile Coloured Plates, and numerous Wood Engravings. Cloth, 31s. 6d. ; half-morocco, 42s.

Decisive Events in History. By THOMAS ARCHER. With Sixteen Illustrations. Boards, 3s. 6d. ; cloth, 5s.

Decorative Design. By CHRISTOPHER DRESSER, Ph.D. Illustrated. 5s.

Deserted Village Series, The. Consisting of *Éditions de luxe* of the most favourite poems of Standard Authors. Illustrated. 2s. 6d. each.

SONGS FROM SHAKESPEARE.	GOLDSMITH'S DESERTED VILLAGE.
MILTON'S L'ALLEGRO AND IL PENSEROSO.	WORDSWORTH'S ODE ON IMMORTALITY, AND LINES ON TINTERN ABBEY.

Dickens, Character Sketches from. SECOND and THIRD SERIES. With Six Original Drawings in each, by F. BARNARD. In Portfolio, 21s. each.

Diary of Two Parliaments. By W. H. LUCY. Vol. I. : The Disraeli Parliament. Vol. II. : The Gladstone Parliament. 12s. each.

Dog, The. By IDSTONE. Illustrated. 2s. 6d.

Dog, Illustrated Book of the. By VERO SHAW, B.A. With 28 Coloured Plates. Cloth bevelled, 35s. ; half-morocco, 45s.

Domestic Dictionary, The. Cloth, 7s. 6d.

Doré's Adventures of Munchausen. Illustrated by GUSTAVE DORÉ. 5s.

Doré's Dante's Inferno. Illustrated by GUSTAVE DORÉ. 21s.

Doré's Don Quixote. With about 400 Illustrations by DORÉ. 15s.

Doré's Fairy Tales Told Again. With Engravings by DORÉ. 5s.

Doré Gallery, The. With 250 Illustrations by DORÉ. 4to, 42s.

Doré's Milton's Paradise Lost. Illustrated by DORÉ. 4to, 21s.

Edinburgh, Old and New. Three Vols. With 600 Illustrations. 9s. each.

Educational Year-Book, The. 6s.

Egypt : Descriptive, Historical, and Picturesque. By Prof. G. EBERS. Translated by CLARA BELL, with Notes by SAMUEL BIRCH, LL.D., &c. Two Vols. With 800 Original Engravings. Vol. I., £2 5s. ; Vol. II., £2 12s. 6d. Complete in box, £4 17s. 6d.

Electricity in the Service of Man. With nearly 850 Illustrations. 21s.

Electrician's Pocket-Book, The. By GORDON WIGAN, M.A. 5s.

Encyclopædic Dictionary, The. A New and Original Work of Reference to all the Words in the English Language. Ten Divisional Vols. now ready, 10s. 6d. each ; or the Double Divisional Vols., half-morocco, 21s. each.

Energy in Nature. By WM. LANT CARPENTER, B.A., B.Sc. 80 Illustrations. 3s. 6d.

England, Cassell's Illustrated History of. With 2,000 Illustrations. Ten Vols., 4to, 9s. each.

English History, The Dictionary of. Cloth, 21s. ; Roxburgh, 25s.

English Literature, Library of. By Prof. HENRY MORLEY. Five Vols., 7s. 6d. each.

VOL. I.—SHORTER ENGLISH POEMS.
VOL. II.—ILLUSTRATIONS OF ENGLISH RELIGION.
VOL. III.—ENGLISH PLAYS.
VOL. IV.—SHORTER WORKS IN ENGLISH PROSE.
VOL. V.—SKETCHES OF LONGER WORKS IN ENGLISH VERSE AND PROSE.

Five Volumes handsomely bound in half-morocco, £5 5s.

English Literature, The Story of. By ANNA BUCKLAND. 3s. 6d.

English Literature, Morley's First Sketch. Revised Edition, 7s. 6d.

English Literature, Dictionary of. By W. DAVENPORT ADAMS. *Cheap Edition*, 7s. 6d. ; Roxburgh, 10s. 6d.

English Poetesses. By ERIC S. ROBERTSON, M.A. 5s.

Æsop's Fables. With about 150 Illustrations by E. GRISET. Cloth, 7s. 6d.; gilt edges, 10s. 6d.

Etching. By S. K. KOEHLER. With 30 Full-Page Plates by Old and Modern Etchers. £4 4s.

Etiquette of Good Society. 1s. ; cloth, 1s. 6d.

Eye, Ear, and Throat, The Management of the. 3s. 6d.

False Hopes. By Prof. GOLDWIN SMITH, M.A., LL.D., D.C.L. 6d.

Family Physician, The. By Eminent PHYSICIANS and SURGEONS. Cloth, 21s. ; half-morocco, 25s.

Fenn, G. Manville, Works by. Cloth boards, 2s. each.

SWEET MACE.
DUTCH, THE DIVER.
MY PATIENTS. Being the Notes of a Navy Surgeon.

THE VICAR'S PEOPLE.
COBWEB'S FATHER.
THE PARSON O' DUMFORD.
POVERTY CORNER.

Ferns, European. By JAMES BRITTEN, F.L.S. With 30 Fac-simile Coloured Plates by D. BLAIR, F.L.S. 21s.

Field Naturalist's Handbook, The. By the Rev. J. G. WOOD and THEODORE WOOD. 5s.

Figuier's Popular Scientific Works. With Several Hundred Illustrations in each. 3s. 6d. each.

THE HUMAN RACE.
WORLD BEFORE THE DELUGE.
REPTILES AND BIRDS.

THE OCEAN WORLD.
THE VEGETABLE WORLD.
THE INSECT WORLD.
MAMMALIA.

Fine-Art Library, The. Edited by JOHN SPARKES, Principal of the South Kensington Art Schools. Each Book contains about 100 Illustrations. 5s. each.

TAPESTRY. By Eugène Müntz. Translated by Miss L. J. Davis.
ENGRAVING. By Le Vicomte Henri Delaborde. Translated by R. A. M. Stevenson.
THE ENGLISH SCHOOL OF PAINTING. By E. Chesneau. Translated by L. N. Etherington. With an Introduction by Prof. Ruskin.
THE FLEMISH SCHOOL OF PAINTING. By A. J. Wauters. Translated by Mrs. Henry Rossel.

THE EDUCATION OF THE ARTIST. By Ernest Chesneau. Translated by Clara Bell. (Not illustrated.)
GREEK ARCHÆOLOGY. By Maxime Collignon. Translated by Dr. J. H. Wright.
ARTISTIC ANATOMY. By Prof. Duval. Translated by F. E. Fenton.
THE DUTCH SCHOOL OF PAINTING. By Henry Havard. Translated by G. Powell.

Fisheries of the World, The. Illustrated. 4to. 9s.

Five Pound Note, The, and other Stories. By G. S. JEALOUS. 1s.

Flowers, and How to Paint them. By MAUD NAFTEL. With Coloured Plates. 5s.

Forging of the Anchor, The. A Poem. By Sir SAMUEL FERGUSON. LL.D. With 20 Original Illustrations. Gilt edges, 5s.

Fossil Reptiles, A History of British. By Sir RICHARD OWEN, K.C.B., F.R.S., &c. With 268 Plates. In Four Vols., £12 12s.

Four Years of Irish History (1845-49). By Sir GAVAN DUFFY, K.C.M.G. 21s.

Franco-German War, Cassell's History of the. Two Vols. With 500 Illustrations. 9s. each.

Fresh-Water Fishes of Europe, The. By Prof. H. G. SEELEY, F.R.S. Cloth, 21s.

From Gold to Grey. Being Poems and Pictures of Life and Nature. By MARY D. BRINE. Illustrated. **7s. 6d.**

Garden Flowers, Familiar. FOUR SERIES. By SHIRLEY HIBBERD. With Coloured Plates by F. E. HULME, F.L.S. **12s. 6d.** each.

Gardening, Cassell's Popular. Illustrated. 4 vols., **5s.** each.

Gladstone, Life of W. E. By BARNETT SMITH. With Portrait, **3s. 6d.** *Jubilee Edition*, **1s.**

Gleanings from Popular Authors. Two Vols. With Original Illustrations. 4to, **9s.** each. Two Vols. in One, **15s.**

Great Industries of Great Britain. Three Vols. With about 400 Illustrations. 4to., cloth, **7s. 6d.** each.

Great Painters of Christendom, The, from Cimabue to Wilkie. By JOHN FORBES-ROBERTSON. Illustrated throughout. **12s. 6d.**

Great Northern Railway, The Official Illustrated Guide to the. **1s.**; or in cloth, **2s.**

Great Western Railway, The Official Illustrated Guide to the. *New and Revised Edition.* With Illustrations, **1s.**; cloth, **2s.**

Gulliver's Travels. With 88 Engravings by MORTEN. *Cheap Edition*, **5s.**

Gun and its Development, The. By W. W. GREENER. With 500 Illustrations. **10s. 6d.**

Health, The Book of. By Eminent Physicians and Surgeons. Cloth, **21s.**; half-morocco, **25s.**

Health, the Influence of Clothing on. By F. TREVES, F.R.G.S. **2s.**

Health in School. By CLEMENT DUKES, M.D.B.S. **6s.**

Heavens, The Story of the. By Sir ROBERT STAWELL BALL, F.R.S., F.R.A.S. With Coloured Plates and Wood Engravings. **31s. 6d.**

Heroes of Britain in Peace and War. In Two Vols., with 300 Original Illustrations. Cloth, **5s.** each.

Horse Keeper, The Practical. By GEORGE FLEMING, LL.D., F.R.C.V.S. With Illustrations. Crown 8vo, cloth, **7s. 6d.**

Horse, The Book of the. By SAMUEL SIDNEY. With 25 *fac-simile* Coloured Plates. *Enlarged Edition.* Demy 4to, **35s.**; half-morocco, **45s.**

Horses, The Simple Ailments of. By W. F. Illustrated. **5s.**

Household Guide, Cassell's. With Illustrations and Coloured Plates. *New and Cheap Edition*, in Four Vols., **20s.**

How Women may Earn a Living. By MERCY GROGAN. **1s.**

India, The Coming Struggle for. By Prof. VAMBÉRY. **5s.**

India, Cassell's History of. By JAMES GRANT. With about 400 Illustrations. Library binding. One Vol., **15s.**

India: the Land and the People. By Sir J. CAIRD, K.C.B. **10s. 6d.**

Indoor Amusements, Card Games, and Fireside Fun, Cassell's Book of. Illustrated. **3s. 6d.**

Invisible Life, Vignettes from. By JOHN BADCOCK, F.R.M.S. Illustrated. **3s. 6d.**

Irish Parliament, The; What it Was and What it Did. By J. G. SWIFT MACNEILL, M.A. **1s.**

Italy. By J. W. PROBYN. **7s. 6d.**

Kennel Guide, The Practical. By Dr. GORDON STABLES. Illustrated. **2s. 6d.**

Khiva, A Ride to. By the late Col. FRED. BURNABY. **1s. 6d.**

Kidnapped. By R. L. STEVENSON. **5s.**

Ladies' Physician, The. A Guide for Women in the Treatment of their Ailments. By a Physician. **6s.**

Land Question, The. By. Prof. J. ELLIOT, M.R.A.C. 10s. 6d.

Landscape Painting in Oils, A Course of Lessons in. By A. F. GRACE. With Nine Reproductions in Colour. *Cheap Edition*, 25s.

Law, About Going to. By A. J. WILLIAMS, M.P. 2s. 6d.

Letts's Diaries and other Time-saving Publications are now published exclusively by CASSELL & COMPANY. (*A list sent post free on application.*)

Liberal, Why I am a. By ANDREW REID. 2s. 6d. *People's Edition.* 1s.

London & North-Western Railway Official Illustrated Guide. 1s. ; cloth, 2s.

London, Greater. By EDWARD WALFORD. Two Vols. With about 400 Illustrations. 9s. each.

London, Old and New. Six Vols., each containing about 200 Illustrations and Maps. Cloth, 9s. each.

London's Roll of Fame. With Portraits and Illustrations. 12s. 6d.

Longfellow's Poetical Works. Illustrated throughout, £3 3s.; *Popular Edition*, 16s.

Love's Extremes, At. By MAURICE THOMPSON. 5s.

Luther, Martin: the Man and his Work. By Dr. PETER BAYNE. Two Vols. 24s.

Mechanics, The Practical Dictionary of. Containing 15,000 Drawings. Four Vols. 21s. each.

Medicine, Manuals for Students of. (*A List forwarded post free.*)

Midland Railway, Official Illustrated Guide to the. *New and Revised Edition.* 1s. ; cloth, 2s.

Modern Artists, Some. With highly-finished Engravings. 12s. 6d.

Modern Europe, A History of. By C. A. FYFFE, M.A. Vol. I., from 1792 to 1814. 12s. Vol. II., from 1814 to 1848. 12s.

Music, Illustrated History of. By EMIL NAUMANN. Edited by the Rev. Sir F. A. GORE OUSELEY, Bart. Illustrated. Two Vols. 31s. 6d.

National Library, Cassell's. In Weekly Volumes, each containing about 192 pages. Paper covers, 3d. ; cloth, 6d. (*A List sent post free on application.*)

Natural History, Cassell's Concise. By E. PERCEVAL WRIGHT, M.A., M.D., F.L.S. With several Hundred Illustrations. 7s. 6d.

Natural History, Cassell's New. Edited by Prof. P. MARTIN DUNCAN, M.B., F.R.S., F.G.S. With Contributions by Eminent Scientific Writers. Complete in Six Vols. With about 2,000 high-class Illustrations. Extra crown 4to, cloth, 9s. each.

Nature, Short Studies from. Illustrated. 5s.

Nimrod in the North ; or, Hunting and Fishing Adventures in the Arctic Regions. By F. SCHWATKA. Illustrated. 7s. 6d.

Nursing for the Home and for the Hospital, A Handbook of. By CATHERINE J. WOOD. *Cheap Edition.* 1s. 6d. ; cloth, 2s.

Oil Painting, A Manual of. By the Hon. JOHN COLLIER. 2s. 6d.

Our Homes, and How to Make them Healthy. By Eminent Authorities. Illustrated. 15s. ; half-morocco, 21s.

Our Own Country. Six Vols. With 1,200 Illustrations. 7s. 6d. each.

Painting, Practical Guides to. With Coloured Plates and full instructions :—Animal Painting, 5s.—China Painting, 5s. —Figure Painting, 7s. 6d.—Flower Painting, 2 Books, 5s. each.—Tree Painting, 5s.—Water-Colour Painting, 5s.—Neutral Tint, 5s.—Sepia, in 2 Vols., 3s. each.—Flowers, and how to Paint them, 5s.

Paris, Cassell's Illustrated Guide to. 1s. ; cloth, 2s.

Parliaments, A Diary of Two. By H. W. Lucy. The Disraeli Parliament, 1874—1880. 12s. The Gladstone Parliament. 12s.

Paxton's Flower Garden. By Sir Joseph Paxton and Prof. Lindley. Three Vols. With 100 Coloured Plates. £1 1s. each.

Peoples of the World, The. In Six Vols. By Dr. Robert Brown. Illustrated. 7s. 6d. each.

Perak and the Malays, "Sarong" and "Kris." By Major Fred McNair. With Illustrations. 10s. 6d.

Phantom City, The. By W. Westall. 5s.

Photography for Amateurs. By T. C. Hepworth. Illustrated. 1s. ; or cloth, 1s. 6d.

Phrase and Fable, Dictionary of. By the Rev. Dr. Brewer. *Cheap Edition, Enlarged*, cloth, 3s. 6d. ; or with leather back, 4s. 6d.

Picturesque America. Complete in Four Vols., with 48 Exquisite Steel Plates and about 800 Original Wood Engravings. £2 2s. each.

Picturesque Canada. With 600 Original Illustrations. Two Vols. £3 3s. each.

Picturesque Europe. Complete in Five Vols. Each containing 13 Exquisite Steel Plates, from Original Drawings, and nearly 200 Original Illustrations. £10 10s. The Popular Edition is published in Five Vols., 18s. each.

Pigeon Keeper, The Practical. By Lewis Wright. Illustrated. 3s. 6d.

Pigeons, The Book of. By Robert Fulton. Edited and Arranged by L. Wright. With 50 Coloured Plates, 31s. 6d. ; half-morocco, £2 2s.

Poems and Pictures. With numerous Illustrations. 5s.

Poets, Cassell's Miniature Library of the :—

Burns. Two Vols. 2s. 6d.	Milton. Two Vols. 2s. 6d.
Byron. Two Vols. 2s. 6d.	Scott. Two Vols. 2s. 6d. [2s. 6d.
Hood. Two Vols. 2s. 6d.	Sheridan and Goldsmith. 2 Vols.
Longfellow. Two Vols. 2s. 6d.	Wordsworth. Two Vols. 2s. 6d.

Shakespeare. Twelve Vols., in Case, 15s.
• *The above are also publishing in cloth. 1s. each Vol.*

Police Code, and Manual of the Criminal Law. By C. E. Howard Vincent, M.P. 2s.

Popular Library, Cassell's. Cloth, 1s. each.

The Russian Empire.	The Story of the English Jacobins.
The Religious Revolution in the 16th Century.	Domestic Folk Lore.
English Journalism.	The Rev. Rowland Hill: Preacher and Wit.
The Huguenots.	Boswell and Johnson : their Companions and Contemporaries.
Our Colonial Empire.	The Scottish Covenanters.
John Wesley.	History of the Free-Trade Movement in England.
The Young Man in the Battle of Life.	

Poultry Keeper, The Practical. By L. Wright. With Coloured Plates and Illustrations. 3s. 6d.

Poultry, The Illustrated Book of. By L. Wright. With Fifty Coloured Plates. Cloth, 31s. 6d. ; half-morocco, £2 2s.

Poultry, The Book of. By Lewis Wright. *Popular Edition.* 10s. 6d.

Quiver Yearly Volume, The. With about 300 Original Contributions by Eminent Divines and Popular Authors, and upwards of 250 high-class Illustrations. 7s. 6d.

Rabbit-Keeper, The Practical. By Cuniculus. Illustrated. 3s. 6d.

Rainbow Series, Cassell's, of New and Original Novels. Price 1s. each.

As it was Written. By S. Luska.	A Crimson Stain. By A. Bradshaw.

Morgan's Horror. By G. Manville Fenn.

Rays from the Realms of Nature. By the Rev. J. Neil, M.A. 2s. 6d.

Red Library, Cassell's. Stiff covers, 1s. each; cloth, 2s. each; or half-calf, marbled edges, 5s. each.

Old Mortality.
The Hour and the Man.
Scarlet Letter.
Poe's Works.
Pride and Prejudice.
Last of the Mohicans.
Heart of Midlothian.
Last Days of Pompeii.
Yellowplush Papers.
Handy Andy.
Washington Irving's Sketch-Book.

Last Days of Palmyra.
Tales of the Borders.
American Humour.
Sketches by Boz.
Macaulay's Lays and Selected Essays.
Harry Lorrequer.
Old Curiosity Shop.
Rienzi.
The Talisman.
Pickwick (2 Vols.)

Representative Poems of Living Poets, American and English. Selected by the Poets themselves. 15s.

Royal River, The : The Thames from Source to Sea. With Descriptive Text and a Series of beautiful Engravings. £2 2s.

Russia. By D. MACKENZIE WALLACE, M.A. 5s.

Russo-Turkish War, Cassell's History of. With about 500 Illustrations. Two Vols., 9s. each.

Sandwith, Humphry. A Memoir by T. H. WARD. 7s. 6d.

Saturday Journal, Cassell's. Yearly Volume. 6s.

Science for All. Edited by Dr. ROBERT BROWN, M.A., F.L.S., &c. With 1,500 Illustrations. Five Vols. 9s. each.

Sea, The : Its Stirring Story of Adventure, Peril, and Heroism. By F. WHYMPER. With 400 Illustrations. Four Vols., 7s. 6d. each.

Sent Back by the Angels. And other Ballads. By FREDERICK LANGBRIDGE, M.A. Cloth, 4s. 6d.

Shaftesbury, The Earl of, K.G., The Life and Work of. By EDWIN HODDER. With Portraits. Three Vols., 36s.

Shakspere, The Leopold. With 400 Illustrations. Cloth, 6s.

Shakspere, The Royal. With Steel Plates and Wood Engravings. Three Vols. 15s. each.

Shakespeare, Cassell's Quarto Edition. Edited by CHARLES and MARY COWDEN CLARKE, and containing about 600 Illustrations by H. C. SELOUS. Complete in Three Vols., cloth gilt, £3 3s.

Shakespeare's Romeo and Juliet. *Édition de Luxe.* Illustrated with Twelve Superb Photogravures from Original Drawings by F. DICKSEE, A.R.A. £5 5s.

Shakespearean Scenes and Characters. With 30 Steel Plates and 10 Wood Engravings. The Text written by AUSTIN BRERETON. 21s.

Sketching from Nature in Water Colours. By AARON PENLEY. With Illustrations in Chromo-Lithography. 15s.

Skin and Hair, The Management of the. By MALCOLM MORRIS, F.R.C.S. 2s.

Smith, The Adventures and Discourses of Captain John. By JOHN ASHTON. Illustrated. 5s.

Sports and Pastimes, Cassell's Book of. With more than 800 Illustrations and Coloured Frontispiece. 768 pages. 9s. (Can be had separately thus : Outdoor Sports, 7s. 6d. ; Indoor Amusements, 3s. 6d.)

Steam Engine, The Theory and Action of the : for Practical Men. By W. H. NORTHCOTT, C.E. 3s. 6d.

Stock Exchange Year-Book, The. By THOMAS SKINNER. 10s. 6d.

Stones of London, The. By E. F. FLOWER. 6d.

" Stories from Cassell's." A Series of Seven Books. 6d. each ; cloth lettered, 9d. each.

Sunlight and Shade. With numerous Exquisite Engravings. 7s. 6d.

Surgery, Memorials of the Craft of, in England. With an Introduction by Sir JAMES PAGET. 21s.

Telegraph Guide, The. Illustrated. 1s.

Thackeray, Character Sketches from. Six New and Original Draw-ings by FREDERICK BARNARD, reproduced in Photogravure. 21s.

Trajan. An American Novel. By H. F. KEENAN. 7s. 6d.

Transformations of Insects, The. By Prof. P. MARTIN DUNCAN, M.B., F.R.S. With 240 Illustrations. 6s.

Treasure Island. By R. L. STEVENSON. Illustrated. 5s.

Treatment, The Year-Book of. A Critical Review for Practitioners of Medicine and Surgery. 5s.

Twenty Photogravures of Pictures in the Salon of 1885, by the leading French Artists.

" Unicode ": the Universal Telegraph Phrase Book. 2s. 6d.

United States, Cassell's History of the. By EDMUND OLLIER. With 600 Illustrations. Three Vols. 9s. each.

Universal History, Cassell's Illustrated. Four Vols. 9s. each.

Vicar of Wakefield and other Works by OLIVER GOLDSMITH. Illustrated. 3s. 6d.

Wealth Creation. By AUGUSTUS MONGREDIEN. 5s.

Westall, W., Novels by. *Popular Editions.* Cloth, 2s. each.

RALPH NORBRECK'S TRUST.

THE OLD FACTORY. | RED RYVINGTON.

What Girls Can Do. By PHYLLIS BROWNE. 2s. 6d.

Wild Animals and Birds: their Haunts and Habits. By Dr ANDREW WILSON. Illustrated. 7s. 6d.

Wild Birds, Familiar. First and Second Series. By W. SWAYSLAND. With 40 Coloured Plates in each. 12s. 6d. each.

Wild Flowers, Familiar. By F. E. HULME, F.L.S., F.S.A. Five Series. With 40 Coloured Plates in each. 12s. 6d. each.

Winter in India, A. By the Rt. Hon. W. E. BAXTER, M.P. 5s.

Wise Woman, The. By GEORGE MACDONALD. 2s. 6d.

Wood Magic: A Fable. By RICHARD JEFFERIES. 6s.

World of the Sea. Translated from the French of MOQUIN TANDON, by the Very Rev. H. MARTYN HART, M.A. Illustrated. Cloth. 6s.

World of Wit and Humour, The. With 400 Illustrations. Cloth, 7s. 6d.; cloth gilt, gilt edges, 10s. 6d.

World of Wonders. Two Vols. With 400 Illustrations. 7s. 6d. each.

Yule Tide. Cassell's Christmas Annual, 1s.

MAGAZINES.

The Quiver, for Sunday Reading. Monthly, 6d.

Cassell's Family Magazine. Monthly, 7d.

" Little Folks" Magazine. Monthly, 6d.

The Magazine of Art. Monthly, 1s.

Cassell's Saturday Journal. Weekly, 1d.; Monthly, 6d.

Catalogues of CASSELL & COMPANY'S PUBLICATIONS, which may be had at all Booksellers', or will be sent post free on application to the publishers :—

    CASSELL'S COMPLETE CATALOGUE, containing particulars of One Thousand Volumes.

    CASSELL'S CLASSIFIED CATALOGUE, in which their Works are arranged according to price, from *Sixpence to Twenty-five Guineas.*

    CASSELL'S EDUCATIONAL CATALOGUE, containing particulars of CASSELL & COMPANY'S Educational Works and Students' Manuals.

CASSELL & COMPANY, LIMITED, *Ludgate Hill, London.*

Bibles and Religious Works.

Bible, The Crown Illustrated. With about 1,000 Original Illustrations. With References, &c. 1,248 pages, crown 4to, cloth, 7s. 6d.

Bible, Cassell's Illustrated Family. With 900 Illustrations. Leather, gilt edges, £2 10s.

Bible Dictionary, Cassell's. With nearly 600 Illustrations. 7s. 6d.

Bible Educator, The. Edited by the Very Rev. Dean PLUMPTRE, D.D., Wells. With Illustrations, Maps, &c. Four Vols., cloth, 6s. each.

Bible Work at Home and Abroad. Volume. Illustrated. 3s.

Bunyan's Pilgrim's Progress (Cassell's Illustrated). Demy 4to. Illustrated throughout. 7s. 6d.

Bunyan's Pilgrim's Progress. With Illustrations. Cloth, 3s. 6d.

Child's Life of Christ, The. With 200 Illustrations. 21s.

Child's Bible, The. With 200 Illustrations. 143*rd Thousand.* 7s. 6d.

Church at Home, The. A Series of Short Sermons. By the Rt. Rev. ROWLEY HILL, D.D., Bishop of Sodor and Man. 5s.

Day-Dawn in Dark Places; or, Wanderings and Work in Bech-wanaland. By the Rev. JOHN MACKENZIE. Illustrated. 3s. 6d.

Difficulties of Belief, Some. By the Rev. T. TEIGNMOUTH SHORE, M.A. *New and Cheap Edition.* 2s. 6d.

Doré Bible. With 230 Illustrations by GUSTAVE DORÉ. Cloth, £2 10s.

Early Days of Christianity, The. By the Ven. Archdeacon FARRAR, D.D., F.R.S.
LIBRARY EDITION. Two Vols., 24s.; morocco, £2 2s.
POPULAR EDITION. Complete in One Volume, cloth, 6s.; cloth, gilt edges, 7s. 6d.; Persian morocco, 10s. 6d.; tree-calf, 15s.

Family Prayer-Book, The. Edited by Rev. Canon GARBETT, M.A., and Rev. S. MARTIN. Extra crown 4to, cloth, 5s.; morocco, 18s.

Geikie, Cunningham, D.D., Works by :—
HOURS WITH THE BIBLE. Six Vols., 6s. each.
ENTERING ON LIFE. 3s. 6d.
THE PRECIOUS PROMISES. 2s. 6d.
THE ENGLISH REFORMATION. 5s.
OLD TESTAMENT CHARACTERS. 6s.
THE LIFE AND WORDS OF CHRIST. Two Vols., cloth, 30s. *Students' Edition.* Two Vols., 16s.

Glories of the Man of Sorrows, The. By Rev. H. G. BONAVIA HUNT, F.R.S., Ed.: Evening preacher at St. James's, Piccadilly. 2s. 6d.

Gospel of Grace, The. By a LINDESIE. Cloth, 3s. 6d.

"Heart Chords." A Series of Works by Eminent Divines. Bound in cloth, red edges, One Shilling each.

My Father.	My Aspirations.	My Hereafter.
My Bible.	My Emotional Life.	My Walk with God.
My Work for God.	My Body.	My Aids to the Divine Life.
My Object in Life.	My Soul.	My Sources of Strength.
	My Growth in Divine Life.	

Helps to Belief. A Series of Helpful Manuals on the Religious Difficulties of the Day. Edited by the Rev. TEIGNMOUTH SHORE, M.A., Chaplain-in-Ordinary to the Queen. Cloth, 1s. each.

CREATION. By the Lord Bishop of Carlisle.	MIRACLES. By the Rev. Brownlow Maitland, M.A.
THE DIVINITY OF OUR LORD. By the Lord Bishop of Derry.	PRAYER. By the Rev. T. Teignmouth Shore, M.A.
THE MORALITY OF THE OLD TESTA-MENT. By the Rev. Newman Smyth, D.D.	THE RESURRECTION. By the Lord Archbishop of York.
	THE ATONEMENT. By the Lord Bishop of Peterborough.

Life of Christ, The. By the Ven. Archdeacon FARRAR, D.D., F.R.S.
ILLUSTRATED EDITION, with about 300 Original Illustrations.
Extra crown 4to, cloth, gilt edges, 21s. ; morocco antique, 42s.
LIBRARY EDITION. Two Vols. Cloth, 24s. ; morocco, 42s.
BIJOU EDITION. Five Volumes, in box, 10s. 6d. the set.
POPULAR EDITION, in One Vol. 8vo, cloth, 6s. ; cloth, gilt edges,
7s. 6d. ; Persian morocco, gilt edges, 10s. 6d. ; tree-calf, 15s.

Marriage Ring, The. By WILLIAM LANDELS, D.D. Bound in white
leatherette, gilt edges, in box, 6s. ; morocco, 8s. 6d.

Moses and Geology ; or, The Harmony of the Bible with Science.
By SAMUEL KINNS, Ph.D., F.R.A.S. Illustrated. *Cheap Edition*, 6s.

Music of the Bible, The. By J. STAINER, M.A., Mus. Doc. 2s. 6d.

New Testament Commentary for English Readers, The. Edited
by the Rt. Rev. C. J. ELLICOTT, D.D., Lord Bishop of Gloucester
and Bristol. In Three Volumes, 21s. each.

Vol. I.—The Four Gospels.

Vol. II.—The Acts, Romans, Corinthians, Galatians.

Vol. III.—The remaining Books of the New Testament.

Old Testament Commentary for English Readers, The. Edited
by the Right Rev. C. J. ELLICOTT, D.D., Lord Bishop of Gloucester
and Bristol. Complete in 5 Vols., 21s. each.

Vol. I.—Genesis to Numbers.	Vol. III.—Kings I. to Esther.
Vol. II.—Deuteronomy to Samuel II.	Vol. IV.—Job to Isaiah.
	Vol. V.—Jeremiah to Malachi.

Patriarchs, The. By the late Rev. W. HANNA, D.D., and the Ven.
Archdeacon NORRIS, B.D. 2s. 6d.

Protestantism, The History of. By the Rev. J. A. WYLIE, LL.D.
Containing upwards of 600 Original Illustrations. Three Vols., 27s.

Quiver Yearly Volume, The. 250 high-class Illustrations. 7s. 6d.

**Revised Version—Commentary on the Revised Version of the New
Testament.** By the Rev. W. G. HUMPHRY, B.D. 7s. 6d.

Sacred Poems, The Book of. Edited by the Rev. Canon BAYNES, M.A.
With Illustrations. Cloth, gilt edges, 5s.

St. George for England ; and other Sermons preached to Children. By
the Rev. T. TEIGNMOUTH SHORE, M.A. 5s.

St. Paul, The Life and Work of. By the Ven. Archdeacon FARRAR,
D.D., F.R.S., Chaplain-in-Ordinary to the Queen.
LIBRARY EDITION. Two Vols., cloth, 24s. ; morocco, 42s.
ILLUSTRATED EDITION, complete in One Volume, with about 300
Illustrations, £1 1s. ; morocco, £2 2s.
POPULAR EDITION. One Volume, 8vo, cloth, 6s. ; cloth, gilt edges,
7s. 6d. ; Persian morocco, 10s. 6d. ; tree calf, 15s.

Secular Life, The Gospel of the. Sermons preached at Oxford. By
the Hon. W. H. FREMANTLE, Canon of Canterbury. 5s.

Sermons Preached at Westminster Abbey. By ALFRED BARRY,
D.D., D.C.L., Primate of Australia. 5s.

Shall We Know One Another ? By the Rt. Rev. J. C. RYLE, D.D.
Bishop of Liverpool. *New and Enlarged Edition.* Cloth limp, 1s.

Simon Peter: His Life, Times, and Friends. By E. HODDER. 5s.

**Twilight of Life, The. Words of Counsel and Comfort for the
Aged.** By the Rev. JOHN ELLERTON, M.A. 1s. 6d. .

Voice of Time, The. By JOHN STROUD. Cloth gilt, 1s.

𝕰𝖉𝖚𝖈𝖆𝖙𝖎𝖔𝖓𝖆𝖑 𝖂𝖔𝖗𝖐𝖘 𝖆𝖓𝖉 𝕾𝖙𝖚𝖉𝖊𝖓𝖙𝖘' 𝕸𝖆𝖓𝖚𝖆𝖑𝖘.

Alphabet, Cassell's Pictorial. 3s. 6d.

Algebra, The Elements of. By Prof. WALLACE, M.A. 1s.

Arithmetics, The Modern School. By GEORGE RICKS, B.Sc. Lond. With Test Cards. (*List on application.*)

Book-Keeping. By THEODORE JONES. For Schools, 2s.; cloth, 3s. For the Million, 2s.; cloth, 3s. Books for Jones's System. 2s.

Chemistry, The Public School. By J. H. ANDERSON, M.A. 2s. 6d.

Commentary, The New Testament. Edited by the Lord Bishop of GLOUCESTER and BRISTOL. Handy Volume Edition. St. Matthew, 3s. 6d. St. Mark, 3s. St. Luke, 3s. 6d. St. John, 3s. 6d. The Acts of the Apostles, 3s. 6d. Romans, 2s. 6d. Corinthians I. and II., 3s. Galatians, Ephesians, and Philippians, 3s. Colossians, Thessalonians, and Timothy, 3s. Titus, Philemon, Hebrews, and James, 3s. Peter, Jude, and John, 3s. The Revelation, 3s. An Introduction to the New Testament, 3s. 6d.

Commentary, Old Testament. Edited by Bishop ELLICOTT. Handy Volume Edition. Genesis, 3s. 6d. Exodus, 3s. Leviticus, 3s. Numbers, 2s. 6d. Deuteronomy, 2s. 6d.

Copy-Books, Cassell's Graduated. *Eighteen Books.* 2d. each.

Copy-Books, The Modern School. *Twelve Books.* 2d. each.

Drawing Books, Cassell's New Standard. 7 Books. 2d. each.

Drawing Books, Superior. 4 Books. Price 5s. each.

Drawing Copies, Cassell's Modern School Freehand. First Grade, 1s.; Second Grade, 2s.

Drawing Copies, Cassell's New Standard. Seven Books. 2d. each.

Electricity, Practical. By Prof. W. E. AYRTON. Illustrated. 5s.

Energy and Motion: A Text-Book of Elementary Mechanics. By WILLIAM PAICE, M.A. Illustrated. 1s. 6d.

English Literature, First Sketch of, *New and Enlarged Edition.* By Prof. MORLEY. 7s. 6d.

Euclid, Cassell's. Edited by Prof. WALLACE, M.A. 1s.

Euclid, The First Four Books of. In paper, 6d.; cloth, 9d.

French Reader, Cassell's Public School. By GUILLAUME S. CONRAD. 2s. 6d.

French, Cassell's Lessons in. *New and Revised Edition.* Parts I. and II., each 2s. 6d.; complete, 4s. 6d. Key, 1s. 6d.

French-English and English-French Dictionary. *Entirely New and Enlarged Edition.* 1,150 pages, 8vo, cloth, 3s. 6d.

Galbraith and Haughton's Scientific Manuals. By the Rev. Prof. GALBRAITH, M.A., and the Rev. Prof. HAUGHTON, M.D., D.C.L. Arithmetic, 3s. 6d.—Plane Trigonometry, 2s. 6d.—Euclid, Books I., II., III., 2s. 6d.—Books IV., V., VI., 2s. 6d.—Mathematical Tables, 3s. 6d.—Mechanics, 3s. 6d.—Optics, 2s. 6d.—Hydrostatics, 3s. 6d.— Astronomy, 5s.—Steam Engine, 3s. 6d.—Algebra, Part I., cloth, 2s. 6d.; Complete, 7s. 6d.—Tides and Tidal Currents, with Tidal Cards, 3s.

German-English and English-German Dictionary. *Entirely New and Revised Edition.* 3s. 6d.

German Reading, Modern. By Prof. HEINEMANN. 1s. 6d.

German Reading, First Lessons in. By A. JAGST. Illustrated. 1s.

German of To-day. By Dr. HEINEMANN. 1s. 6d.

Handbook of New Code of Regulations. By JOHN F. MOSS. 1s.

Historical Course for Schools, Cassell's. Illustrated throughout. I.—Stories from English History, 1s. II.—The Simple Outline of English History, 1s. 3d. III.—The Class History of England, 2s. 6d.

Latin-English and English-Latin Dictionary. By J. R. BEARD, D.D., and C. BEARD, B.A. Crown 8vo, 914 pp., 3s. 6d.

Little Folks' History of England. By ISA CRAIG-KNOX. With 30 Illustrations. 1s. 6d.

Making of the Home, The: A Book of Domestic Economy for School and Home Use. By Mrs. SAMUEL A. BARNETT. 1s. 6d.

Marlborough Books:—Arithmetic Examples, 3s. Arithmetic Rules, 1s. 6d. French Exercises, 3s. 6d. French Grammar, 2s. 6d. German Grammar, 3s. 6d.

Music, An Elementary Manual of. By HENRY LESLIE. 1s.

Natural Philosophy. By Prof. HAUGHTON, F.R.S. Illustrated. 3s. 6d.

Popular Educator, Cassell's. *New and Thoroughly Revised Edition.* Illustrated throughout. Complete in Six Vols., 5s. each.

Physical Science, Intermediate Text-Book of. By F. H. BOWMAN, D.Sc., F.R.A.S., F.L.S. Illustrated. 3s. 6d.

Readers, Cassell's Readable. Carefully graduated, extremely interesting, and illustrated throughout. (*List on application.*)

Readers, Cassell's Historical. Illustrated throughout, printed on superior paper, and strongly bound in cloth. (*List on application.*)

Readers for Infant Schools, Coloured. Three Books. Each containing 48 pages, including 8 pages in colours. 4d. each.

Reader, The Citizen. By H. O. ARNOLD FORSTER, with Preface by the late Right Hon. W. E. FORSTER, M.P. 1s. 6d.

Readers, The Modern Geographical, illustrated throughout, and strongly bound in cloth. (*List on application.*)

Readers, The Modern School. Illustrated. (*List on application.*)

Reading and Spelling Book, Cassell's Illustrated. 1s.

Right Lines; or, Form and Colour. With Illustrations. 1s.

School Manager's Manual. By F. C. MILLS, M.A. 1s.

Shakspere's Plays for School Use. 5 Books. Illustrated, 6d. each.

Shakspere Reading Book, The. By H. COURTHOPE BOWEN, M.A. Illustrated. 3s. 6d. Also issued in Three Books, 1s. each.

Spelling, A Complete Manual of. By J. D. MORELL, LL.D. 1s.

Technical Manuals, Cassell's. Illustrated throughout:—Handrailing and Staircasing, 3s. 6d.—Bricklayers, Drawing for, 3s.—Building Construction, 2s.—Cabinet-Makers, Drawing for, 3s.—Carpenters and Joiners, Drawing for, 3s. 6d.—Gothic Stonework, 3s.—Linear Drawing and Practical Geometry, 2s.—Linear Drawing and Projection. The Two Vols. in One, 3s. 6d.—Machinists and Engineers, Drawing for, 4s. 6d.—Metal-Plate Workers, Drawing for, 3s.—Model Drawing, 3s.—Orthographical and Isometrical Projection, 2s.—Practical Perspective, 3s.—Stonemasons, Drawing for, 3s.—Applied Mechanics, by Sir R. S. Ball, LL.D., 2s.—Systematic Drawing and Shading, 2s.

Technical Educator, Cassell's. Four Vols. 6s. each. *New and Cheap Edition,* in Four Vols., 5s. each.

Technology, Manuals of. Edited by Prof. AYRTON, F.R.S., and RICHARD WORMELL, D.Sc., M.A. Illustrated throughout:—The Dyeing of Textile Fabrics, by Prof. Hummel, 5s.—Watch and Clock Making, by D. Glasgow, 4s. 6d.—Steel and Iron, by W. H. Greenwood, F.C.S., Assoc. M.I.C.E., &c., 5s.—Spinning Woollen and Worsted, by W. S. Bright McLaren, 4s. 6d.—Design in Textile Fabrics, by T. R. Ashenhurst, 4s. 6d.—Practical Mechanics, by Prof. Perry, M.E., 3s. 6d.—Cutting Tools Worked by Hand and Machine, by Prof. Smith, 3s. 6d.—Practical Electricity, by Prof. W. E. Ayrton, 5s. *Other Volumes in preparation. A Prospectus sent post free on application.*

CASSELL & COMPANY, LIMITED, *Ludgate Hill, London.*

𝔅ooks for 𝔜oung 𝔓eople,

Under Bayard's Banner. By HENRY FRITH. Illustrated. 5s.

The King's Command. A Story for Girls. By MAGGIE SYMINGTON. Illustrated. 5s.

The Romance of Invention. By JAMES BURNLEY. Illustrated. 5s.

The Tales of the Sixty Mandarins. By P. V. RAMASWAMI RAJU. With an Introduction by Prof. HENRY MORLEY. Illustrated. 5s.

A World of Girls: The Story of a School. By L. T. MEADE. Illustrated. 3s. 6d.

Lost among White Africans: A Boy's Adventures on the Upper Congo. By DAVID KER. Illustrated. 3s. 6d.

Perils Afloat and Brigands Ashore. By ALFRED ELWES. Illustrated. 3s. 6d.

Freedom's Sword: A Story of the Days of Wallace and Bruce. By ANNIE S. SWAN. Illustrated. 3s. 6d.

Strong to Suffer: A Story of the Jews. By E. WYNNE. Illustrated. 2s. 6d.

The Merry-go-Round. Original Poems for Children. Illustrated throughout. 5s.

Heroes of the Indian Empire; or, Stories of Valour and Victory. By ERNEST FOSTER. Illustrated. 2s. 6d.

In Letters of Flame: A Story of the Waldenses. By C. L. MATÉAUX. Illustrated. 2s. 6d.

Through Trial to Triumph. By MADELINE B. HUNT. Illustrated. 2s. 6d.

Sunday School Reward Books. By Popular Authors. With Four Original Illustrations in each. Cloth gilt, 1s. 6d. each.

Rhoda's Reward; or, "If Wishes were Horses."

Jack Marston's Anchor.

Frank's Life-Battle; or, The Three Friends.

Rags and Rainbows: a Story of Thanksgiving.

Uncle William's Charge; or, The Broken Trust.

Pretty Pink's Purpose; or, The Little Street Merchants.

"Golden Mottoes" Series, The. Each Book containing 208 pages, with Four full-page Original Illustrations. Crown 8vo, cloth gilt, 2s. each.

"Nil Desperandum." By the Rev. F. Langbridge.

"Bear and Forbear." By Sarah Pitt.

"Foremost if I Can." By Helen Atteridge.

"Honour is my Guide." By Jeanie Hering (Mrs. Adams-Acton).

"Aim at the Sure End." By Emilie Searchfield.

"He Conquers who Endures." By the Author of "May Cunningham's Trial," &c.

The New Children's Album. Fcap. 4to, 320 pages. Illustrated throughout. 3s. 6d.

The History Scrap Book. With nearly 1,000 Engravings. 5s.; cloth, 7s.6d.

"Little Folks" Half-Yearly Volume. With 200 Illustrations and several Pictures in Colour. 3s. 6d.; or cloth gilt, 5s.

Bo-Peep. A Book for the Little Ones. With Original Stories and Verses, Illustrated throughout. Boards, 2s. 6d.; cloth gilt, 3s. 6d.

The World's Lumber Room. By SELINA GAYE. Illustrated. 3s. 6d.

The "Proverbs" Series. Original Stories by Popular Authors, founded on and illustrating well-known Proverbs. With Four Illustrations in each Book, printed on a tint. 1s. 6d. each.

Fritters. By Sarah Pitt.

Trixy. By Maggie Symington.

The Two Hardcastles. By Madeline Bonavia Hunt.

Major Monk's Motto. By the Rev. F. Langbridge.

Tim Thomson's Trial. By George Weatherly.

Ursula's Stumbling-Block. By Julia Goddard.

Ruth's Life-Work. By the Rev. Joseph Johns.

The "Cross and Crown" Series. Consisting of Stories founded on incidents which occurred during Religious Persecutions of Past Days. With Illustrations in each Book, printed on a tint. 2s. 6d. each.

By Fire and Sword: A Story of the Huguenots. By Thomas Archer.

Adam Hepburn's Vow: A Tale of Kirk and Covenant. By Annie S. Swan.

No. XIII.; or, The Story of the Lost Vestal. A Tale of Early Christian Days. By Emma Marshall.

The World's Workers. A Series of New and Original Volumes. With Portraits printed on a tint as Frontispiece. 1s. each.

General Gordon. By the Rev. S. A. Swaine.

Charles Dickens. By his Eldest Daughter.

Sir Titus Salt and George Moore. By J. Burnley.

Florence Nightingale, Catherine Marsh, Frances Ridley Havergal, Mrs. Ranyard ("L.N.R."). By Lizzie Aldridge.

Dr. Guthrie, Father Mathew, Elihu Burritt, George Livesey. By the Rev. J. W. Kirton.

David Livingstone. By Robert Smiles.

Sir Henry Havelock and Colin Campbell, Lord Clyde. By E. C. Phillips.

Abraham Lincoln. By Ernest Foster.

George Muller and Andrew Reed. By E. R. Pitman.

Richard Cobden. By R. Gowing.

Benjamin Franklin. By E. M. Tomkinson.

Handel. By Eliza Clarke.

Turner, the Artist. By the Rev. S. A. Swaine.

George and Robert Stephenson. By C. L. Matéaux.

The "Chimes" Series. Each containing 64 pages, with Illustrations on every page, and bound in Japanese morocco, 1s.

Bible Chimes.
Daily Chimes.

Holy Chimes.
Old World Chimes.

Books for Boys. Cloth gilt, 5s. each.

"Follow My Leader;" or, the Boys of Templeton. By Talbot Baines Reed.

For Fortune and Glory: a Story of the Soudan War. By Lewis Hough.

The Champion of Odin: or, Viking Life in the Days of Old. By J. Fred. Hodgetts.

Bound by a Spell: or, the Hunted Witch of the Forest. By the Hon. Mrs. Greene.

Price 3s. 6d. each.

On Board the "Esmeralda:" or, Martin Leigh's Log. By John C. Hutcheson.

For Queen and King: or, the Loyal 'Prentice. By Henry Frith.

In Quest of Gold: or, Under the Whanga Falls. By Alfred St. Johnston.

The "Boy Pioneer" Series. By EDWARD S. ELLIS. With Four Full-page Illustrations in each Book. Crown 8vo, cloth, 2s. 6d. each.

Ned in the Woods. A Tale of Early Days in the West.

Ned on the River. A Tale of Indian River Warfare.

Ned in the Block House. A Story of Pioneer Life in Kentucky.

The "Log Cabin" Series. By EDWARD S. ELLIS. With Four Full-page Illustrations in each. Crown 8vo, cloth, 2s. 6d. each.

The Lost Trail. | Camp-Fire and Wigwam. | Footprints in the Forest.

Sixpenny Story Books. All Illustrated, and containing Interesting Stories by well-known Writers.

Little Content.
The Smuggler's Cave.
Little Lizzie.
Little Bird.
The Boot on the Wrong Foot.
Luke Barnicott.
Little Pickles.
The Boat Club. By Oliver Optic.

Helpful Nellie: and other Stories.
The Elchester College Boys.
My First Cruise.
Lottie's White Frock.
Only Just Once.
The Little Peacemaker.
The Delft Jug. By Silverpen.

The "Baby's Album" Series. Four Books, each containing about 50 Illustrations. Price 6d. each; or cloth gilt, 1s. each.

Baby's Album.
Dolly's Album.

Fairy's Album.
Pussy's Album.

Illustrated Books for the Little Ones. Containing interesting Stories. All Illustrated. **1s.** each.

Indoors and Out.
Some Farm Friends.
Those Golden Sands.
Little Mothers & their Children.

Our Pretty Pets.
Our Schoolday Hours.
Creatures Tame.
Creatures Wild.

Shilling Story Books. All Illustrated, and containing Interesting Stories.

Thorns and Tangles.
The Cuckoo in the Robin's Nest.
John's Mistake.
Pearl's Fairy Flower.
The History of Five Little Pitchers.
Diamonds in the Sand.
Surly Bob.
The Giant's Cradle.

Shag and Doll.
Aunt Lucia's Locket.
The Magic Mirror.
The Cost of Revenge.
Clever Frank.
Among the Redskins.
The Ferryman of Brill.
Harry Maxwell.
A Banished Monarch.

"Little Folks" Painting Books. With Text, and Outline Illustrations for Water-Colour Painting. **1s.** each.

Fruits and Blossoms for "Little Folks" to Paint.
The "Little Folks" Proverb Painting Book.
The "Little Folks" Illuminating Book.

Pictures to Paint.
"Little Folks" Painting Book.
"Little Folks" Nature Painting Book.
Another "Little Folks" Painting Book.

Eighteenpenny Story Books. All Illustrated throughout.

Three Wee Ulster Lassies.
Little Queen Mab.
Up the Ladder.
Dick's Hero; and other Stories.
The Chip Boy.
Raggles, Baggles, and the Emperor.
Roses from Thorns.
Faith's Father.

By Land and Sea.
The Young Berringtons.
Jeff and Leff.
Tom Morris's Error.
Worth more than Gold.
"Through Flood—Through Fire;" and other Stories.
The Girl with the Golden Locks.
Stories of the Olden Time.

The "Cosy Corner" Series. Story Books for Children. Each containing nearly ONE HUNDRED PICTURES. **1s. 6d.** each.

See-Saw Stories.
Little Chimes for All Times.
Wee Willie Winkie.
Pet's Posy of Pictures and Stories.
Dot's Story Book.
Story Flowers for Rainy Hours.

Little Talks with Little People.
Bright Rays for Dull Days.
Chats for Small Chatterers.
Pictures for Happy Hours.
Ups and Downs of a Donkey's Life.

The "World in Pictures." Illustrated throughout. **2s. 6d.** each.

A Ramble Round France.
All the Russias.
Chats about Germany.
The Land of the Pyramids (Egypt).
Peeps into China.

The Eastern Wonderland (Japan).
Glimpses of South America.
Round Africa.
The Land of Temples (India).
The Isles of the Pacific.

Two-Shilling Story Books. All Illustrated.

Stories of the Tower.
Mr. Burke's Nieces.
May Cunningham's Trial.
The Top of the Ladder: How to Reach it.
Little Flotsam.
Madge and her Friends.
The Children of the Court.
A Moonbeam Tangle.
Maid Marjory.

The Four Cats of the Tippertons.
Marion's Two Homes.
Little Folks' Sunday Book.
Two Fourpenny Bits.
Poor Nelly.
Tom Heriot.
Through Peril to Fortune.
Aunt Tabitha's Waifs.
In Mischief Again.

Half-Crown Story Books.

Little Hinges.
Margaret's Enemy.
Fen's Perplexities.
Notable Shipwrecks.
Golden Days.
Wonders of Common Things.
Little Empress Joan.
Truth will Out.

At the South Pole. *Cheap Edition.*
Soldier and Patriot (George Washington). [hood.
Picture of School Life and Boyhood.
The Young Man in the Battle of Life. By the Rev. Dr. Landels.
The True Glory of Woman. By the Rev. Dr. Landels.

Library of Wonders. Illustrated Gift-books for Boys. 2s. 6d. each.

Wonderful Adventures.
Wonders of Animal Instinct.
Wonders of Architecture.
Wonders of Acoustics.

Wonders of Water.
Wonderful Escapes.
Bodily Strength and Skill.
Wonderful Balloon Ascents.

Gift-Books for Children. With Coloured Illustrations. 2s. 6d. each.

The Story of Robin Hood.
Playing Trades.

Reynard the Fox.
The Pilgrim's Progress.

Three and Sixpenny Library of Standard Tales, &c. All Illustrated and bound in cloth gilt. Crown 8vo. 3s. 6d. each.

Jane Austen and her Works.
Mission Life in Greece and Palestine.
The Dingy House at Kensington.
The Romance of Trade.
The Three Homes.
My Guardian.
School Girls.

Deepdale Vicarage.
In Duty Bound.
The Half Sisters.
Peggy Oglivie's Inheritance.
The Family Honour.
Esther West.
Working to Win.
Krilof and his Fables. By W. R. S. Ralston, M.A.
Fairy Tales. By Prof. Morley.

The Home Chat Series. All Illustrated throughout. Fcap. 4to. Boards, 3s. 6d. each. Cloth, gilt edges, 5s. each.

Half-Hours with Early Explorers.
Stories about Animals.
Stories about Birds.
Paws and Claws.

Home Chat.
Sunday Chats with Our Young Folks.
Peeps Abroad for Folks at Home.
Around and About Old England.

Books for the Little Ones.

The Little Doings of some Little Folks. By Chatty Cheerful. Illustrated. 5s.
The Sunday Scrap Book. With One Thousand Scripture Pictures. Boards, 5s.; cloth, 7s. 6d.
Daisy Dimple's Scrap Book. Containing about 1,000 Pictures. Boards, 5s.; cloth gilt, 7s. 6d.

Little Folks' Picture Album. With 168 Large Pictures. 5s.
Little Folks' Picture Gallery. With 150 Illustrations. 5s.
The Old Fairy Tales. With Original Illustrations. Boards, 1s.; cloth, 1s. 6d.
My Diary. With 12 Coloured Plates and 366 Woodcuts, 1s.

Books for Boys.

Kidnapped. By R. L. Stevenson. 5s.
King Solomon's Mines. By H. Rider Haggard, 5s.
The Phantom City. By W. Westall. 5s.
Famous Sailors of Former Times. By Clements Markham. Illustrated. 2s. 6d.
Treasure Island. By R. L. Stevenson. Illustrated. 5s.

Modern Explorers. By Thomas Frost. Illustrated. 5s.
Cruise in Chinese Waters. By Capt. Lindley. Illustrated. 5s.
Wild Adventures in Wild Places. By Dr. Gordon Stables, M.D., R.N. Illustrated. 5s.
Jungle, Peak, and Plain. By Dr. Gordon Stables, R.N. Illustrated. 5s.

CASSELL & COMPANY, Limited, London; Paris, New York and Melbourne.